LOVE
FINALLY

M Reid

LOVE
FINALLY

by

Nakiesia Reid

Copyright © 2009 Nakiesia Reid

Published by: Voices Books & Publishing

P.O. Box 3007

Bridgeton, MO 63044

www.voicesbooks.homestead.com

Printed in the United States of America

This book is a work of fiction. Names, characters, places and incidents are products of the author's imagination or are used fictitiously. Any resemblance to actual events or locales of persons living or dead, is entirely coincidental.

All rights reserved. No part of this publication may be reproduced, stored in a retrieval system, or transmitted in any form or by any means, electronic, mechanical, recording or otherwise, without the prior written permission of the author.

Library of Congress Catalog Card No.: Pending

ISBN 10: 0-9841665-1-3

ISBN 13: 978-0-9841665-1-0

Acknowledgements

Never in a million years did I think that I would write a book. As a sophomore in high school, I read Omar Tyree's, *Flyy Girl* for the first time and from that day on, I always imagined bringing characters to life like he did.

Here I am twelve years later, bringing my own characters to life. I must first thank God because if he hadn't blessed me with this written talent, I wouldn't be able to share it with you. He has truly kept me through this journey and I am so grateful. To my wonderful parents, thank you for birthing me. Mommy, who would've known that by you introducing me to reading the newspaper at the tender age of three, would amount to this moment? *The Nancy Drew and Hardy Boys* books that you continuously provided were the start to this journey. I didn't become a doctor like I thought I would, but I'm somewhat glad because I found my true passion as a writer. Thank you for your encouragement and for not giving up on me. Daddy, thank you for believing in my vision. Your kind words in my time of hopelessness have kept me going. I am truly appreciative. I love you both and I am so ever grateful for your unconditional support. You are the best parents that anyone could ask for. Muah!

I know that if I don't include you, I will never hear the end of it, so to my wonderful sister, Nella Reid, I want to thank you for your generous assistance. I know I nagged you throughout me writing this book, but your criticism and honesty were what I needed to make it happen. I love you!

My best friend, Jamelia, what would I do without you? I am thankful for the friendship that we share because no matter what, you always had my back. I look forward to many more years of friendship. I couldn't have asked for a better person to share what we share with. You know I got you! Oh and I love you like my sister! (LOL).

Lisa! My, my, my. Our encounter was not a mistake, but a divine set up by God! You have been there since the beginning of my decision to write this book and you have been my number one supporter ever since. I thank you so, so much. Your help was not taken for granted. You pushed me to follow through on my dream and as you can see, I took your advice because we did it! Yeah!!!! (LOL) Thank you for everything.

Brenda, my publisher, this book would not come alive if it weren't for your help. Thank you for taking a chance on this unknown author. You believed in me and I will never forget it. We are in this for the long haul! You have been so patient and helpful. Thank you for working with me on this path to our success. You are the best!

To my readers, you are the reason I write. Thank you for allowing me to share my dream with you. For all of you who chose to purchase this book, thank you for the support and I hope that you all will continue supporting me. This will not be that last you read of me so continue to look out for future books of mine. You all play a part in making things happen. Let's continue to read together and spread love to one another. If I forgot to mention anyone specifically, please forgive me, but you know I love you just the same.

Love and Blessings,

Nakiesia Reid

Love Finally

Chapter 1

She dug her French manicured nails into the small of his back and soft moans escaped her lips when he traced his tongue against the sensitive parts of her body. "Ummm." He thrusted his thick hardened flesh inside her womanhood. "Mmmm...yeah daddy. Just like that." He pumped harder and their hips moved in a simultaneous rhythm. It was an explosion waiting to happen. His body stiffened and her insides burned for him to go deeper and deeper as she wrapped her legs around his muscular mid section to keep him in position. Grabbing a fold of the red silk sheets, her back arched as he began to take her to the point of no return. "OH YES...OH..."

RING...RING...

Carla opened her eyes due to the loud rings and looked down to see her hands squeezed between her thighs. "FUCK! I was almost there," she fumed. Upset that her orgasmic dream was interrupted, Carla stretched her arm and reached for the handset on her nightstand. Without looking at the caller ID, she quickly answered with the intention to hurry and get whoever it was off the line.

"Hello," she panted. Her dream seemed so real that it had her temporarily out of breath and beads of sweat lined her forehead.

"Hey stranger, how have you been?" the deep baritone voice on the other end of the receiver asked.

Carla raised her head from the pillow and looked at the clock that sat on her night stand. It read 11:45 p.m. It had been raining all day and she didn't realize how long she'd fallen asleep. Becoming annoyed, she plopped her head back down on the pillow and blurted, "Who is this? I really don't have time for any bullshit guessing games tonight."

Just when I was about to have a fucking orgasm, she thought.

"Calm down, Carla. It's me, Antoine."

Carla cut her eyes and wished he could've seen her do it through the phone. *Damn! Why didn't I check the caller ID before I answered,* she thought.

"Oh, it's you. What do you want?" Her voice was filled with attitude. She hoped that he would sense the manner and hang up.

"Is this a bad time?" Antoine asked. He sensed that Carla wasn't too thrilled with hearing his voice. But that didn't discourage him from wanting to strike up a conversation.

Not giving an immediate response, Carla paused and then Antoine asked, "So, how have you been doing? I mean, we haven't spoken in months…"

"As a matter of fact, this is a bad time. I thought I told you to lose my number and not to call me anymore." Her voice got loud.

It all happened two months ago when Carla saw an ad for internet hook ups and decided to give it a try. According to the results from the input data, it was suggested that Antoine would be a perfect match for her. It was her first time doing anything like that, but the desperate need for a man had Carla testing all her options. She always saw the commercials on TV, and thought that maybe the shit would work for her too. "Hell, I don't see the harm in this," she remembered herself saying after she'd click the 'accept' link on her Mac Notebook laptop.

She'd immediately sent Antoine an email and they planned to meet up at the movie theatre to watch the latest Tyler Perry production. They'd exchanged photos and phone numbers via the internet and from the looks of his picture, Carla knew that he wasn't the typical man that she would date, but figured she would test the waters and try him out. In his photo, Antoine rocked shoulder length dreads and his brown complexion made him resemble a thugged out version of Eric Benet. He flaunted a warm inviting smile and there was something about his dark, mysterious eyes that intrigued her. Within the first week of them getting acquainted, it reached the point where they would converse on the phone every night and she had to admit that Antoine had a way with words. He would tell her things like, "I fall asleep with your picture under my pillow at night" or "I can't wait to treat you like the queen you are." She had to admit that he was flattering. Maybe it was the lack of not having a man in her life that made her naively buy into it. Before she knew it, Antoine was feeding her from the palm of his hands. It wasn't until he stood her up for another woman, that Carla realized how much of a gamester he was.

    Carla decided to have nothing to do with Antoine after he stood her up for their movie date. Not only did he stand her up, but the low down geezer had the nerve to bring another bitch to the movies on the same night he planned with her. After waiting for an hour and a half, the movie was already rolling. She called him 'til her damn fingers hurt and not once did he have the decency to pick up. Fed up, Carla decided she was not going to wait any longer. She walked outside of the AMC theatre and her eyes popped open when she spotted Antoine standing in line hugged up with a chocolate colored skin, blue weave wearing hood rat. *"That's what I get for trying that damn internet dating gimmick"*, she'd mumbled. Her first impulse was to walk over to him and give him a piece of her mind, but he wasn't worth it. He wasn't her man, but she couldn't believe he had played her like that. Instead, she held her head straight, not wanting him to see her, and ran all the way to the parking lot. Carla knew that she could do better than him. Furthermore, she is a dime piece. She could've had any man she wanted, but she had standards and was not willing to settle for just anything or anyone. That would be the last time she tried internet dating.

    "I'm busy, I gotta go."

    "Please, hear me out Carla. I know I messed up and I'm calling to see if there's anything...."

    "Not interested." She cut him off. After saying those two words, Carla mashed the end button and slammed her handset on the base, without giving him a chance to finish his sentence. The only thing Antoine would hear is the automated operator telling him, "If you would like to make a call please hang up and try your call again."

Carla plopped down on her pillow. She was pissed that her sleep was interrupted by foolishness. As she continued to lay in the dark, the faint moon tried to shine some light in through her curtain less window. She could see that the rain was beginning to slow its pour and droplets ran down her window pane. The thought of Antoine caused her to grow frustrated. Carla diverted her eyes up at the ceiling. *I can't believe that Negro had the audacity to call me. The incident happened two months ago and now he decides to call. He needs to go somewhere else with his trick ass.*

Climbing out of bed, Carla was delighted to see that the sun was finally out. She loved the way the rainy weather relaxed her, but too much of that shit would've put her in a depressive state. She walked over to her bedroom window and her gaze was fixed on how quickly the roads were dried. *This would be a good day to run some errands,* she ruminated. Wearing hot pink, silk pajama pants with a matching top, Carla walked into her kitchen and grabbed the peach flavored yogurt from the refrigerator. She removed a spoon from the kitchen drawer, walked towards her living room and sat on her leather sofa. Carla's posh two bedroom, two bath condo in the upscale area of Buckhead, Atlanta, was exquisite. Her living room was adorned with white furniture and glass tables. The floor was that of marble tiles and crystal chandeliers hung high in the ceiling. She knew the all white arrangement was playing it safe, but she also found it to be classy. A few paintings of legendary jazz singers like Billie Holiday and Nina Simone graced her walls.

Let's see if there is anything good on TV today, she wondered. Carla picked up the remote from her glass center table, and before she had the chance to get comfortable, turn the TV on and dunk the spoon into her yogurt; her house phone rang. She made sure to check the caller ID first this time and picked up on the second ring.

"Hello," she answered, already knowing who it was.

"Whassup, heifer? I hope you have some clothes on," the voice said and screamed excitedly through the phone.

"Good morning to you too," Carla said sarcastically. "It is 9:30 in the morning, ain't shit open right now. Where the hell are we going? Better yet, what are you so damn happy about?"

"You better quit drilling me. Go wash yo stank ass and get ready within the next twenty minutes. I'm coming to pick you up. I'm treating you to breakfast," Tamika, her best friend, told her.

"I guess I'll just wait until you get here to find out what this is all about. See you in twenty." *Click.*

Excitement and curiosity flooded Carla all at once. She jumped up off of the sofa and ran to the bathroom to take a shower. She was excited that Tamika was coming to rescue her from her boredom, but she was also looking forward to whatever plans Tamika had up her sleeves. Whenever Carla and Tamika got together, they were bound to have a good time.

Tamika Johnson and Carla Milford have been best friends since childhood. They were both from well off families and grew up in the same neighborhood. They attended the same schools; even college. Although their personalities were complete opposites, they were always able to maintain a stable friendship. They were always there for each other through thick and thin. When Carla's father passed away four years ago, Tamika was the person she cried to and confided in. From heart breaks to drama filled relationships, Tamika always had Carla's back. Their bond and love filled friendship was one thing they had in common and it kept them together. Simply put, Tamika was her ace boon coon and vice versa. Nothing and no one came between them.

Carla stepped out of the glass encased shower and onto her red and black oriental rug. She stood in front of the floor length mirror that hung behind the door and admired her curves. Her skin was drenched with water and she scrutinized every aspect of her caramel complexion, almond shaped, hazel eyes, and light brown hair. Carla appreciated every detail of her five-feet five inches frame and all one hundred and forty-five pounds. Her D cup breasts were full, perky and hardly required a bra for support. She was blessed with a twenty-six inch waistline, plump round ass, and dimples that would make any man wanna get lost in them. Her former love interest and high school sweetheart, whom she now refers to as "what's-his-name", always told her that her facial features were a mixture between Nia Long and Sanaa Lathan. She often wondered why their ten year relationship went sour, but the thought of him and the pain he'd cause; made her hardly want to make mention of him. She just wanted him and their past to remain a simple pigment of her imagination. Purchasing the condo and moving away after their break-up, was the start of her journey to a new life and finding love again.

There was a thumping sound that broke her concentration. She quickly snapped out of her deep, self admiration and ran into her master bedroom. "Shit." She looked at the time. "Tamika will be here any minute." She panicked and hurried to her walk-in closet which was filled with all the latest fashion designs. Carla scanned the huge space and grabbed a yellow tube dress with gold trimming from the hanger. Getting dressed in front of the mirror, Carla seductively pulled her thongs up over her thighs and gently positioned the string between her agile, apple bottom butt cheeks. Her body was banging and she almost "touched herself". *Damn! I'm turning myself on;* she thought and continued to watch her own movements in the mirror. Her hands were itching to grab her battery operated rabbit from her hiding spot to have a five minute quickie of self satisfaction, but she quickly dismissed the idea and started to lather her silky skin with amber rose scented, Victoria's secret lotion.

After slipping into her yellow tube dress, Carla gave herself two thumbs. She did a model spin to check her image one last time and her ensemble the stamp of approval. She then hurried to apply her makeup. The gold MAC eyeliner showed up her eyes and the neutral color lip gloss made her lips look juicy enough to make a man want to suck on them like they were popsicles. She'd bought the set last weekend from Saks Fifth Avenue and she had to admit that it was money well spent. Carla brushed a honey colored bronzer over her flawless skin to add glow to her already fabulous face. The girl had skills when it came to fashion and makeup. Well let's just say she was always on point with fashion, but recently mastered the art of makeup. Her image meant a lot to her. She went to the extreme of enrolling in a Mary Kay makeup application course so that the she could learn how to apply her makeup the professional way. Carla had to give herself credit, because she'd come a long way. Last year this time, she was paying a makeup artist to do the job for her. She could remember the first time she called herself trying to apply makeup and ended up looking like Bozo the clown. Carla brushed her shoulder length hair up in a ponytail and placed her Gucci shades on top of her head.

BANG…BANG….

"HERE I COME," Carla yelled from inside her bathroom. She grabbed her brown signature leather bag, slid on her gold wedges and headed towards the door. When she slowly opened the door, loud screams greeted her.

"AAAHHH!!!!" Tamika screamed to the top of her lungs and filled the empty hallway with her vocals. She longed to see her best friend. Two weeks seemed like a long time to be away from each other. They embraced in a tight squeezed hug, looked each other over to check out their fabulous gears, and then they walked towards the elevator.

"That yellow looks good on you", Tamika complimented while they waited for the elevator.

"And you look very diva-ish," Carla said in return. Tamika wore a blue and white, butterfly print spaghetti strapped chiffon dress that flowed to her ankles with a pair of white flats, and a hobo settled over her shoulder. Every strand of her hair was neatly in place as usual and her skin glowed like the early rising sun. She was the sophisticated resemblance of Lalah Hathaway minus the dreads and with the exception that Tamika could not hold a tune to save her life. Fact was she had it going on and some. Simply put, Tamika was a beautiful full- figured woman.

On the ride down to the lobby, Carla decided to tell Tamika about the phone call she received from Antoine last night. Tamika burst out with laughter when Carla told her how she hung up on him.

"That fool knew he was wrong for what he did, you should've told him to drop dead and go to hell," Tamika said before they laughed in unison.

The elevator doors opened when it reached the lobby and Tamika flipped her wrist up and glanced at her diamond crusted watch. The blinged out accessory looked good on her. "It's only 11:30, so we still have time to catch the breakfast menu," she said while walking out of the building. Carla waved to her door man and they proceeded to the parking lot. As they approached the car, Tamika unlocked the doors with her key less remote. "I'll drive, because I'm treating you today," Tamika added. They climbed into her 2008 black BMW 750Li and when she turned the key into the ignition, Chrisette Michelle's "Epiphany" CD blazed through the speakers.

"That's my jam," Carla yelled over the music and they drove off enjoying the cool air that pumped from the A/C vents.

Pulling up to the Chicken&Waffles restaurant, they could smell the aroma of the food from outside the building.

"This must be a very special occasion," Carla stated.

They promised only to dine at the Waffle joint with each other whenever they had something special to celebrate. There was only one reason for this rule: the food was the bomb! They tried not to eat there too often or else they would grow tired of it fast. The place was packed as usual, but Tamika had already called ahead of time to make reservations. She found out the hard way when they tried to dine there for her birthday four months ago. They showed up expecting to have dinner and celebrate, only to find out that the place was filled to capacity. They were extremely disappointed and ended up eating out at TGI Fridays. She refused to have that happen to her a second time, so she got smart this time around and called in advance.

Tamika gave her name at the front desk, and the woman led them to a reserved table for two. They took their seats across from each other and Carla wanted to know what was going on.

"So, what is this..."

"Good morning," a voice interrupted. "My name is Tony and I am going to be your server today. May I start you both off with something to drink?"

Damn! This brotha is fione! Carla lusted and licked her lips. *I can drink him any day!*

Tony resembled the movie actor, Djimon Hounsou, from that movie, *Black Diamonds.* He made a fashion statement with his salt and pepper goatee and he stood about 6'1, but was built like a NFL player. He had wide shoulders, muscular arms and an ass that a woman couldn't help but to imagine wrapping her legs around. His pearly whites glistened and were straightly lined. Carla swore that she could see her reflection in them. Tony had what one would call a "million dollar smile". He was dark chocolate just like she liked her men and there was nothing sexier than a chocolate colored brotha wit a sexy ass smile. She was beginning to realize why white women mostly dated dark skinned brothers, like Heidi Klum and Seal for example. *Guess it's true what they say, "The blacker the berry, the sweeter the juice,"* she thought and yearned to take his full lips into her mouth. She was so busy fantasizing, that she almost forgot where she was.

"And what may I get for you ma'am?" Tony's voice caught her off guard.

"I'm...I'm sorry. I'll have a glass of pink lemonade please." Carla stammered and felt flushed. She prayed that he didn't catch her sweating him, but it was too late because Tony was already checking her out from his peripheral. He thought she was very attractive.

"Ladies, I shall return with your drink orders shortly," he promised and walked off.

"What was that all about?" Tamika inquired.

"What do you mean?" Carla played dumb.

"I saw you checking that man out! He is attractive."

"Guurrl…ain't he fine? He can be my boy toy any day. This Kat needs a serious tune up and he looks fit for the job!" Carla pretended to have a hot flash and fanned herself.

"Ewww…That's more than I needed to know." Tamika shooted up her lips at Carla.

"Whatever, but anyway, why did you drag me out of my house this morning and bring me up in here? What's the occasion?" Carla asked.

"When you and the waiter dude hit it off with each other, you're going to be thankful that I dragged you here" Tamika joked and they exchanged laughter. "But for real, I took us here for a reason and you…."

"Here are your drinks ladies. This first round is on the house. Compliments of me," Tony told them and winked at Carla.

Carla almost creamed in her panties. Even the sound of his voice was beginning to turn her on. *It's a shame for a man to be that fucking fione and it's not illegal!*

"Are you ready to order?" He asked them.

"Yes." They answered at the same time then laughed.

"I can tell that you two are probably either best friends or sisters," he guessed, but truth is, he wanted to strike a conversation with Carla. The line he used was corny, but most women always fell for the corny ones.

"How could you tell?" Carla asked.

"The way you both answered at the same time," Tony responded. He knew that wasn't the best answer, but it was the first thing that came to mind.

"We *are* best friends. Always have been since childhood," Tamika interjected and stated proudly before looking down at her menu.

"That must be something special to have such a long friendship," Tony added. "So, what can I get you ladies to eat?" he asked.

"I'll have the number five: four wings and three stacked waffles," Tamika placed her order.

Tony turned to face Carla. "What are you having?"

Carla pretended to stare at the menu a little while longer. *I'll have you if you let me,* she wished. "Actually, I would like to have the number eight: six wings, four stacked waffles and cheese grits."

"I like a woman with a healthy appetite." Tony smiled and walked away. He was flirting with her.

Carla smirked, not wanting him to see her blush. She liked it when Tony smiled at her.

"Before we get interrupted again, can you hurry and tell me your reason?" she nagged Tamika.

"Let me just come out with it, I'M ENGAGED!!" Tamika squealed.

"OH MY GOSH!!" Carla screamed in astonishment. Her loud outburst caused others to stare in their direction. Carla felt slightly embarrassed and lowered her voice. "Are you serious!?"

"Serious as a heart attack."

"I am so happy for you." Carla stood up from her chair and walked to the other side of the table to hug her best friend.

Tears stung Tamika's eyes. Ever since the fifth grade, they always dreamed and spoke of the day when they would get married and have children of their own. Seeing that "THE" day is now here for Tamika, Carla kept hope alive that her day would soon come.

"Marcus and I are going to pick out my ring next week. It was the most romantic proposal," she explained. "He waited until I came home from work last night. Red and white rose petals met me at the front door and guided me to the bathroom which was lit with vanilla scented candles," she bragged and continued to paint the scene for Carla. "The Jacuzzi tub was filled with warm bubble water with a few rose petals afloat. He treated me to a relaxing sponge bath followed by a full body massage. He then dried me off, picked me up and laid me gently on the bed. He had me for dinner and dessert. After we tired ourselves out, he held me in his arms, looked me in my eyes, and asked me to marry him." Tamika couldn't help but blush after she recapped her passionate moment with Marcus.

"Sounds like Marcus is the real deal," Carla said with a pinch of jealousy. She was indeed happy for Tamika, but also wished she had a man of her own. Carla has dated her share of guys, but it was just her luck that none of them turned out to be the man she dreamed about. All she ever wanted was a man who was attractive, kept a steady job, treat her right and good credit was a must. Oh and not to forget, one who knows how to fuck her brains out. Was she asking for too much?

Marcus and Tamika have been dating for two years now. They met at a business training that she attended two years ago to represent the marketing company she works for. Marcus was her training instructor and the whole time he taught the class, he couldn't take his eyes off of her. In his eyes, Tamika was the most beautiful woman he had ever seen. Tamika was not as petite as Carla, but she knew how to hold her own. She was more on the tall side, standing five feet nine inches at one hundred sixty-five pounds, with ambiguous curves that were more to love. Her bluntly cut bob crowned her face and displayed her eccentric cheek bones. On that particular day, Tamika's mocha complexion made her skin look cool like early winter breeze. Once he concluded the training session, Marcus built up confidence to approach her. He'd spotted her walking to the parking garage and ran to catch up with her. He formally introduced himself and his thick eye brows had her hooked. Tamika was always a sucker for men with thick eye brows, whatever that was about. To make a long story short, numbers were exchanged and now here they were, engaged to be married two years later.

Tony returned with their breakfast which they might as well call brunch, because it was well going on 1:00 p.m.

"How does everything taste?" Tony checked in on the girls.

"It's finger licking good," Carla answered and seductively licked all ten of her fingers to demonstrate.

Tony was already intrigued by her. And she knew it. "Will this be together or separate?" he asked regarding method of payment for their food.

"It's all on one check," Tamika spoke up.

Tony returned with the tab and Carla slipped him her number on a piece of napkin. He thought that was a pretty bold move of her, but he liked a woman who knew what she wanted and wasn't afraid to go after it. Tony took the signature napkin and slipped it in his pocket.

"I want to thank you ladies for coming. Take care and hope you come again," he told them, and then went off to serve another table.

I need you to make me cum alright. Carla could not stop having sexual related thoughts about Tony. He was the black stallion that she hoped to ride.

Tamika laid the money on the table and they left the restaurant with their stomachs full.

They sat in the car and pondered their next destination. Tamika reached for her CD case in the backseat and search for Mary J Blige's 'Stronger' album. After retrieving the silver disc, she popped it in the deck.

"You feel like getting a pedicure?" she asked Carla. "It's such a beautiful day and I want us to catch up and make the best of it."

"That sounds good! My feet could sure go for a pedicure right now. Put this bat mobile in drive and let's go!" Carla goofed.

With sheer confirmation, Tamika turned up the volume and slammed the gas pedal to the floor while Carla reclined her chair and crammed her mind with nasty thoughts about Tony. She anticipated the sexual fun she hoped to have with him. Sure, Tony was *fine* and all, but she wouldn't dare get serious with a man who worked as a waiter. How ridiculous would that be? At this point, he was only good enough for her to fuck his brains out, have him do the same and send his ass home. They drove out of the parking lot with the sounds of Mary J. bumping in the background and proceeded to join the heavy traffic on the busy Peach Tree Rd. in downtown Atlanta.

USA Nails was the spot to be. Those Asian Natives knew how make your damn feet have an orgasm. Their prices were a little steep, but Carla and Tamika didn't mind paying because it was worth every penny. The place was normally crowded on Saturdays, but to their surprise, it was abnormally quiet when they arrived. This was a good sign for them because it meant that they would be in and out of there before they could blink their eyes. The usual wait time on any given Saturday was two hours, so today they were feeling lucky. They walked in and the smell of nail polish and acrylic assaulted their nose. They requested the TITANIUM special, which includes a full leg scrub, exfoliation, hot towel wrap, foot massage, new

Love Finally

titanium polish look that all the celebrities were wearing, with a relaxing glass of wine as added bonus. They even crack your Damn toes and that shit felt soooo good. They sat in the massage chair and the technicians went to work on their feet. Tamika's cell phone rang, playing the ring tone, "TRUST" by Keyshia Cole.

"Hello." She answered on the first ring. "Okay babe..... I guess I'll see you in a few..."

Carla looked over at Tamika with disappointment. She knew that it had to be Marcus who called and she was not ready for their girls' day out to be over.

"That was Marcus," Tamika said to confirm what Carla was thinking. "He wants me to meet up with him at his brother's house in an hour, but he didn't say what for."

"So that means our day together is over?" Carla pouted.

"Carla, I'm sorry. I promise to make it up to you. This was so unexpected," Tamika expressed.

"It's okay... I understand. I just hoped that we could've hung out a little longer," Carla told her. They each slipped their technician a ten dollar tip after paying for the service, and then sat under the ultra violet lights to allow their polished toes to dry.

On the ride to Carla's condo, she hated that she had to go home without the presence of a male's biceps and triceps to console her. Carla wished there was a man to call her own at home waiting for her. She was happy for Tamika, no doubt, but now that Tamika and Marcus were engaged, it meant that they wouldn't be in each other's company as much anymore. When they pulled up in front of Carla's building, both ladies said their good-byes and she watched as Tamika drove off to go meet up with Marcus.

Carla took the elevator to the tenth floor and entered her condo. Feeling lonely, she decided to take a hot bath before her nap. Carla glanced at the clock that read 4:00 p.m. It was still early, but there was not a whole lot to do around the house. She lived alone, but hardly spent any time there so how much of a mess could she make? Cleaning was done on a bi-weekly basis and after scanning how spotless everything was, Carla ran her bath water and poured in honey suckle bath oil. She undressed and stepped into her Jacuzzi tub one foot at a time. She eased her body under the water and the warmth felt good against her skin. Carla tried to relax, but the mood was not to her liking. She stepped out of the tub and walked her wet body into the living room. She then inserted a Luther Vandross CD in the stereo system, lit the apple cinnamon candles in her bedroom, and poured a glass of merlot from the bottle she stored in the wine rack. "*Ah*". She took a sip and savored the refreshing taste.

Upon returning to the bathroom with the wine glass in hand, she tested the water with her right big toe (making sure the water did not get cold). Carla re-entered the tub and exhaled as she relaxed to Luther in the background. With her eyes closed, Carla retreated to fantasize about Tony. She imagined straddling across his strong, muscular thighs, engaging in wet, heated kisses and sucking the sweet nectar from his tongue. A ringing sound startled her and interrupted her fantasy. She quickly opened her eyes and realized that her mind was playing tricks on her. She had wishful thinking that Tony would call.

The water was getting cold, so Carla stepped out of the tub, reached in to pull the lever up and drained her bath water. She grabbed the plush bath towel that hung behind the bathroom door, wrapped her shivering body, and then walked into her bedroom. Carla walked over to the dresser and pulled out the sexiest pair of lingerie that she owned. The black and red laced ones she'd bought last year on Valentine's Day. She slipped into the lace garment and found pleasure in the sex appeal it gave. *It's ok to go to bed sexy without a man lying next to me,* she thought. She grabbed the baby oil from her dresser and gently oiled her skin, loving the way it made her skin feel and smell. She simultaneously inhaled the fresh scent and closed her eyes, followed by a short exhale. She so longed for a man's touch.

Chapter 2

The telephone startled her awake. *"Why must people insist on calling me when I'm asleep?"* she grumbled, with her eyes still closed. Carla removed the cover from her face, rubbed her small fist in her eyes, and removed the handset from the cradle. She glanced at the caller ID this time and saw her mother's home number flashing across the screen.

"Hello," she answered in a sleepy voice.

"Rise and shine my darling," her mother, Ellen, said cheerfully.

"Good morning mother."

"Are you going to make it to church this morning? You know, the reverend is having a singles seminar today." Her mother added.

Knowing where the conversation was headed, Carla thought back on what her mother said to her just three weeks ago: "When are you going to get married and give me some grandbabies?" Ellen had asked her.

Carla was an only child born to Ellen and Carl Milford. Ellen worked as a surgeon, but retired when Carl passed away. Before Carl passed on, he was a magistrate judge for thirty years. What a coincidence that Carla ended up becoming a lawyer, the apple didn't fall too far from the tree. When her husband passed away just four years ago of a sudden heart attack, Ellen took it hard. She fell into a deep state of depression and when she did finally recover, (after a few counseling sessions) Ellen has been pressuring Carla to get married and start a family.

"I'm still a little tired mom. I doubt I'll be making it to church today, but I'll definitely make it to bible study on Wednesday. May I call you back when I'm officially awake?"

"Okay dear, get some rest and we'll talk later." Ellen was well aware that her daughter was obviously trying to avoid the conversation.

I don't see what the rush is, I'm only twenty-eight and there's plenty of time to have kids and get married. My mother needs to back off a bit. She rolled over and tried to fall back asleep, but it was useless. Carla mounted out of bed and walked into the bathroom to freshen up. She gazed at herself in the mirror that stood over the sink. She stroked her cheeks with the back of her hand. Sure she looked refined now, but it occurred to her that she wouldn't remain twenty-eight forever. Carla knew that her mother was right, but the thought of heartbreak and settling with the wrong guy was something she would have to say "no deal" to. She let off a sigh and threw on a navy blue silk robe and strolled into the kitchen to brew some coffee.

She opened the double French doors that led outside onto the back terrace and was pleased to see that it was another beautiful, sunny day. As she stood on the terrace, she allowed the sun to beat on her face and inhaled the fresh air. "Nothing beats the smell of nature," she spoke into the air. With her arms folded under her breasts, Carla walked back inside and decided that she would stay indoors to relax and rest up for the next work day. Her mind was made up about not going to church, so the next best thing was to watch it on TV.

Walking into the living room, Carla snuggled onto her white sofa with the remote in her left hand and the cup of coffee in her right. She flipped through the hundreds of channels that her satellite dish provided, and hoped there would be a service on that was worth watching. When she stopped on the WORD channel, there a minister preached about spending quality time with God. "You have to seek the kingdom of God first and all things will be added after," he shouted into the microphone and paced back and forth on the pulpit. "Life is short," the minister continued to preach. "And we must learn to love thy neighbor as thy self." The sermon was already thirty minutes in, but the words he spoke captivated her.

When the television service ended, Carla slid off the sofa and walked back out onto the terrace, where she sat down to enjoy the view of the golf course and the lake that was stationed behind her building. She reflected on the preacher's words form the television and began to think about her own life and her future. In two years she would be the big '30' and Carla wondered how long it would really be before she does actually find a man whom she could become serious with. The clock on her eggs was running out and the thought just became overwhelming.

She returned inside and ordered Chinese food. "Ummm...yes, I would like to place an order for delivery. I'll have a pint of shrimp lo mein with two spring egg rolls and a quart of sweet and sour chicken. How long before it's delivered? Thirty minutes is perfect." She ran to take a quick shower and then searched for a movie to order from pay per view while she waited on her food. *Not easily broken*, starring her long time crush, Morris Chestnut, was on the playlist. Carla quickly selected it and was in luck because it just started.

KNOCK.....KNOCK.....

With a silk scarf tied around her mane and wearing yellow cotton pants (with the word 'PINK' written across her ass), with a white tank top, Carla ran to the door. "Hi," she greeted the delivery guy.

"You order shrimp lo mein, spring egg roll and sweet sour chi'ken?" He repeated her order with his Chinese accent.

"Yes."

"You pay $15.95," he told her after handing her the bag and held his hand out for the cash.

Carla handed him a twenty and told him to keep the change. The guy thanked her and left. She closed the door and ran to her living room to get comfortable so that she could take pleasure in watching the movie and eating her food. Tonight would be her dinner and a movie night to enjoy her solitude.

The movie finally ended and fatigue was weighing in on her. Carla was stuffed from the Chinese food. *Damn, niggeritis is kicking in,* she thought and yawned. After watching the movie, it only made her desire having a man in her life even more so than before. She envied the love that Dave, (played by Morris Chestnut), and Clarice, (played by Taraji Henson), had for each other. Yes they fought like hell, but it was the love that they developed in the end that Carla hoped for in her own life. She often dreamed about finding a love of her own, but she wanted a man that would love her genuinely and support her no matter what. *If only men like that really exist,* she mused. In Atlanta, the market for men has become pitiful. It seemed like all the good ones were either locked up, married, dead, or.... yes, you guessed it, GAY! You never knew who was who these days and Carla would be damned if she risked messing around with some brotha that was probably married and on the 'DL', living a double life. In the city of Atlanta, the odds were pretty high. To save herself the humiliation, she stuck to the old saying, "patience is a virtue," but how much patience should one have? Her pussy was longing to be filled with a good piece of dick and she had her hopes on Tony being the one to fill her up. Carla jumped in her queen sized sleigh bed and pulled up the covers.

Her Jennifer Hudson ringtone alarmed her just when she was about to get comfortable. Carla became baffled. It was going on midnight and any phone calls at this hour could only mean one of two things. (A) Ellen had trouble falling asleep or (B) someone was seeking a late night booty call. She picked up her new BlackBerry storm, touch screen phone and saw an unfamiliar number. Hesitant, she pressed the talk button.

"Hello."

"Good evening, May I speak with Carla?" The smooth male voice asked.

She recognized the voice instantly and a huge KOOL-AID smile came across her face. If she smiled any harder, her cheeks

Love Finally

would touch her ears. *I can't believe he actually called... and he has phone etiquette. Let the games begin.* Carla intended to make Tony her fuck buddy. Nothing more, nothing less. No strings attached. She would welcome him into her world to enjoy the sweetness of her cum lacking punany, and then send him about his business. It may sound sleazy, but a girl has to do what a girl has to do in order to get what she wanted and what she craved at the moment was a huge dick to satisfy all her sexual needs. Getting serious with anyone below her rank was a huge NO-NO in her book.

"Yes, this is she. I think evening has passed because it looks like nighttime outside to me," she joked.

Tony chuckled. "There's nothing like a beautiful woman with a sense of humor. So I take it you know to whom you are speaking?"

"How could I not? That voice is one of a kind." She answered in a sultry tone.

"Oh really? That's the first any woman has ever told me that."

"You can't be serious?! Maybe those women you talk to can't hear very well."

"That could very well be possible, or is it that you hear something they don't?"

"So, Tony, tell me a little about yourself." Carla wanted to get right to it. If she planned on sexing the brotha, a little background check is essential. She didn't want a stalker on her hands. Her pussy had power, at least that's what she's been told, and she couldn't risk giving him a taste of her love, only to find out that he would become hooked and then become psychotic. That was not a risk she was willing to gamble, so she needed to screen him. Her last fuck told her that she needed to hang a sign that read: *ENTER WITH CAUTION! PUSSY POWER IN ACTION!* She smiled at the thought and knew that her wet, tight dick hugger was the shiznick.

"Where do I start? Let's see, I'm an only child. My mother passed away seven years ago and my father went behind her two years later. I have no children. I'm single, so you don't have to worry about baby mama drama. I spend most of my time working at the restaurant. I love sports. Ummm...I enjoy traveling. I'm a real laid back kind of guy. I like to be spontaneous...not big on making plans. Half of the time, plans don't pan out the way we expect them to. My life unfolds as I go. I'm an open book. You care to tell me about yourself?"

"Wow! First, I want to say sorry about your parents." Carla expressed her condolence.

"Thanks...I appreciate that."

She cleared her throat. "Well, I too am an only child. My father also passed away... four years ago. I'm single, no kids. To think of it, I don't get out much. I mean, my life is pretty simple."

"Looks like we have a few things in common. I would never imagine that we've encountered similar experiences...you know, losing a parent and all. In this life you never know who you're likely to meet..."

"Such a small world. We can be so different, but yet so similar." She countered. There was brief silence.

"So, you never mentioned what you do for a living," Tony mentioned and broke the silence.

"Well, if you must know, I am an attorney at Simon & Hurst law firm in downtown Atlanta." Carla knew that men were usually intimidated by a successful woman. She did not want to judge Tony and place him that same category. By all means, she barely knew the guy, but she hoped her profession would not be an issue. Carla graduated from Georgia State University Law School two years ago and landed her first job as an associate attorney at Simon & Hurst law firm, one of the top law firms in Atlanta. Her father never got the chance to see his baby girl walk across the stage, but nevertheless; Carla knew that if he were alive, he would've been proud of her accomplishments.

"'If I must know? Whoa...a little feisty aren't we? That's pretty impressive, a lawyer huh? So what's that like?" Tony asked.

"Just like any other job, there's the good, bad, and ugly. It can be stressful at times but also rewarding. Anyway, enough about me. So why is a handsome brotha like yourself single?"

"So you like to get straight to the point huh?"

"Why not? Sometimes foreplay gets in the way. Rather get it over and done with." She seductively responded.

Her every word kept Tony more intrigued. "That's cute. I like that. Why am I single you asked? I'm gonna simply put it like this, I have yet to find a woman to love me unconditionally, one who is attracted to the man on the inside and not looking for an arm trophy. You're an attractive woman...I could ask you the same thing."

"Let's just say I chose to be single," she lied. Truth was, she hasn't had any luck finding love. "I have come to the conclusion that there is no need to force love. If the right one comes along, the chemistry and energy between the two will be inevitable." *How the hell did we end up talking about love? I am by no means looking for love with his ass. All I want is some dick right about now,* she mused.

"Wow, didn't realize that it had gotten this late." Tony's voice echoed through the phone. "I know you probably have an early start tomorrow and I apologize for keeping you up this late. That's probably not a good first impression. Perhaps the conversation had me carried away."

"You have absolutely nothing to apologize for. I enjoyed our conversation. But like you said, it is late and I do need to get some rest. Maybe we can do this again sometime? Take care and have a good night." Carla pressed the end button and plugged her cell phone up to charge.

Carla jumped up when her alarm clock sounded and quickly hit the snooze button to quiet the loud beeps. "Damn, is it time to wake up already?" She opened her eyes and yawned and stretched her arms, wishing she could go back to sleep for a few more hours. Forcing herself out of bed, she walked towards the bathroom and looked at herself in the mirror, dreading that she stayed up so late.

Traffic was always ridiculous on highway 20, but it was two times worst on a Monday morning. It's normally a thirty minute drive each way, from her condo to the office; but for some weird reason, on Monday mornings, the drive would take her an hour to get there. Carla showered quickly and rushed to get dressed. She hurried to the closet and pulled her black knee length, ruffled neck line dress over her head and slipped her feet into a pair of black, five inch leather pumps. She untied her silk scarf, combed her wrapped hair down and did a complete makeup application. She then grabbed her black bag that hung on her closet door handle and dashed towards the front door.

Once it reached the ground floor, the elevator doors opened up and Carla sped up her pace in search of her vehicle. When she located it, she unlocked the doors and climbed into her 2009 metallic grey, Range Rover Sport SUV and drove off in the direction of the rising sun with voice of John Legend booming from her stereo.

"Good morning," she spoke as she entered through the revolving glass doors.

"Hi, Carla, I placed some messages on your desk." Sarah, the receptionist informed her. Sarah, a slim Caucasian with brown hair and thin reading glasses stationed on the bridge of her nose, was dressed in a satin white buttoned shirt and a polyester black skirt. She has been with the firm for five years and became Carla's personal receptionist once she was brought on board two years ago.

"Messages already?" Carla looked at the time. It was only 8:15 a.m.

"No, they were from Friday evening after you left."

"Oh...okay. Thanks." Carla proceeded towards her office while Sarah watched; admiring her curves with each step she took.

Carla walked into her office and placed her bag on top of her polished oak wood desk. She sat down in her burgundy leather rolling chair and pulled herself forward. The first thing she did was read the hand written messages that Sarah left on her desk and they were all irrelevant, so she crumpled the small rectangular leaflets and tossed them in the trash. Carla then pulled out her appointment book from her desk drawer and retrieved the files for each client from the file cabinet. She planned on leaving the office early to go home and catch up on her sleep.

"Carla, Mr. Stevenson would like to speak with you on line one." Sarah buzzed through the intercom.

"Put him through, I'm expecting his call."

Mr. Stevenson, one of Carla's clients, was facing a misdemeanor DUI charge that could potentially land him six months in jail. "Mr. Stevenson, how are you? You're right on time for our phone appointment. Everything is looking good. I spoke with the judge on your behalf and he's willing to place you on six months probation to replace any jail time." Carla looked over his file and continued to explain to Mr. Stevenson what he needed to do in order to complete the Judge's requirements. Their conversation lasted for another twenty minutes before she hung up her line.

Her last appointment was scheduled for 3:30 p.m., so Carla took the time to catch up on some paper work before taking her lunch break. She planned to stop by Neiman Marcus to purchase a pair of Michael Kors pumps that she'd been eyeing for the past week.

"Carla, you have a delivery up here at the front desk." Sarah informed her through the intercom.

"Delivery?! Are you sure that it's for me?"

"Positive. The delivery guy asked specifically for you."

A puzzled look swept across her face. "Okay, I'll be right up." *A delivery? I wonder what it is and who it's from.* She walked up to Sarah's desk and saw a huge vase with what looked like two dozen pink and white roses.

"Is that my delivery?" She asked and pointed to the vase as her eyebrows came together.

Sarah eyed the beautifully mixed arrangement. "Yes. So, who's the lucky guy?" Sarah asked nosily.

Carla shot her a look like "why are you in my damn business?", but politely responded, "Your guess is as good as mine. Did the delivery guy say where they were from?"

"No, but it looks like someone thinks you're special. They're really beautiful." Sarah commented.

"Thanks." Carla picked up the vase and returned to her office. She sat the vase on her desk and inhaled their fresh scent. The roses smelled like they were recently cut from a rose bush garden. She continued to wonder who sent them. This was the first time anyone delivered anything to her place of employment. She spun the vase around and noticed a card clipped to the mouth. She removed the card and sat on the edge of her desk and read:

I really enjoyed our conversation last night. I felt so bad about keeping you up late. Here's a token of my deepest apology. You seem like a person I would like to get to know more about. What do you say about me taking you to dinner sometime? 404-762-8111 Call me. I hope you enjoy the roses....Yours Truly, Tony Simmons.

Carla was touched. Butterflies filled her stomach. Never in a million years would she expect for Tony to send her roses. They'd just met and they haven't even been on their first date. He was wearing her down and she knew it. *I still don't see myself getting serious with him. My mother would have a heart attack if I told her I was dating a waiter. The roses are a nice gesture, but I'm sticking to the idea of only being fuck buddies. The moment he decides to think he wants to be serious, I am kicking his ass to the curb then I'm ghost*

Love Finally

.*How did he know my work address anyway? He probably googled it after I told him the name of the company. It's amazing what a person can do on the internet these days.* Carla closed the card and re-clipped it to the mouth of the vase. Tony was making a good impression on her, but she was in denial about wanting to find love with him. After being hurt time after time, Carla found it hard to open up her heart to any man and became fearful when she felt herself falling in love. She figured it would be best to not get attached and that way it will be easier to walk away.

Peering up at the clock that hung above her office door, Carla realized that it was time for lunch. She stood up from her desk and grabbed her hand bag.

"I'll be an hour longer for lunch," she yelled over her shoulder to Sarah as she headed out the revolving doors.

"Okay…I'll hold your calls," Sarah yelled back, her eyes glued to Carla's backside.

Carla hopped into her SUV and decided she wanted something light to eat. Subway was around the corner from her office and it would give her enough time to eat, go to the mall, and be back in time for her 3:30 p.m. appointment.

"Your dress is flattering." A random guy complimented as she walked into the deli. Carla thanked him and noticed him checking her out while she joined the line. She ordered a six-inch Italian BLT on toasted monetary cheddar bread and a bottled water. She paid for her sandwich and sat in a nearby empty seat by the window.

She took a bite out of the sub and wondered if she should still go through with having sex with Tony. She feared that he would get too attached from their sexual encounter and hurting his feelings by telling him that it was only a sex thing, was the last thing she wanted to do because he seemed like a nice guy. *Wait a minute, am I out of my frigging mind? Hell yes I'm going through with it. Men these days don't care about hurting women's feelings. I'm in need of some dick and I am going to get some. Hell, who says he's not out for the same thing?* She finished her lunch and walked out of the deli.

Carla entered the mall, which seemed busy for a Monday and in the middle of the day for that matter. *Do these people have jobs?* She pondered, but wondered if they thought the same thing about her. She proceeded to Neiman Marcus and when she approached the shoe department, Carla felt like a kid in a candy store. She had a fetish for shoes that was undeniable. Carla spotted the pair she wanted after checking over other pairs and a sales clerk approached her.

"May I get that in your size?" The pale colored man asked in a rusty tone.

"Oh...yes a size eight please." She hoped they had her size because they ran a half size small.

"Here you are ma'am." The frail framed clerk handed her the shoe box. "Let me know if you desire anything else." He told her then walked off.

Carla tried the shoe and they fit her like a glove to a hand. *Perfect!*

"Does it fit okay?" The clerk asked when he walked over to check in.

"They're perfect!" She exclaimed. She placed the shoes back into the shoe box and dashed towards the cashier.

"Will this be all for you today?" The red head cashier asked and popped her gum.

"Uh. Where is your dress department?"

"Our ladies department is upstairs on the second floor." The cashier directed.

"Can I check the shoes out up there as well?"

"Sure."

Love Finally

"Okay. I think I'll take a moment to look around up there...thanks." Carla grabbed her shoe box and ran towards the escalator. She thought about taking Tony up on his dinner invitation and wanted a dress to fit the occasion. She hasn't been on a date in a while and if he was paying, then why not? Time was now against her. Carla had forty five minutes before she was due back at the office. She hurried to the dress section on the second floor, but she didn't have to search. The second she turned the corner, the perfect dress was staring her in the face. "Wow! This is beautiful." She whispered. Carla removed the dress from the rack and held it up against her like it was her newly found best friend. It was a multicolored, silk material, open back, V-cut out dress with turquoise, black and white flower print with a hint of yellow trailing the outline. The dress was a definite attention grabber. The low, open V-cut out would expose her back, leaving something for the imagination. The dress along with the shoes was a must have. Without looking at the price tag, Carla grabbed it from the rack.

"Did you find everything okay?" the elderly lady asked.

"Yes. I did."

"Your total today is $368.87," the cashier informed her after scanning the items. Carla took out her debit card and swiped it.

"Would you like your dress to remain on the hanger? It is beautiful."

"Thank you." She smiled and knew that it was indeed the perfect dress. "That would be nice if you could," Carla told her then returned the debit card into the vacant slot inside her wallet.

"Here you go young lady. Have a nice day." The elderly cashier handed her the bag with her dress and Carla hurried out of the store to meet up with her client.

"Any messages Sarah?" Carla asked as she entered the building.

"Yes, there were two messages that I forwarded to your voicemail."

With only fifteen minutes remaining before her client arrived, Carla hurried to her office to review the file. She bounced down in her rolling chair, took a sip of her bottled water and took a deep breath to regain her composure. *Shopping with limited time can be so overwhelming;* she thought and screwed the lid onto the plastic bottle. Carla removed the file labeled THOMPSON, in big bold letters, from her file cabinet and placed it on her desk. In the middle of her review, Sarah informed Carla that Mrs. Thompson had arrived.

Mrs. Thompson was a widow and now a single mother of her sixteen year old son, Oliver. Supposedly, her husband died two months ago while on top of a woman he was having an affair with. It seems that while engaging in sexual intercourse with his mistress, of twenty one years of age, the fifty two year old, Mr. Thompson, had a sudden stroke while still inside her and his heart somehow stopped beating. According to Mrs. Thompson, the doctors said that Mr. Thompson took one too many male enhancement drug. Mrs. Thompson entered the office and Carla stood up from her chair to greet her.

"Hello Mrs. Thompson. So good to see you again," She said then extended her right arm to shake hands.

"It's always good to see you," Mrs. Thompson assured her while returning the handshake.

"Have a seat if you will," Carla instructed.

They sat down to discuss the case involving Mrs. Thompson's sixteen year old son, Oliver, who was facing a life sentence for a first degree murder charge. Three months ago when Mrs. Thompson discovered attorney, Carla Milford, through an ad in the yellow pages, she took a great liking to Carla's welcoming smile and judging by Carla's compassion for her job, she knew that she'd picked the right lawyer for her son's case. Mrs. Thompson explained what happened on the day that Oliver Thompson was arrested: "Oliver said that he was hanging out with some friends and the leader of the crew, Max, decided to rob another young man that they knew from the neighborhood. Oliver told me that he stayed behind and waited for them. He said that he only saw when the rest of his friends came running around the corner and he followed after them. He said that Max confessed to shooting the kid after robbing him, but the police charged Oliver because he was present on the scene when the kid was shot and accused him of being an accessory."

Their meeting lasted for an hour and a half before Mrs. Thompson departed the office. Carla stayed behind to type the final notes regarding the case. She powered down her computer and looked at her watch to see that it was 6:30 p.m. She stayed longer than expected, but figured it was earlier than most nights when she would leave the office. After gathering her things, she headed towards the parking lot. Carla hopped in her Range and drove towards the highway in silence.

On the way home, Carla decided to stop at Mother's Soul Food Kitchen, to pick up dinner. It was getting late and cooking was not something she did regularly. She entered the restaurant and was greeted by a staff member, Jane. Because she frequented the restaurant, Carla was well known by the staff.

"Hey there Carla, long time no see! How's it going?" Jane asked.

"Everything is going well, Jane."

While waiting for her food, they engaged in small talk. Jane decided to broadcast that she had a hopeless love life and Carla was not in the mood to discuss such thing. She did not need someone to dump their sad story on her to convince her that finding true love was hopeless. She decided to tune Jane out and let her words go in one ear and out the other. As Jane continued to babble, Carla thought of ways to seduce Tony in her bed.

Chapter 3

Upon entering the cozy place she called home, Carla kicked off her pumps at the front door and walked into the kitchen. She then walked into her bedroom and hung her newly purchased dress in her closet and placed her new pair of shoes alongside the rest of her collection. Feeling starved, she returned to the kitchen and fixed her plate. Carla plopped down onto her red, suede dining chair and dug into the macaroni casserole, fried chicken, and potato skins that was placed in front of her. In the middle of her meal, her house phone rang.

"Hello." She answered with a mouth full of food.

"Hey boo! How was your day at the office?" Tamika asked loudly.

Carla quickly swallowed. "Long and tiring, but somewhat enjoyable," she answered. "How about you? How was your day?"

"I didn't go in today. Marcus did me in for the kill last night, so I had to call in sick! A sistuh gotta recuperate, if you know what I mean," Tamika explained with laughter.

"Dang! Sounds like you guys put it down!" Carla teased.

"He put it down, in, up, around." Tamika laughed. "Guurrl, that brotha knows how to maneuver his joystick in all the right places! You don't want to know the half."

"Spare me the details." They shared a hearty laugh and Carla began to imagine what it would be like to make love with Tony.

"So what's up with you and dude from the Waffle House? Did he call you yet?" Tamika inquired.

"You mean Tony?" Carla made sure Tamika knew his name.

Love Finally

"E-X-C-U-S-E ME!" Tamika said jokingly. "So, did *TONY* call you?" She emphasized.

"He sure did." Carla blushed. The sound of his name was beginning to fill her stomach with butterflies.

"OOOHHH! Now you know you have to spill the details!"

"I swear, you are a mess. Anyway, we only talked about our backgrounds and stuff. You know, trying to feel each other out. Nothing out of the norm for a first time conversation."

"So boring!!! Does he have any kids? Is he single? I need to make sure the brotha ain't bringing no baby mama drama into my best friend's life."

Carla laughed at Tamika. "The answer is HELL NO! AND HELL YES! You act like you're screening him for a day time position."

"You have to know these things up front. Nuccas these days think they can take us females for a joy ride on their emotional rollercoaster. I have seen you get hurt too many times and I refuse to let him make a fool out of you. Not that I'm trying to get up in his business, but I'm just looking out for my girl," Tamika told her. "So you still plan on giving it up to him?"

"Hell yeah! If I wait any longer, it will be a brush fire waiting to happen in my dry wilderness."

"Tony has no idea what he's up against with your sexually repressed ass, huh?" Tamika joked. "So when are you two going to hook up?"

"Maybe this weekend. He invited me for dinner."

"Sounds like he's interested."

"Yeah and he even sent me roses today."

"Did he really? He sounds like a potential winner. I don't even know him, but I think I like him already."

"We'll see."

"Don't hurt him too much." Tamika laughed. "Hey, let's do lunch on Wednesday. Tomorrow is going to be hectic, now that I have to play catch up," Tamika suggested.

"Sounds good," Carla confirmed and ended their call. She decided to take a quick shower to relax. As she stepped out of the glass enclosure, Carla heard her Jennifer Hudson ringtone singing, "If this isn't love..." She ran out of the bathroom to answer her cell phone. The short run caused her to breathe heavily. She made a mental note to see her trainer and visit the gym ASAP!

"Hello," she answered still trying to catch her breath.

"You sound busy," Tony remarked.

"No, I was in the shower and I ran to answer the phone."

"I see. So, how was your day?" Tony asked.

"It got better once I received your roses. They were beautiful. I must say thank you."

"Don't mention it. It was the least I could do after keeping you up so late."

"You didn't have to go through the trouble..."

"Trust me, if I thought that it was trouble, I wouldn't have bothered. But you deserved them. I imagine you eventually made it through the day anyhow."

"Yes, I had a fairly smooth day. It wasn't as tiring as I expected, but it was cool for a Monday."

"I know it's getting late, but I was wondering if you already ate dinner?" Tony asked, hoping she would say no.

"Yeah, I picked something up on my way home from work. Did you have something in mind?"

"Since you already ate, I was thinking that maybe we can talk over an ice cream cone. You think there's some room left for such?"

"Are you kidding? I love ice cream!"

"Great! How about I come to pick you up? It will give you a break from driving."

"Sounds inviting. I'm cool with that," Carla said. She was impressed by his offer. She gave him directions to her place and they agreed to meet up within the hour. Carla hurried to pick out an outfit. Anxiety struck her. She felt like a teenage girl going on a first date with her first crush. Wanting to be comfortable and not overly dressed, she decided to wear a pair of denim skinny jeans that hugged her curves, with a green and white striped tube top and a pair of white sandals. She pulled her hair up in a bun to expose her high cheek bones and long eye lashes.

There was a sudden knock at the door. "He's here!" Her voice was filled with excitement. She grabbed her matching white purse and dashed for the front door. Carla's heart beat became rapid. She placed her hand over her chest to calm it. She took a deep breath, exhaled slowly, and then opened the door. For Carla, it was as if time had stood still and a rush of feelings that she hadn't felt in years, suddenly came over her. A feeling she hadn't felt since the first time she fell in love. She tried to shake the feeling and was surprised when Tony greeted her with a big brown teddy bear and a jar filled with Hershey almond kisses.

"These are my favorite," she referred to the chocolate. "The bear is lovely. Thank you." She leaned in to give him a hug then pulled herself back to retrieve her gifts.

They stepped inside the elevator and on the ride down, Carla gave Tony a once over. His orange 'Polo' shirt and semi baggy blue jeans fit his body with perfection. His dark complexion glowed amongst the orange color. He noticed how much sexier he looked outside of his work uniform. His low hair cut and neatly trimmed goatee gave his flawless skin a youthful appearance. There were no visible bumps, which indicated that he took good care of his skin. It was either that or he just maintained a healthy diet. Whatever the case was, he was doing something right. There was no doubt that he was a handsome man. Tony's designer fragrance diffused throughout the small spaced elevator and the scent nearly sends Carla into a frenzy. It was one of those scents that made a woman's hormones run wild. Having him standing in front of her and thinking about what she wanted to do with him sexually, drenched Carla's panties with her natural juices.

    The elevator doors opened and snapped Carla back into reality. "After you." Tony motioned for her to walk in front of him as he held the elevator doors opened. They walked through the parking lot and were in search of his car. Carla tried to imagine what kind of vehicle he drove. Her imagination was short lived when he pressed the unlock button on his keyless remote and the lights flashed on his black Mercedes ML 350 4Matic SUV. He was driving the latest model and Carla's eyes widened. She wondered how a waiter could afford such a luxury vehicle based on what she assumed to be his estimated $20,000 dollar annual salary. She was impressed, but shrugged her shoulders and quickly dismissed the thought. It wasn't important. All she cared about at the moment was to ride a good piece of dick. Tony was not her man nor did she plan on him becoming her man. However he got his money was his business, as far as she was concerned. Tony opened the passenger door and waited for Carla to get in.

    "You are such a gentleman aren't you?" Carla sat her body in the soft, grey leather seat and buckled her seat belt. Tony shut the door once she was seated comfortably and then walked around to the driver's side. He hopped in the SUV and turned the key to start the engine. They listened to it purr like a kitten before Tony switched on his CD player.

    "This is one of my all time favorite!" Carla exclaimed when she heard Jaheim's "Makings of a Man" CD playing through the speakers.

    "I guess that's another thing we have in common, because this album also happens to be one of my favorite R&B albums," Tony said then looked at her and smiled. Carla blushed and looked away. His eyes were so entrancing. "You have beautiful eyes." Tony complimented.

"Thank you." She turned again to look at Tony and caught him staring at her. They made eye contact and it felt like he was looking through her soul. A burning desire came over her and her inner thigh became moist.

"Did I tell you how gorgeous you look tonight?" Tony asked and broke her daze.

"I don't recall, but thank you. You look nice as well." She said shyly. His compliment gave her tingles and made her nipples harden. They continued to drive in silence until they pulled up to the ice cream parlor.

"Welcome to Cold Stone." The melodious staff greeted them as they entered the parlor. They walked up to the encased glass that had all the various ice cream flavors stored behind it.

"What's your favorite flavor?" Tony asked as he expected her to say vanilla.

"Pistachio. What's yours?"

"Okay. That's different. Me, I'm a cookies and cream guy," he told her while making a silly face.

Carla couldn't help but to laugh. Tony had a sense of humor and he was slowly growing on her. They were served with their cones and Tony paid the cashier. They sat and talked about their lives at present and their hopes for the future. They continued to ramble and lost track of time.

"It's getting late," Tony informed her after checking the time on his phone. "I wouldn't forgive myself if I kept you up late two nights in a row."

They retreated to his truck and he drove Carla home.

On the ride home, Carla made the decision that she would make her move on Tony. They pulled up in the parking lot and she invited him upstairs. Her schedule was clear for tomorrow so it wouldn't hurt if she called out sick. She had a feeling that Tony would sex her into exhaustion anyway, so a day of rest would be just what her body needed.

"This is nice!" Tony complimented as he stepped over the threshold and entered her condo. "Did you do all of the decorations yourself or did you hire someone?" He joked.

"You are so full of humor tonight huh? I'm delighted that you take pleasure in my hard labor," she told him. "May I offer you something to drink?"

"Nah, I'm cool for now." Tony continued to admire her décor. "So, I see you have a thing for jazz?" He took notice of the pictures that hung on her wall.

"Why don't you join me on the sofa?" Carla shifted to the left and tapped a spot next to her for him to sit. They talked for a moment, but during the conversation, Carla couldn't keep her eyes off of his lips and she wanted very much to take them into her mouth. Tony was caught off guard when she pulled his face into hers and hungrily sucked on his bottom lip until it became numb. They continued to explore each other's mouth and their kiss grew into passionate, wet, deep tangling of the tongues. They darted their tongues in and out of each other's mouths before she climbed on top of him and straddled her thighs across his, just like she fantasized. Their kisses grew deeper and their tongues continued to intertwine. Carla made panting noises when she briefly came up for air. She then planted soft kisses on his forehead and worked her way down to his neck. Tony tilted his head back and melted with each peck of her lips against his skin. His manhood was fully erect. He lifted his head forward and gripped Carla firmly by her waist. She was filled with heat between her thighs. She slowly climbed off of Tony and took him by the hands to lead him to her bedroom.

When they entered her master room, Tony swept her up in his arms and gently laid her on top of the handmade quilt. Carla quickly lifted the tube top over her head, as if time were against her. She attempted to remove her jeans, but Tony stopped her before she could undo her button.

"Why don't you relax and let me do that for you?" He whispered. Tony kneeled in front of her and pulled her jeans off one leg at a time. Carla reclined on her back and took pleasure in him undressing her. Once she was totally undressed, she propped herself up on her elbows, in her nude state, and observed Tony as he took off his shirt and slid out of his pants, causing them to fall to the floor. Her body craved to feel him inside her. His sexy, dark build had her tempted to touch. Carla's eyes traveled to his erect manhood and she admired the thick nine inches of flesh that stood at attention. It stood out like a prize trophy and he was well endowed. She snickered as she anticipated the fun she would have taking all nine inches of Tony into her mouth, milking him until he was dry. Of course, she wouldn't go down on him on their first sexual encounter, but it was surely tempting. Tony leaned in towards her and she traced his muscular cuts with her index finger. Lying on her back, Tony took her feet into his hands and massaged them before rolling her onto her stomach to perform a back massage. Carla buried her face into the sheets as he kneads the tip of his fingers into her shoulder blades.

"That feels sooo good." She spoke into the sheets causing her words to sound frayed. Carla pinched herself to see if she was dreaming. It had been months since she was intimate with a man, and Tony touched her in all the right places. He released his touch from her back and gently entered her from behind. Carla's body squirmed. She felt like a virgin all over again as he plunged his erect flesh inside her. "UGH!" She cried out with each thrust that filled her vagina walls. Carla sank her nails into the sheets and a single tear fell from her eye as she enjoyed each stroke that he delivered. Tony hit her "g" spot like no man has before. The intensity of his thrusts became unbearable.

"I'm about to cum," she whispered. Tony held her tightly around the waist and she backed her ass up on him. He spread her ass cheeks and forced himself all the way inside her. She closed her eyes and the forceful thrust made her see stars, moons, and a galaxy beyond outer space. Carla felt his legs shudder, signaling an orgasm and that was her cue to release her warm juices all over him. They erupted together and the creamy juices trickled down her thighs and unto her sheets. Carla didn't mind because he had taken her to ecstasy and back, giving her climax after climax. Tony's legs fell weak, his body stiffened and he collapsed onto her back. Not totally spent, Tony slid his body off of Carla and lay next to her. With sweat dripping from their bodies and their hearts pounding from the vigorous love making they just executed, they took a moment to regain their equanimity.

Thirty minutes past and their blood levels returned to normal. She started to play with his dick and massaged his balls to get him aroused. Tony's semi-soft member rose at attention and he climbed on top of her "Are you ready for round two?"

Chapter 4

Last night felt unreal. Carla opened her eyes and saw Tony sleeping next to her. *It wasn't a dream after all,* she mused. Tony had taken her to heights she had never been before. They created sexual magic in her bedroom and she looked forward to making every night light up like the fourth of July, with his enticing dick slanging pleasures.

Careful not wake Tony, Carla snuck out of bed and removed the cordless from the cradle and walked out into the living room to call the office to notify them of her absence.

"Hi, Sarah. It's Carla. Listen, I want you to hold all of my calls today. I'm a little under the weather, so I won't be in."

"Sorry to hear that. I hope you feel better. See you tomorrow?" Sarah asked with a hint of disappointment.

"Good morning." Carla's sultry tone echoed against the four white walls as she strutted her naked body into the bedroom and saw Tony sitting at the edge of her bed. He wore nothing except a pair of cotton briefs, exposing his wide, ripped, muscular chest. He sat there looking like a Greek god and Carla couldn't get over how *foine* he was. She returned the cordless on the charger and stood in front of him with her legs spread apart and posed with her hands on her hips. Tony's eyes traced the outline of her sexy, thick, petite frame. She was surely an eye candy. Tony pulled her between his thighs and put his arms around her waist.

"Did you enjoy last night?" He asked and peered up into her hazel eyes.

Carla lowered her head and kissed him on the tip of his nose. "More than you ever know."

She sat on his left thigh and Tony cupped her breast, taking each marble shaped nipple into his mouth. The warm sensation from his tongue running back and forth against her nipple, made her pussy throb. He licked, sucked and toyed with her nipples until she begged him to stop. He released her nipples and told her to stand up. He gently pushed her, causing her to fall backwards onto the bed. Tony kneeled in front of her, held her thighs apart and licked the outline of her vagina lips. The warm sensation from his tongue sends her into a whirlwind of gratification. He sucked on her clit and glides his finger in and out of her slippery vagina, drowning in her moisture. Carla moaned and Tony noticed her arousal. He stuck his tongue deep inside her and searched her walls, eating her like she was his last meal. Carla rotated her hips on his tongue, and Tony pulled her closer to his mouth to oblige her. After giving her tongue service for what seemed like hours, Tony brought Carla to a climax that would always keep her coming back for more.

"I really enjoyed every minute with you." Tony told her while he pulled his shirt down over his head.

Lying on her side with her knees bent and the pillow between them, Carla propped herself up on her elbow and rested her head in her palm. She watched Tony dress himself and reflected on the passionate love they made the night before and the intricate tongue action she'd just received.

"So did I." She hoped to make a nightly practice out of their rendezvous. Tony put on his shoes and she got up off the bed to retrieve her terry cloth robe that hung behind the bathroom door. She walked him to the front door and he softly kissed her lips.

"I'll call you later," Tony said before he turned to walk off into the direction of the elevator.

Carla watched his every stride until he disappeared. Her sexual escapade with Tony was just what her body needed. In Carla's mind, Tony was now a life time fuck buddy until she found someone to settle down with. Things were starting to look up for Carla. She was a successful attorney, single, beautiful, childless, drama free and now she could experience great sex. She closed her front door and walked into her bedroom to change her linen. She opened the curtains and blinds to let the sunlight brighten inside her dimly lit condo. The day was too beautiful to waste and Carla was in a good mood, so she decided to go out and have breakfast. After a soothing hot shower, Carla dressed herself in a high waist denim jean shorts, a baby blue tank top and a pair of nine west sandals. She undid her bun, straightened her hair with the flat iron, and applied lip gloss to her naturally pink lips.

On her drive to IHOP, Carla cruised to the mellow sounds of Gerald Levert's album. Her thoughts drifted to Tony and his immaculate love making skills and she found herself catching feelings for her new chocolate, masculine lover. "I can't be serious," she spoke over the lyrics.

When she pulled up to the restaurant, she turned off the engine, unbuckled her seat belt and stepped out onto the pavement. Carla entered through the door and a knock off Rupaul look-alike greeted her.

"Good morning. Welcome to IHOP. How many?"

Carla flashed her a smile. "Just one."

The lean, curly blonde hair staff grabbed a menu from beneath the desk and instructed Carla to follow her.

"Come with me this way."

Carla walked behind her and the woman switched her hips so hard, it looked like her hips were going to pop out of its socket. "You can have a seat and your waiter will be with you shortly."

"Thanks."

Carla took her seat and blondie placed the menu on the table in front of her. "We have a $3.99 special today which includes any three pancakes of your choice with a glass of orange juice," the woman informed her then returned to her post to greet other customers as they entered the door.

Carla took a moment to search the room. She couldn't believe her eyes when she looked over to the opposite side of the room and spotted Antoine sitting in a booth, hugged up with a brunette, Caucasian, trailer trash. Carla shook her head at the sight. "Bastard," she mumbled beneath her breath. She questioned his taste in women, and wondered if he used the internet to trick all of the women he encountered. Carla quickly disregarded it because he was none of her concern. She only pitied the women that fell for his corny ass lines. She was grateful that she never gave him the satisfaction of sleeping with her and figured he did her a favor when he stood her up. She quickly held her head down and returned her eyes to the menu in front of her, hoping that Antoine didn't see her.

After browsing the menu for a few seconds, a Mickey Mouse sound alike approached her table. Carla looked up and was surprised to see that the voice did not match the person standing in front of her.

"Have you decided on your selection? I'm Mike by the way and I'll be your server so if you need anything just give me a shout." Mike was a skinny, spiked hair, surfer looking, young white guy with a nonchalant look on his face.

"Do you know about the pancake special we have right now? It's only $3.99 which is a pretty good deal."

"Sounds like you're in the wrong line of business, Mike. Maybe you should be a salesman. You are such a fast talker. Anyway, I'm gonna pass on the special and order the international combo. I would like my eggs scrambled with bacon instead of sausage, but a cup of hot tea would be good for starters."

"Would that complete your order?"

"Yup. That'll do it for now."

Mike picked up the menu and walked off. Carla stared off into the crowd and her thoughts drifted to Tony. She actually enjoyed his company and his conversation. Her cell phone vibrated in her bag and she quickly retrieved it. Weirdly, she hoped it was Tony. She had only been away from him for two hours and already, she found herself missing him. Carla looked at the caller ID and saw that it was her mother calling. She was not in the mood to be lectured or interrogated about her life, so she pressed the ignore button and figured she would return the call later.

Love Finally

"Here is your hot tea. The sugar is to your left. Your food should be up shortly." Mike handed her a napkin and off he went.

Her cellular device vibrated once more. Again, she looked at the caller ID, but this time, it was Tony calling.

"Hello." Carla was actually excited to hear his voice.

"Hey beautiful, what are you up to?"

Carla blushed. "I'm at IHOP," she answered in her little girl voice. "The day is too beautiful to stay locked up in the house."

"So the beautiful lady is enjoying this beautiful day. I'm not mad at that. I wish I could've been there with you."

"Where did you learn to be so charming?"

"All credit goes to my mother."

"She taught you well. So what's on your agenda?" She asked.

"I'm on my way to work, but I couldn't stop thinking about you."

"Awww....that was sweet of you. Well, don't work too hard."

"Haha. I'll try not to. Enjoy your breakfast."

"I plan to. I see the waiter returning with my food, so call me later." Carla ended her call and Mike placed the hot plate in front of her.

"Here you go. May I get you anything else?" Mike asked.

"This will do for now." Carla dug into her meal and enjoyed every bite.

After she paid the tab, Carla left the building and got into her truck. She sat for a while with the A/C blowing and meditated on how she wanted to spend the rest of her day. Playing hooky from work was not something she often did, but she was determined to enjoy the day to its capacity. It was Tuesday and most people were on their jobs. Shopping was out of the question. Carla was financially equipped to splurge, but she was smart about saving her money. She had enough clothes and shoes to clothe an entire nation. Whatever she would buy from this point on would've been out of want and not out of need. She thought about going to watch a movie, but none of the latest big screen productions tickled her fancy. After careful thought, Carla decided to stop by her next best place, Barnes and Nobles. When all else fails, a good book would always put her mind at ease. Carla turned off the A/C, slid back her sunroof, inserted Jay Z's 'Blue Print album', and drove off allowing the cool breeze to blow through her hair.

Walking into Barnes and Nobles, Carla immediately started to browse the shelves for a good love story. There was one that caught her eye. It was written by an author she never heard of before, but it sounded interesting enough to read. Love stories with some drama were Carla's favorite. She often hoped her life would end up like most of the stories she read, finding true love.

After going up and down the aisles, nothing else stood out to her so she settled for a *Vibe* magazine featuring Lisa Ray on the cover. Starbucks was located in the back of the store and a grande caramel frappuccino with whipped cream was just what the doctor ordered. Carla purchased the frappuccino and sat down to read the magazine to find out the latest scoop on the celebs. She continued to gulp down a few more frappuccinos and read more magazines until she concluded that enough time was spent in the bookstore. It was going on 4:00 p.m. and beating the rush hour traffic would be in her best interest, so Carla proceeded to the checkout line to pay for her book.

Thankful to be home, she entered her abode and locked the door behind her. "There's no place like home," she blurted. Filled with energy, Carla was in the mood to prepare a home cooked meal. Rib eye steak, mashed potatoes and green beans was what she craved. She removed the packaged meat from the refrigerator and then removed the canned green beans, and bagged Irish potatoes from the pantry and placed them in the stainless steel, under mounted sink.

Carla ran to her bedroom to change into something comfortable. "Maybe I should invite Tony over for dinner." She wanted a valid reason to see him again so that she could once again experience his thick nine inch flesh. Carla slid the jean shorts down her thighs and replaced it with a pair of grey sweats. Wanting to show off her cooking skills, Carla reached for her cell phone to send Tony a text message. *Dinner on me tonight...B @ my door by 8 p.m. and don't be late. C ya then! Carla.*

Music was her therapy, so Carla inserted a throwback album by Sade into her surround sound stereo system. It was something about good musical lyrics that took her away from reality. She proceeded to the kitchen and tied an apron around her waist. *I have to look the part and dress the part,* she thought. Carla moved to the music and imagined herself as a chef for the evening.

She'd slaved over the stove for a few hours and prepared a finger licking meal. The delicious smell made Carla proud of her efforts. With only an hour before Tony was scheduled to end his shift, Carla cleaned up well and ran her bath water. While relaxing in the tub, it dawned on her that Tony did not reply to her text message to confirm if he was actually going to show up. This began to worry her, but Carla managed to keep her cool and enjoyed the silky feel of the crisp bubbles against her skin.

After her bath, Carla grabbed her favorite bath and body works scented lotion from her dresser and smoothed it onto her body. As her ass cheeks jiggling with each step, Carla walked over to her drawer and retrieved a pair of black laced boy shorts; which she quickly draped over her thighs. She paired the boy shorts with a black half bra and threw on her black silk robe. Carla tied the robe tightly around her waist and exposed little cleavage.

She walked back into the bathroom to fix her hair and examined her profile in the mirror, turning from one side to the next. Carla looked like a pinup girl who was getting ready to do a photo shoot; the only thing missing was a pair of black thigh highs. With Sade still playing in the background and the lights dimmed, a romantic mood was unquestionably in motion.

There were three light knocks at the door and Carla jumped. The knocks caught her by surprise. She assumed that Tony received her text and decided to show up unannounced, knowing that she was already expecting him. Carla ran out of the bathroom and into her closet to slide on a pair of five inch patent leather novelty heels. She glanced at the clock to see that it was exactly 8 p.m. "That's him alright."

Tugging on her robe to make sure that it was securely tied, she walked towards the front door. She ran her fingers through her hair, gained her composure, and slowly pulled the door towards her. The moment she opened the door, a familiar fragrance filled her nostrils. It was the same scent that she smelled on the elevator the night before. She inhaled and instantly felt invigorating. Tony stood in her doorway dressed in an all white linen suit, looking like he just stepped out of a GQ magazine. His hair was freshly cut, displaying his crisp lined edges, and he held a bottle of red wine in his hands. Carla had to soak up the divine sight in front of her before she was able to speak.

"I'm glad you could make it." She managed to say.

"This is one dinner invitation I could not turn down."

Carla continued to block the doorway, not realizing that Tony was still waiting to come inside. She couldn't help herself. Tony was a Greek god and he was too *foine* to not be admired. Tony cleared his throat and broke her stare. "Are you going to ask me in or are we just gonna stand here and stare at each other all night while the food gets cold?"

"Oh dear! I am so sorry. Please, come in." Carla made way for Tony as he entered through the door. Was she catching feelings for this man? His sexy ass voice gave her chills.

"Nice shoes. Looks like I'm a little over dressed," He joked as he walked past her and took notice of the fact that she only wore a bra and panty underneath her robe.

Carla smiled, knowing what he was hinting at. "No, I'm just underdressed, but your suit looks very nice. This will just be dessert after your main course," she referred to her garment. She locked the door and followed behind him.

"Something smells delectable." The scrumptious smell attacked Tony as he entered the living room. He sniffed his nose in the air and turned his attention to the delectable smell. "I hope it tastes just as good," he teased.

"You'll just have to taste it to find out," she said with an inviting smile.

Tony handed her the wine and took a seat on the sofa. Carla took the bottle of wine and walked into the kitchen. "You're going to be taken aback by this finger licking meal that I prepared," she yelled to him as she fixed his plate.

Carla walked out of the kitchen holding the plate above her head. "Dinner is served." She cautiously laid the plate on the table then pulled out a dinning chair, motioning with her finger for Tony to come and have a seat at the dining table.

"Looks like I'm in for a treat," Tony said about the meal and treatment he was receiving. He took his seat and rubbed his hands together. The presentation of the well prepared meal gave him no doubts that it would taste just as delicious as it looked.

"I hope you came with an empty stomach," Carla stated as she placed the napkin in his lap.

"I did indeed."

Tony enjoyed the way Carla was catering to him and at that moment, he made up his mind that he wanted her to be his woman. Tony knew he wanted her the moment they locked eyes with each other at the restaurant, but having the chance to experience her for himself, Tony would be damned if he allowed her to slip through his fingers. "You sure know how to make a man feel good."

"You have catered to me, so please allow me to return the favor." Carla pulled up a chair next to Tony and started to feed him like he was a toddler in a high chair. Tony was ecstatic and took pleasure in the moment.

"That was superb!" Tony praised her cooking. He took the napkin from his lap and wiped his mouth before washing down the meal with a glass of homemade sweet tea.

Carla stood up from her chair and trotted to her linen closet. She rummaged around for the vanilla scented candles that she stored in the box on the floor. After finding them, Carla put a candle in each room of her condo. She clicked off her lights and let the glow from the candles permeate throughout her living space. She walked back into the dining room and saw that Tony was still sitting around the dining table.

"Do you have room for dessert, or did you have enough to eat?" She asked seductively and looked at him with alluring eyes. Tony locked into her stare and became mesmerized. The only thought that crossed his mind, was ripping her clothes off. Carla loosened the tie on her robe and allowed it to fall on the floor. The sight caused Tony's manhood to grow through his pants.

"Dessert is always welcomed," He uttered and almost choked on his words.

"I'll be right back." Carla walked into the kitchen and Tony's eyes followed her ass cheeks as they switched up and down with each step. She grabbed a can of whipped cream with a bowl of pre-sliced strawberries from the fridge and walked out of the kitchen and back into the dining room shaking the can in her right hand, and held the bowl of strawberries in her left.

She stood in front of Tony with her legs spread apart and he followed her legs with his eyes as if they could lead him straight to heaven. He sat and watched in awe as she squirted whipped

Love Finally

cream into her mouth. She rested the can on the table and then gave him her mouth to indulge in the creamy sweet flavor. Tony sucked Carla's tongue dry, and then she pulled her mouth away from him. She then sat on his lap, undid her bra (letting it fall to the floor), and squeezed whipped cream, this time, on both nipples. She instructed Tony to devour them. Tony followed her instructions and sucked her nipples like his life depended on it. He came up for air and Carla fed him a slice of strawberry that she placed between her lips.

"Follow me," she told him after their lips met for a brief kiss. Carla climbed off of Tony, picked up the whipped cream and the bowl of strawberries from the table, and led him to the living room. She lay down on the carpet and delicately placed the thinly sliced strawberries on her body, making a trail from between her breasts down to the opening of her moistened valley.

"Why don't you dig in?" She whispered.

Tony kneeled down beside Carla, licked along her trail and took each strawberry into his mouth. Carla watched as his mouth slid down her belly and the suction from his tongue and lips against her skin made her back arch and her toes curl. The waters in her valley were beginning to run deep. Tony used his tongue to play with her navel.

"That tickles." Carla giggled and returned to laying flat on her back.

Tony moved back up her body and covered her mouth with his. He sat up on his knees, unbuttoned his shirt, and slid off his pants. Tony was well aroused and sprouted long and hard like a baseball bat. Once he completely undressed, Tony leaned over Carla and slid her boy shorts down her thighs with his mouth, allowing it to dangle around her ankles. Carla bent her knees upward and finished the job by pulling it off her feet. Tony unbuckled her heels and threw them in the corner by the fireplace. Tony stood up and pulled Carla up with him. He wrapped his arms around Carla's waist, pulling her body into his and they swayed their naked bodies to the sweet voice of Sade. After their brief waltz, Carla jumped up on Tony and wrapped her legs around his mid section.

"Let's start in the kitchen," She whispered into his ear.

Tony agreed to her suggestion and allowed the glow from the candles to lead. He placed her on top of the counter and goose bumps filled her arms from the cool feel against her bottom. Tony stood between her legs. They leaned into each other and kissed aggressively while he palmed her breasts in the process.

They tongue wrestled for what seemed like hours. He picked Carla up from the counter and she wrapped her arms around his neck, wrapped her legs around his waist, and then lowered herself down on his stiff shaft. The tightness of her vagina made Tony grit his teeth and Carla loved the way he filled her insides. She began to ride him slowly in a jockey style position. She picked up her pace with each stroke and continued to ride him like she was nearing the finish line of a horse race.

Tony gripped her tighter around the waist and you could hear her ass slapping against his thighs. She continued to rock her hips faster and faster in a breathless rhythm bouncing up and down and he caressed her round, mounted ass until she reached one mind blowing orgasm after another.

"UGGGHHH" She made a loud cry for she's never felt anything like this before. Carla was exhausted. She breathed heavily and her head fell upon Tony's shoulder. He continued to hold her tightly as she managed to catch her breath.

"You are the best lover I've ever had," She told him and kissed his lips. Tony carried her back out into the living room, laying her flat on her back on the carpeted floor in front of the unlit fireplace. He retrieved a blanket from her bedroom and threw it over her naked body. Carla curled up in the fetal position and Tony lay next to her. They faced each other and he looked deeply into her eyes. He pulled her closer into him and Carla loved his tenderness towards her.

"Carla, I know that we've only known each other for a short period of time, but the feelings that I have developed for you can no longer go unmentioned. I feel like I've waited for you all my life and

Love Finally

you finally appeared," He explained. "Thank you for accepting me with opened arms and for allowing me to feel comfortable around you."

His words took her by surprise and she became speechless. She didn't want to hurt Tony's feelings. Her intention with him was only a sexual relationship. She saw him as a sexual icon. *Is it a bad thing that I only find him good enough to have sex with and not good enough to settle with?* Carla paused for a moment and thought hard before she replied. "I had no idea that you felt that way." There was silence between them. Tony sat up and rested his head against the headboard. She did the same.

"I can't deny the fact that I have fallen for you, Carla, and I'm not quite sure where we stand with each other at this point, but I want to make you my woman. My one and only. Would you do me the honor of making you that woman in my life?"

Carla's heart sank like a rollercoaster dropping ten feet. This was all so sudden. She was not prepared for this. Butterflies filled her stomach. Her heart wanted to say yes but her head told her no. She played tug of war in her head. *Oh my goodness, why is this happening now? This was not the initial plan...no, no, Carla think fast.* She panicked. *He was only supposed to be a fuck buddy. What the hell have I gotten myself into? I can't dare get serious with a waiter. I'm a damn attorney for crying out loud. What the hell are people going to think when they find out that attorney Carla Milford is dating a lousy waiter? OH HELL NO!*

Chapter 5

Last night couldn't have been more awkward. Carla told Tony that she needed time to think and they needed more time to get to know each other. She was relieved when he agreed and decided to take things slow. Tony took her by surprise when he disclosed his feelings toward her and it was exactly what she was afraid would happen. Now she didn't know how to act toward this man. Yes, she was catching feelings just the same, but she didn't want him to know that. Things were already getting complicated too soon. She'd stayed up during most of the night contemplating on what to do about the situation. Should she give him a chance or should she just do away with him altogether? Sure he seemed like a nice guy, but what if he wasn't cracked out to be all of what he seemed? This wouldn't be as easy as she thought. Grant it, she was looking for love, but Tony did not come with the complete package. He had the looks and knew how to give her pleasure, but he held the wrong profession. Why were the rules to this game so damn difficult?

Carla jumped up when Tony tapped her shoulders lightly. Little did he know that she'd only gotten three hours of sleep. While he was comfortably snoozing, she was heavily thinking.

"What time is it?" she asked and rubbed her eyes. "It's time for you to wake up."

"I can't believe that it's that time already," she said and rolled on her side.

"You're probably going to have a busy day at the office, considering that you were out yesterday."

"Yeah, I can only imagine. It is going to be very busy especially because I have to try a case in court tomorrow."

She dragged herself up from the floor and headed to the shower. The reality of last night did not completely settle within her mind. She was aware of what took place and what was said, but she was still trying to make sense of it all. Carla brushed her teeth and tried to let it all sink in. She stepped into the shower and the hot water massaged her back. Lost in thought, Carla jumped when Tony suddenly swung the bathroom door open.

"Is everything ok?" He asked.

"Yeah. I'm just going to rinse off and I'll be out in a sec." Carla smiled about the fact that he was concerned about her. *Being his woman probably won't be so bad.* Carla hurried out of the shower and threw on a pair of grey slacks along with a rose pink buttoned up long sleeve shirt. She put in her two-carat diamond studs, one in each ear, and completed her look with a pair of three inch rose pink pumps.

"You look very sophisticated this morning." Tony complimented her and began to get himself dressed.

"Thank you."

Tony smiled and preceded to the kitchen to brew her some coffee. Carla grabbed her handbag and Tony handed her the thermos filled with coffee as they headed out the door. They walked to the parking lot and he helped Carla into her truck. He kissed her forehead and told her to drive safely. After shooting him down, she couldn't believe that he was still so generous. He could've been arrogant and say to hell with her and on to the next, but why didn't he? She was curious to know what was it about her that caused him to catch feelings so fast.

They parted ways and Carla drove off in the direction of Interstate 20.

Carla entered the doors and hurried to her office. The red blinking light on her office phone caught her attention. The light only blinked when the voicemail was full. Curious to know who was in such demand of her, Carla pressed the play button. "Carla, it's me Antoine. I saw you yesterday. You looked good girl...." *Beep.* "Carla,

Antoine again. Please call me.....″ *Beep.* "I am sorry for the millionth time. Look, we need to talk..." *Beep.*

"Such a whore," She mumbled as she listened to his sorry ass pleas. Disappointed to hear that most of the messages were from Antoine, Carla quickly deleted them. Apparently, he spotted Carla at IHOP the day before and wanted to know if they could meet for dinner so that he could clear the air, so to speak. Finally taking her seat, Carla went straight to work. She was due in court on the next day with Mrs. Thompson and Oliver and she needed to catch up on what she missed yesterday.

"Good morning."

Carla looked up and saw Sarah standing in her door way. "Hi Sarah! I didn't see you at your desk when I walked in a few moments ago."

"Oh, yeah. I had to go into the storage closet to retrieve some archived files that John asked about."

"Ummm. Speaking of John, is he here today?" Carla asked.

"No, he's actually out. Something about a conference meeting in San Francisco, but he's due back by tomorrow," Sarah informed Carla.

"Darn! I'm always missing him. I needed his input on this case I'm working on for tomorrow. Hopefully I will do a good job pulling it off..."

"I'm sure you will. By the way, are you feeling better today?"

"Huh? Oh, much better...thanks for asking. I just needed to get some rest." Carla swore her cheeks were fire red after almost getting caught in her lie.

"Good. I'm glad that all is well. I'll be at my desk if you should need anything," Sarah said then pushed her glasses up on her face and sashayed down the hallway.

Love Finally

In the middle of contemplating on her upcoming case and keenly reviewing her notes, Carla's office phone rang. She took a deep breath and hoped it wasn't Antoine. She picked up the receiver and answered with hesitation.

"Hey girlfriend!" Tamika's voice squealed through the phone set.

"You are such the morning person. It is 8:30 a.m., what the hell did you have for breakfast, a red bull? Because you sound like you grew some wings," Carla teased. She was relieved when she heard Tamika's voice.

"You know it chile. But moving on, are we still on for lunch today?"

"No doubt," Carla assured her. "What time are we meeting up?"

"I'll come and pick you up around 1:30 p.m. Wanna go to our favorite spot, Mexicana Tex? I'm so in the mood for tacos."

"Sounds good to me, I can just taste a fajita right now."

"So it's a date. See you then," Tamika said before they hung up. Tamika worked three blocks away from Carla and due to their busy schedules and the fact that she now had a fiancé in her life, they hardly have the chance to do lunch dates like they use to, so they would get together whenever they could.

As Carla returned to reviewing her notes, the thought of her mother crossed her mind. She picked up the receiver and dialed Ellen's number.

"Good morning mother," she spoke after Ellen answered on the third ring.

"Hi cupcake! How are you? I tried calling you yesterday, but I guess you were probably busy with work."

"I did see your miss call. Sorry I didn't get the chance to call you back sooner. I was really busy yesterday and I was so beat when I got home last night," Carla comprised.

"So how is work coming along?"

"I'm working on a case that I have to try in court tomorrow, so you know how that goes."

"Well you know what I always say honey, do your best because your best is all you have."

"Thanks Momma. So what are your plans for today?"

"The usual. You know, pay some bills. Run errands, and make a stop by the grocery store to pick up a few items."

"Why don't you save yourself the headache and pay your bills online?"

"Oh Carla, you know I don't fool around with that internet stuff. Besides I don't mind getting out. It gives me something to do, you know."

"Thought I would save you some trouble. Well, I was just calling to see what you were up to. Guess I'll get back to work now."

"Okay baby. Have a good day and I will talk to you later. I love you Carla."

"Love you too Mama." It occurred to Carla that she must make it her business to spend more time with her mother. Ellen could be somewhat overbearing at times, trying to tell Carla how to live her life, but Carla realized that that's what mothers do. Ellen wanted the best for her only daughter and Carla was all she had.

"Carla, Tamika is holding for you on the back line," Sarah informed her.

"Put her through, Sarah. Thanks."

"This is Carla speaking."

Love Finally

"Are you ready? I'm leaving the office in like thirty seconds."

"Yeah. I'm wrapping up now, so I should be ready when you get here." Carla was so caught up in her review, that she completely lost track of time. She returned the files in the file cabinet and walked towards the lobby to wait on Tamika.

Carla was excited about having lunch with her best friend. When Tamika's car pulled up, Carla quickly made a run for it.

"Hey girl! You look nice! That pink really looks good on you," Tamika complimented Carla when she entered the car.

Carla settled in and placed her handbag on the floor beside her feet.

"Thank ya!" She looked over at Tamika and noticed a new hairdo. "I love the hair!" Carla exclaimed as she continued to take notice of Tamika's new hair cut. Tamika's hair was always naturally glossy and jet black in color. The edgy bob she once sported was now transformed into a short cut like Halle Berry. The new cut showed up her heart shaped face and enhanced her rosy cheeks.

"Who did it 'Mika? That shit is hot! It really fits your face. You go girl!" Carla snapped her fingers.

"My stylist Lilly did it. I told her to give me something different for a change and she hooked a sistah up! All the love making me and Marcus did, I'm surprised it's not sweated out," Tamika laughed and patted her tightly curled hair.

They drove off and Tamika reached out to adjust the vent for the A/C. The beam from the sun made a reflection and it caught Carla's attention. She looked in the direction of the shiny reflection. "AAHH!" Carla let out a short scream. The sudden outburst frightened Tamika and nearly caused her to rear end the car in front of her.

"What's the matter?" Tamika asked. Her voice now filled with concern.

"I'm sorry." Carla placed her hands over her mouth and her eyes widened at the size of Tamika's diamond. "OH MY GOSH! Tamika you didn't tell me that you finally got your ring! Look at the size of that thing."

Tamika's secret was out. She planned to surprise Carla with the ring at lunch. Tamika tried her best to hide her left hand and failed to realize that she exposed it when she adjusted the vent. "That's what you get for being nosey, *Miss Thang*. I wanted to surprise you at lunch. You know that I wouldn't hold out on you, especially something as special as this. Well, SURPRISE! I got my ring, even though you saw it before I could actually show it to you."

They pulled up to the restaurant and Tamika parked her car into a spot next to the handicap parking. "This is huge!" Carla took Tamika's hand and admired her rock. "Now this is what you call BLING BLING," Carla clowned.

"You are so damn silly." Tamika pulled her hand away.

"Marcus knows what time it is. He knows that he has a good woman by his side and furthermore, you deserve it 'Mika. You are a woman that every man dreams to have as a wife. You are a sure blessing from God. Marcus doesn't know the angel he has on his hands."

"Please don't let me get all teary eyed, Carla. You know that you too are more than every man's dream. I promise that your day will come when you will find a man that is going to cherish the ground you walk on. And when it happens, he will be the man that God designed specifically for you." They hugged without saying a word.

"Please don't let me cry and ruin my makeup. This shit took too long to apply this morning," Tamika blurted. They laughed and released each other.

"Okay Carla, don't forget that we are on corporate America's time. We have just enough time to catch up and grab a bite to eat before I'm due back at the office." They shared their moment then made their way inside the restaurant.

"Hello ladies." A Latino guy welcomed them as if he were expecting their arrival.

"Hi." They replied in harmony.

"Table for two please," Tamika requested and they followed the young man as he led them to their table with two menus in hand.

The girls have eaten at Mexicana Tex a few times too many and they always took pleasure in the brightly colored decorations and the mural of the different cities of Mexico that were painted on the walls. They took their seats and immediately gave their orders, considering that they were pressed for time.

"So when did you actually receive your ring?" Carla quizzed. She wanted to make sure that Tamika wasn't holding out on her.

Tamika held out her left arm, pointed her hand up towards her face and admired the beautiful five carat, Cartier diamond that was a perfect fit for her finger. "He surprised me with it last night. I wasn't expecting him to give it to me until the end of the week! When he opened that black velvet box, I almost jumped through the roof when I saw the size of it."

"Girl, I am still baffled. I still can't get over how huge that thing is. So, did you already set a date for the wedding?"

"Not quite. Marcus said that whatever date I choose is okay by him, but I am seriously considering a winter wedding."

"What if it gets too cold?"

"I mean, everything will be kept indoors where there's heat. It's not like I'm gonna let people freeze…"

"Enough said. So a winter wedding it is. I can't wait."

The server returned with their food. "Too chicken fajitas for you." He placed the plate in front of Carla. "And two soft tacos for you." He placed Tamika's food in front of her and departed their table. They dug right in.

Tamika took a bite out of her taco. "So what's the latest with you and Tony?"

Carla cut her fajitas into little squares and took a fork full to her mouth. She chewed quickly then swallowed. "I'm glad you brought him up. Okay, so we've been hooking up at my place for the past couple of nights and can a sistah brag for a second? The sex is the bomb!"

"By that smirk on your face, I knew you gave up the kitty kat. That's what I'm talking about! It's about time you hooked up with somebody who knows how to handle their business in the bedroom." Tamika high-fived Carla.

"You know I couldn't pass on that good piece of dick! Hell, I haven't had any for what seemed like a decade. Had I waited any longer, my well would've surely run dry...probably grow cobwebs even." Carla laughed.

"So besides his sex game, what else has been going on? Or is it just a sex thing for you? I mean are you feeling dude or what?"

"Well since you took it there, I guess I can say that I am somewhat feeling him, but I am not sure of how to handle the situation."

Tamika lowered her eyebrows. "Okay, you lost me. What situation?"

"See, at first, I figured I would just have fun with him sexually, you know. But the more time I spend with him, the more I'm starting to like him. Last night he told me he wanted things between us to get serious."

Tamika shrugged her shoulders. "So what's the problem?"

Love Finally

"Don't you think that's a little too soon?"

"Who says that there was a time frame on mating? You gave it up on the first night. There are no rules on when to have sex or when to date. If two people have a mutual attraction for each other, then make the damn thing happen."

As Tamika spoke, Carla's thoughts roamed.

"Carla, you can't bullshit me because I know that you are really into this guy. I haven't seen you glow like this in a long time. Okay, sure you only wanted sex, I can understand that. But if your heart is pulling you in another direction, then take a chance and follow it. What's the worst that could happen? If it doesn't work out, then you can say at least you tried. There are plenty of men out there."

"I don't know, 'Mika. I don't want to rush it. The real problem is...well he's a waiter. How is that going to look on my end?"

Tamika cut her off. "I see what you are saying, but it shouldn't be that big of a deal, dear. He's still a human being right? Whether you date a janitor or a waiter, it doesn't make you less of a person, Carla. Being a lawyer shouldn't define who you are as a person and to hell with what other people think. Half of the time they are so busy critiquing others while their own lives are in shambles. If you ask me, I say go for it. Have you taken a good look at that man? Girl he is like a beautiful piece of art. He is damn near close to perfect."

"I have to give it to him, he is fine."

"You never know. Sometimes you have to take chances. These days, anything is possible. I just want you to be happy."

"I couldn't have asked for a better BFF. You always got my back."

"I'm just excited that you finally got a potential candidate. Shiit, I was starting to wonder what the hell was going on. Beautiful women like yourself shouldn't be single."

"That's what you think. Now you have given me more to think about. Well, if I decide to take a chance on him, I hope it won't be another heartbreak story that will lead me to crying on your shoulder again." Carla knocked on the wood table.

"You know I'm always here for you. I just can't believe my girl is going to have a man now! It is long overdue," Tamika teased.

"Don't start jumping to conclusions. I still have to think about it." Carla shook her head and smiled. "It feels good to have a man in my bed though."

"See, look at you. Go on and tell that man you want him." They giggled.

"But let's not get too excited yet. We need to see how things work out for the next couple of weeks first."

"I hear you. Some men can change their minds like women change their panties. They can be so unpredictable sometimes. Wish they would make up their damn minds and know what they want, but I think you have a winner."

Carla nodded in agreement. They finished their meals, paid the check and headed to the car. They settled in and Tamika pulled out of the parking lot.

"I am so excited about your wedding 'Mika. I can't wait to throw you a bridal shower."

Tamika looked over at Carla. "Just make sure you have a sexy ass stripper jumping out of the cake," she said playfully. They talked about the wedding and came up with ideas as they drove to Simon and Hurst law firm.

They pulled up to Carla's place of employment and gave each other a hug before Carla exited Tamika's car. "Lunch was great.

We need to start doing this more often," Carla stated then shut the car door. She hurried to her office to complete her file reviews; as tomorrow is her big day in court with Mrs. Thompson and Oliver.

Evening rolled around and Carla was exhausted. Hunger struck her, so she decided to order out a bowl of spaghetti from Olive Garden. She packed up her belongings, locked up the office.

Thoughts of Tony weighed heavily on her mind as she drove on the highway, allowing the sounds of jazz to mellow her mood. Her Jennifer Hudson's ringtone interrupted her thoughts and she shuffled through her bag to locate the cellular device.

"Hello."

"Hey. Are you still at the office?" Tony's voice had a special effect on Carla. Her heart would melt every time he spoke to her.

"No. I just left. I'm on my way to pick up dinner. Where are you?"

"On my way home. Today was rather hectic. So, did you have a good day today or did you work yourself to death?"

"It was a little of both. Why was your day so hectic?"

"Nothing major, just tedious things, but I'm glad it's over. Looking forward to a better day tomorrow. Speaking of which, I know you are out to have a good day tomorrow because I know you are going to defend the hell out of your case."

"I am a little nervous about it. This case is going to be the epitome of my career. Depending on my performance, it could make or break my career."

"I wouldn't worry too much if I were you. A little birdie told me that you are going to do one hell of a job."

"So sweet. You always know the right things to say."

"I'm only stating the facts."

"I really appreciate that. So you're going home to relax?"

"Yes indeed. Relaxation is well overdue for me at this point."

"Maybe I can treat you to one of my full body massage special sometime."

"I sense that you are trying to persuade me. I would be a fool to turn that down. There's nothing better than having a beautiful, sexy woman touching and rubbing all over my naked body."

Carla chuckled. "You will not be disappointed either. "I have hidden skills," she said and continued to laugh.

"Is that right? Please do show."

"Time will reveal all."

"You couldn't have said it better. I know you're driving and I want you to be focused on the road, so I will call you later when I know you've made it home," Tony told her.

"Okay." They said their good-byes then hung up.

Carla continued her drive to Olive Garden and couldn't stop thinking about how genuine Tony was. Tamika made interesting points, but she needed to go about this relationship thing carefully. Her heart would be on the line here. She pulled up to the restaurant and removed her debit card from her wallet. Carla hopped out of her truck, locked the doors and walked inside. She went to the take out section.

"Hi, I'm here to pick up an order for Carla," she told the short, bald head man behind the counter.

"Let's see." He looked over the rim of his glasses and shuffled through the other take out bags that were on the shelf. "C-A-R- okay, here we are. Your total is $13.95."

Love Finally

Carla presented her debit card and paid for her food. The man handed her the bag and she exited through the doors.

Now that she could finally unwind, Carla ate, showered, and then retired on her couch for an hour of TV time. Family Matters was an all time favorite. She always got a kick out of watching Steve Urkel chase after Laura, only to get rejected time after time. After the first thirty minutes, The TV would soon be watching her. Carla decided to call it a night and turned in early to her bedroom. The telephone rang and alarmed her. She quickly answered with the sound of sleep in her voice.

"Someone sounds tired." Tony pitied her.

"I really am," she said then let out a yawn.

"I'm part to blame," he told her as if scolding himself.

"No one is to blame. I'm a big girl. I know how to handle myself so don't you worry your head. It's not like you held a gun to my head."

"Yeah, more like you held one to mine," Tony joked. "Well, with no further a due, go ahead and get some sleep. I know you have a long day ahead of you and I just wanted to hear your voice before I turned in to bed myself. And by the way, knock 'em dead tomorrow."

"Thanks. Have a good night." Carla fought to keep her eyes opened, but she lost the battle and laid the cordless on her nightstand then pulled the covers up.

Carla woke up earlier than usual. Today was her big day in court and she planned to make it into the office early so that she could retrieve her files and have a quick briefing with Mrs. Thompson before they entered the court room. After fishing through multiple suits, Carla decided to wear her grey skirt suit. It was the same suit she wore two years ago when she tried and won her first case. Considering it to be her lucky suit, Carla took it off the hanger and hoped it still fit because lawd knows she needed to get lucky today. When she pulled the pleated skirt over her thighs, Carla was surprised to see that she had no trouble fitting into the faux wool material. In fact, it fitted her like the first day she wore it two years ago. Elated, Carla pulled the matching suit jacket over her arms and buttoned it.

"Voila," she said as she looked at herself in the mirror. So far, things were starting to go her way. Carla skipped back into her closet and buckled a pair of grey, five inch, snake skin Jimmy Choo heels unto her feet. Taking another look in the mirror, Carla was beginning to feel confident about winning her case; although, deep down she was still a bit nervous.

In her two years of practicing law, this would be the hardest case that Carla would have to defend, considering that her client was just a mere teenager and it was her first murder case. It always broke her heart to see young black men behind bars instead of using their potential to do something great in the world. Most of her major cases consisted of felons involved in drug charges and amazingly enough; she was almost always successful in getting those cases acquitted. Oliver's case on the other hand, would not be as easy because of the State law and the fact that there were witnesses to identify him on the scene. But if she could pull it off and win this case or reduce his sentence, it would be the break she had been waiting for to qualify for partnership with the male dominated, elite law firm that she'd worked her ass off for for the past two years. It hadn't been easy for Carla to earn respect as an attorney, but her determination made her prove her worth. After several consistent wins and her near perfect acquittal rate thus far, the cocky male infested society of attorneys had no choice other than to tip their hats off to her. She earned that right fair and square and dared anyone to try and strip her of it. Taking a deep breath, Carla crossed her fingers and headed out the door.

Driving on the deserted highway at 6:30 a.m. was not typical. She had been so anxious that she didn't realize how early she was. It felt good to drive on the highway and not be bombarded by bright lights and crazy drivers. There was time to spare, so a stop at Dunkin Doughnuts for an egg sandwich and a latte would be just what she needed to start her day. Carla exited off the highway and pulled up to the first Dunkin Doughnuts in sight. She drove up to the drive thru and placed her order. She handed the lady at the window a ten dollar bill, took her food and drink and drove back onto the Interstate. Coasting on the highway, a million and one thoughts crossed Carla's mind about the case. The thought of doubt tried to invade her mind. Carla took the straw from the bag containing her sandwich, and inserted it through the hole in the plastic lid. She took a sip of her latte, injected a gospel CD in the deck and flushed the negative thoughts that tried to make her doubt herself.

When she arrived, the parking lot was empty and her vehicle was the only one present. Carla quickly surveyed the area, grabbed her breakfast, and retrieved her briefcase from the backseat and speed walked to the entrance of the building.

Carla deactivated the company's alarm system and headed to her office. It was 7:15 a.m. and Sarah was due in the office within the next fifteen minutes. Turning on the lights in her office, Carla rested the briefcase on the floor beside her desk, took a seat and proceeded to eat her sandwich.

Once she was through eating, Carla crumbled the brown, Dunkin Doughnuts labeled paper bag, and tossed it into the trash can beneath her desk. She placed her right palm up to her cheek and worried about whether or not she would prevail in her case.

The prosecutor that she was up against, Charles Bryant, has a reputation of being intimidating. She'd done her research on him, but Carla had news for him. Not wanting to toot her own horn, but Carla was not one to be played with. She was born with the gift of gab and once she painted a heartfelt picture for the jury, they would evidently feel sorry for her client and there would be no doubt that Mr. Bryant would learn to respect her just like the others after she kicked his ass and send him home crying to his momma. Carla never had the pleasure of working with the well known Charles Bryant before, but she was determined to bring him down today. She planned to beat him down to his socks.

A prayer would always put her worried mind at ease, so Carla closed her eyes and spoke out loud.

"Lord, thank you for waking me up this morning. I come to you, seeking your guidance and wisdom. I pray that you will comfort my client and his family, as well as the victim's family. As I present myself into the courtroom today, I pray that you fill my mouth with the right words to say. Victory is mine, in Jesus name, amen."

Carla opened her eyes and she immediately felt like all her worries were gone. Looking up at the clock, it was exactly 7:30 a.m. Carla heard Sarah's footsteps along the ceramic tile out in the front lobby. *She's always on time,* Carla thought. She then picked up the phone to call Mrs. Thompson. Carla spoke with Mrs. Thompson and instructed for them to meet up in front of the courthouse within the hour. After taking the remaining thirty minutes to finalize her notes, Carla grabbed her briefcase and made her way to the courthouse.

After fighting for a parking space in the crowded parking garage, Carla swung her Range into a vacant spot between a Lexus coupe and a beat up Ford escort. She hopped out of her SUV, grabbed her briefcase and hurried to the elevator. She was parked on the 5th level and walking down five flights of stairs in a pair of five inch heels was far out of the question. The elevator was slow as molasses. Carla waited for what seemed like forever until the elevator finally opened up. Before she could step her foot inside, the doors started to close, causing her to almost break a heel.

"Shit," Carla blurted. "This slow ass elevator takes forever to open up and now it won't even allow me to step inside," Carla fumed. She was vexed about nearly ruining her $700.00 pair of shoes. She straightened her jacket and rode the elevator to the ground floor. When the doors finally opened up, Carla made a mental note to park in the garage across the street the next time around. She quickly stepped off the elevator, not wanting the doors to close on her again, and dashed across the street in search of Mrs. Thompson.

The courthouse was always busy and full of people going and coming. After squeezing through crowds of people, Carla spotted Mrs. Thompson standing in front of the building by the steps. To her surprise, Mrs. Thompson did not have a look of worry on her face. Instead, her face glowed as she stood there patiently and smiled at each person that walked by her. Carla took a deep breath and approached her. Mrs. Thompson's smile grew wider when she saw Carla walking in her direction.

"Good morning Mrs. Thompson." Carla greeted her with a hug.

"Hi Carla. How are you?"

"Just well, thank you. I wanted to take the time to go over some things with you so that we are on the same page with each other," Carla informed her.

Mrs. Thompson nodded her head. "I'm all ears."

"Do you mind if we have a seat over there in the shade?" Carla asked.

"Not at all."

With Mrs. Thompson in tow, Carla led her to a shaded area where they took a seat on the vacant bench on the side of the building. Carla explained to Mrs. Thompson that she didn't want her to get her hopes up too high, because due to the nature of the case and the severity of the charges, Oliver was bound to do some time behind bars, but she would fight extremely hard to get him out of doing the possible life sentence that he was potentially facing.

It made her cringe inside to know that this case would be the first non acquittal, but she was well aware of that from day one and lessening his sentence would be just as good. She figured anything lesser than a life sentence was worth fighting for. Mrs. Thompson nodded her head at every word Carla spoke and explained that she understood and was just thankful for all the help she could receive. She trusted Carla and knew that Oliver would get the fair trial that he deserved. With Carla being his attorney, Mrs. Thompson knew that justice would be served.

Time was drawing near. Carla and Mrs. Thompson stood up from the bench and walked up the twenty five steps that led them straight into the courthouse. Going through the metal detectors and being searched by the security officers was always a pain in the ass for Carla.

The fucking Robo cops would always take their jobs too seriously and act as if she was the damn criminal. There was one in particular who made her remove her shoes and all her jewelry. He felt her up and asked if she had any weapons or anything of the sort on her body. Carla couldn't believe the nerve of the foul breath, gorilla looking security guard. *Is he fucking kidding me,* she thought. *As tight as my skirt is, does he think I could possibly get away with hiding anything in my clothes? I'm probably the closest he'll ever get to any woman. Well, I guess someone has to make sure this place is safe for all the people visiting, but they could've made a better selection other than this clown.* She was beginning to think that his musky ass enjoyed feeling on her, but if he pulled that shit again next time, she planned to put him in his place.

"No water allowed in the facility ma'am." The broke down version of Wesley Snipes security officer told Mrs. Thompson. Carla turned to face him and wondered if it was in the company's policy for these Robo cops to wear shades on the job and inside the building at that. She considered the look to be tacky and shot him a mean unit. Robo cop noticed her and flashed her a smile. Mrs. Thompson threw out the half filled water bottle and Carla wanted to tell Mr. Officer to kiss her ass. But she remained cool, classy, and lady like.

"Have a great day." She sarcastically told gorilla Wesley. Mrs. Thompson returned from the trash can and flashed him a sarcastic grin. Carla took her belongings from the belt, buckled her shoes back onto her feet and stormed off towards the escalator with Mrs. Thompson in tow.

They entered the courtroom and were shocked by the amount of people that were present. Most of them were family members of the victim. Nervousness started to play its role once again and a nauseous feeling invaded the depths of her belly. Carla looked over at the victim's mother, who had tears running down her cheeks, and could understand the pain she felt from the son that she'd lost. Carla discreetly regained herself and reminded herself that Oliver was her number one priority at this point.

Mrs. Thompson took her seat in the back of the courtroom because she didn't want Oliver to see the anguish she felt within her eyes when the correction officers would bring him out. Carla asked Mrs. Thompson if she would be okay sitting back there and she assured Carla that she would.

Carla then proceeded to the front of the courtroom with her game face on. She walked through the swinging half door and there he stood, prosecutor Charles Bryant. He was neatly dressed in a blue Prada pinned striped pants with a crisp white collared shirt under the matching suit jacket, with a blue tie. On his feet were a pair of shiny gator skin shoes that screamed money. No lie, he was sharp and handsome. His dark complexion was similar to that of Tony's and his fresh hair cut was neat and made him resemble Taye Diggs from the movie, *How Stella Got Her Groove Back*. He looked like he weighed no more than one-hundred ninety pounds and 6'2 in height.

Carla walked over to him and introduced herself. She extended her arm to shake hands with Charles and his overly cocky ass acted as if he was too good to return the handshake. When she returned to her defense table, Carla looked over at Charles and she noticed him whispering into his partner's ear. He must've felt her staring at him because he stopped in the middle of his whisper and looked over at Carla. Their eyes made four and she had a serious look on her face. She wanted him to know that she was not intimidated by him. Charles took her look to be a simple front and gave Carla a devilish grin before he continued his whisper.

In her opinion, Charles seemed arrogant. In her research on him, his ninety-five percent conviction rate was not at all flattering to her because just the same, she was close to never losing a case in her two years of being a licensed attorney. Carla maintained her game face, retrieved her files from her briefcase, and placed them neatly in front of her on the desk.

She took one last look back at Mrs. Thompson, smiled and held up her crossed fingers. Mrs. Thompson returned the smile and crossed her fingers as well.

"Silence. Please rise, Judge Banks presiding." The grey haired bailiff spoke loud and clear to all the people in the courtroom.

Carla stood up as the judge entered the room. The room was so quiet, if someone was standing next to you, you could hear them think.

"You may be seated," Judge Banks stated in a stern tone. Judge Banks resembled Will Smith's uncle, Carl, on the *Fresh Prince of Bel Air*. He looked like a human teddy bear, but he had such a mean demeanor. Carla's palms were beginning to sweat. She always got nervous during a trial. It was probably human nature. She looked around the courtroom and took notice of the jury, and the woman who sat next to the Judge's bench; the one who would be typing every word that was spoken during the trial. She hoped the people of the jury would be fair in their decision making.

While waiting for court to be in session, two police officers walked out with Oliver. He wore an orange jumpsuit and was handcuffed in the front and shackled around his ankles. Seeing her client chained in this manner was heartbreaking for Carla. She wondered how Mrs. Thompson felt about seeing her son like this, bound by chains. As Oliver struggled to walk closer to Carla, she noticed him searching through the audience for his mother. He must've seen her because his frown turned into a hearty smile. His smile made him look so young and innocent. Oliver took a seat next to Carla and Charles Bryant was first to address the court.

After countless hours of cross examinations, accusations, and arguments brought against her client, Carla was relieved when the prosecutor and his partner rested their case. Both Carla and Charles articulated their closing arguments to the jury and her throat was dry from the constant arguing with Charles about his false accusations against Oliver.

"This court is in recess and the jury will deliberate their decision," Judge Banks stated then exited the courtroom.

Oliver was taken back into custody and Carla remained in her seat and watched Charles as he bragged about knowing that he already won. *Such unattractive arrogance,* Carla thought of Charles. Being confident was one thing, but arrogance was a total turn off for Carla, no matter how fine the man was. Forty five minutes passed and everyone returned to the courtroom, including Oliver. The jury was finished deliberating and had come to a final decision.

"Did the members of the jury reach a unanimous verdict?" The judge asked.

"Yes your honor." The seven members of the jury stated in unison. The foreman handed the judge the sheet of paper with their answer.

Judge Banks took the paper and looked at what was decided. He handed the paper back to the foreman and Carla's heart raced like the speed of sound. She dropped her head down, closed her eyes, folded her hands behind her back, and prayed silently that a lesser sentence would work in her favor.

"We the jury, hereby find the defendant, Oliver Thompson not guilty on the first count of first degree murder, not guilty on the second count of premeditated murder, guilty on the third count of being an accessory to the murder."

Carla opened her eyes and couldn't believe her ears. She expected them to find him guilty on all counts. If it wasn't for the state of Georgia and their dumb accessory law, Oliver would have been acquitted. Her eyes lit up like a Christmas tree and Oliver smiled from ear to ear. One family member of the victim became irate and made loud, degrading remarks towards Oliver and Carla.

"Order in the court!" Judge Banks banged his gavel and demanded that the out of control woman be removed from the courtroom. "Order!" Judge Banks pounded the gavel once more to capture everyone's attention. "Mr. Thompson, you are hereby sentenced to three months in jail. The time already served will be credited toward those three months. This court is dismissed." BANG! He pounded the gavel one last time.

When the officers took Oliver out of the court room, he looked back at his mother and he whispered the words "I love you" to her. Carla looked back at Mrs. Thompson, who placed her right hand over her heart and fought to hold back the tears that stung her eyes. People were beginning to clear the courtroom and Carla noticed when Charles slammed a manila folder on the desk. He was obviously angry and wore the look of disappointment on his face. She walked over to him and his partner, shook their hands and congratulated their hard effort. Charles was not pleased. He forced himself to shake Carla's hand, but this didn't bother her, because she ruined the joy of him getting Oliver convicted for life. Not wanting to rub her triumph in his face, Carla walked away with a huge grin on her face. She walked to meet Mrs. Thompson, who was waiting outside the courtroom.

"I want to thank you for all your hard work, Carla."

"Thank you Mrs. Thompson. It was a pleasure working with you and Oliver. He will be out in no time. The one month that he already served is credited so maybe with good behavior, he could possibly be out in thirty days. I am glad that he will have a second chance at life. I know he learned a valuable lesson from all of this. I wish you and your family all the best." They hugged for the last time and went their separate ways.

It had been a long day, and Carla felt drained. "I'm so glad it's all over," she said and slid out of her shoes. Her first stop was in the kitchen. Carla removed a bottle of white wine from the electric wine cooler and poured a glass of Pinot grigio into the crystal wine glass. *I can really go for a massage right now;* she ruminated and continued to drink her glass of wine. She poured a second glass and there was a sudden feeling of emptiness. Carla walked into her bedroom, took the cordless handset from its cradle and gave Tony a call. It was funny how she quickly went from not wanting a fulfilling relationship with Tony to missing his presence every second of every hour. Tony answered on the first ring.

"Hi! How did it go today?" His voice was filled with excitement.

"Wow! Sounds like you were anxiously awaiting my call."

"I was... I mean, today was a big day for you and I am anxious to hear the outcome. I know you did your thing in the court room."

"I'm not one to brag, but let's just say that things worked in my favor. Prayer can be one hell of a thing. I prayed and God listened. My client's potential life sentence was replaced with a three months jail sentence. Can you believe that?"

"I told you that things would work out. We need to celebrate. How about dinner this weekend?"

"That sounds inviting. I might have to take you up on that invite."

"We can go anywhere you like," Tony told her. "Just name the time and place and we have a date."

Carla grinned at his persistence. "Okay. But for now, is there any chance of me seeing you tonight?"

"I'm your genie and your wish is my command. Give me a moment to wash up and I will be over in a few."

"See you when you get here." Carla hung up and then walked into the kitchen to pour another glass of wine. Still dressed in her grey, wool skirt suit minus the matching wool suit jacket, Carla walked back out onto the terrace and took a seat on her wicker chair and looked up in the sky to observe the beautiful arrangement of the twinkling stars. She took a sip of the white wine and enjoyed the fresh air of Mother Nature. Carla heard knocks at the front door. She stood up from the chair and ran inside her condo. She quickly opened the door and Tony greeted her with four 'congratulations' balloons. She gasped and raised an eyebrow.

"What is this all about?" she asked as Tony walked pass her.

"They are for your hard work today," he said as he handed her the balloons and walked past her nonchalantly.

"That was thoughtful of you." She locked the door and followed behind Tony who was now standing in the center of the living room.

"They were well deserved. Good job." Tony kissed her cheek and she accidentally freed the balloons from her hands. Carla watched them float to the ceiling.

"What's this?" Tony noticed the opened doors that led to the terrace and walked outside. "I had no idea that this was out here. This is a gorgeous view. I doubt you sit out here often." He yelled to Carla who was still in the middle of the living room trying to reach for the balloons. Tony looked down and saw the glass of wine on the wicker table. "Maybe I should take that back."

Carla gave up on trying to catch the balloons that were already too high up in the ceiling, and walked back onto the terrace to join Tony. "Take what back?" she asked.

"I was saying that I doubt you took advantage of this view... but I noticed the wine glass. I see someone has already set the mood."

"That's glass number three." Carla walked up behind him, wrapped her hands around his waist, and kissed the back of his arm. She closed her eyes and rested her head in the middle of his back. Yes, she was definitely feeling him. She was too afraid to admit it.

Tony pulled her in front of him, positioning her back towards his chest, and wrapped his arms around her waist instead. They both looked up and watched the stars together.

"It's getting late. Don't you think you should be getting ready for bed?" he asked.

"What, you my daddy now?" Carla teased.

"I didn't mean it in that way; I just don't want you to be tired at work tomorrow."

"I know, I was only teasing. I guess you have a point."

Carla was in fact tired. She's had a long day in court and the liquor was beginning to make matters worse.

"Let's go inside," Tony said and swept her off her feet.

Chapter 6

Carla opened her eyes and saw Tony towering over her. He was watching her sleep.

"TGIF!" He whispered and kissed her forehead. "Did sleeping beauty rest well last night? I've never seen a woman look so beautiful after they wake so early in the morning."

Where did this man come from? He does and says all the right things at the right time.

Carla smiled and stared at him briefly. She then rolled over and turned to lie on her left side; facing the opposite direction of Tony. She didn't want him to see the truth in her eyes. The truth of her falling for him in a way she never expected. She suddenly cupped her head in her hands and made low groans.

"What's the matter babe?"

"I think I'm paying for the one glass too many that I had last night because my head is pounding."

Tony hurried to the kitchen and returned with a glass of water and two gel cap Advil.

"Here, take these. They should help your headache."

Carla sat up in bed and the quilted cover slid down her body, exposing her breasts. Her nipples hardened and stuck out like two whopper chocolate balls. Tony noticed her black pearls and had an instant hard on. Carla became aware of his stimulation and forced a smile through the pain. She swallowed the pills, washed them down with the glass of water, and then curled up in the fetal position. She handed Tony the empty glass and he placed it on the night stand and lay parallel next to Carla in the spooning position. He pulled her into the warmth of his strong arms causing her back to rest against his chest. Her ass rubbed against his stiffened manhood.

"Oooh, looks like someone is excited," she said and continued to back her ass up on him.

"He can help with your headache too." Tony leaned in and kissed the back of Carla's neck.

The feel of his breath against her neck sent tingles down her spine and made her forget about the pain she felt. She took Tony's hand and positioned it at the opening of her slippery tunnel.

"Looks like he's not the only one who's excited," Tony mentioned from the feel of her wetness. He threw the cover onto the floor and fondled Carla until she begged him to enter her. Tony inserted his penis inside her warm, wet womanhood, and the warm feel from his thick flesh was what Carla craved at 7:30 in the a.m.

"Damn. You drive me crazy," Tony crooned at how tight she felt inside and continued to penetrate her until he filled inside of her.

Carla closed her eyes and played with her nipples as Tony cautiously pumped in and out of her in slow motion. She preferred slow love making vs. that aggressive bam slam thank you madam that most men did to get a quick fix.

Carla loved the way that Tony was always in tuned with her feelings. It was like he was in her mind to know what she was thinking. She knew how to get her freak on from time to time, don't get it twisted, but making slow, passionate love with Tony always ended in a mind blowing orgasm. Tony pulled her tightly into his chest and soft moans escaped both of their lips as they released their secretions in unity. Tony knew how to handle Carla; it was like he knew her body better than she did and fulfilled her every need. He never failed to please her sexually and she soaked up every minute of their mind blowing experience.

"How's that head feeling?" Tony asked as she turned to face him with a huge smile on her face.

"I guess the smile on my face tells it all huh?"

"A picture is worth a thousand words."

Carla slid her head down and kissed Tony's navel. The fact that she was due in the office at noon nearly slipped her mind. She was enjoying every minute of Tony's company. There was no doubt that she was totally into him. The idea of him being a waiter was no longer becoming an issue for Carla. She was beginning to fall in love with the man and now cared less about what he did for a living. But how does she stifle her feelings and stick to the initial plan without giving in? At the rate he was going, it would be hard for her to fight what her heart felt for this man.

"I'll be right back." Tony climbed out of bed and walked towards the TV.

"Where are you going?" Carla asked and watched as his dick dangled between his thighs like a pendulum on a grandfather clock.

"I can't go too far...here." Tony walked towards her and handed her the remote. She kept her eyes on his dick with each step he took and imagined how lovely it would be when she decided to deep throat the entirety of his long, thick, nine inches of manhood. Tony noticed that something had her attention so he followed her eyes and realized what she was staring at.

"We can go another round if you want."

Carla looked up at Tony and realized that she was busted. "Trust me, I would love to go another round, but you and I both know that there is not enough time for that. I need to get ready to go into the office." Carla flicked on the TV with the remote and searched for the news channel. Tony glanced at the clock on her nightstand and walked out of the room. As she continued to lie in bed and watch the local tragedies on the channel two action news, a sweet aroma coming from the kitchen distracted her focus from the news reporter's words. Carla was surprised to see Tony returning with a loaded tray containing a plate of scrambled eggs, French toast, bacon, Italian sausage links, assorted fruit on the side, and a cup of hot chocolate.

"Breakfast is served."

Carla sat up and Tony placed the tray beside her. "Oh my gosh...this is a sure surprise. You have some hidden talent. What else can you do that I don't know about?" Carla couldn't imagine that she had all of this food stored in her refrigerator. Breakfast was not something she usually had time to cook, but she would often buy groceries in hope to cooking them.

"You don't expect me to work in a restaurant and not learn a thing or two. Besides, you have a long day ahead of you and breakfast is the most important meal of the day."

"Do you expect me to eat all of this by myself?" she questioned and looked down at the tray.

"It may look like a lot of food, but trust me, you can handle it." Tony sat beside her with the tray in between them. He took a piece of fruit from the tray and fed it to Carla.

"If you keep on spoiling me like this, sooner or later, I won't know how to act." She said and then Tony lifted her chin, pulled her face into his and planted a kiss on her lips.

After breakfast, Carla moseyed out of bed and headed to the shower. She allowed the water to heat up while she pinned her hair up to prevent it from getting wet. The steam began to fog the mirror, which was proof that it was warm enough for her to step inside. Carla stepped into the warm mist and the hot water spraying from the removable showerhead greeted her like rain bursting from a cloud. She embraced it as it sprayed onto her chest and caressed her nipples.

Carla swayed into the bedroom with a brown towel wrapped around her body and plopped down on the bed. Tony had set a comfortable environment for her and she dreaded that she had to leave his presence and go into the office.

"Don't forget that you agreed to us having dinner this weekend," he reminded her.

"Shoot. I almost forgot," she admitted. "There's this nice restaurant that I haven't eaten at in a while. Morton's Steak House...you ever heard of it?" she asked Tony.

"Yeah. I've eaten there a time or two. It's been a while though."

"Great! So that's where we'll have dinner." Carla reached for the telephone to make dinner reservations.

Before she could dial the number, Tony stopped her. "I know the owner of the place. Maybe I can give him a call. It's been a while since we've spoken, but I'm sure he remembers me..."

"But just in case he doesn't, I am going to call and make reservations. Better safe than sorry. Moreover, it can be difficult to get seating in a place like that. They're always booked to capacity so that just goes to show how good their food is."

"Don't forget to add how expensive they are too."

"That they are. Which explains why I don't eat there often, but they never fail to deliver a good meal though."

"Well I'm still going to reach out to my man and see what's up."

"Try and pull your strings, but if all else fails, at least we'll have our reserved seats." Carla smiled and dialed 411 to retrieve the number to the restaurant. Tony treaded to the bathroom to brush his teeth.

"Any luck?" He asked when he returned to the bedroom.

"Talk about luck. We just got the last seating."

"Get out of here! Man, seems like you have to secure seats months in advance to be guaranteed any seating," Tony added.

"Those rich white folks don't play when it comes to having a good piece of steak." Carla joked.

"Do you see what time it is?" Tony asked.

Carla looked at the clock. "Damn. Time flies. I think you're just rubbing it in because you don't have to work today."

Tony attempted to hold his laugh in. "I swear I wouldn't do that." He burst out in laughter after his attempt failed.

Carla threw a pillow at him which initiated a pillow fight between the two that lasted a solid fifteen minutes. She couldn't remember the last time she had that much fun. Carla laughed so hard every time when Tony would try to dodge the pillow that was thrown at him, but it made no sense for him to try because she would strike him every time.

Since she became a lawyer, Carla has been so wrapped up in her work and had forgotten what it was like to loosen up and enjoy life. Tamika always quoted the phrase, "All work and no play makes Carla a dull girl," whenever she refused to take time away from her job. Tony knew how to bring out the kid in her and it was rare for anyone to tap into that side of her. The only person that she could remember doing that, was her father. It was then that Carla knew that Tony was special.

After their short game of pillow fight, Carla undid the fold in her towel and lathered her body with lotion.

"You do that so well." Tony stared at her in admiration with each stroke.

"I would ask you to assist me, but I already know what that would lead to." She smiled and smoothed the body butter onto her legs. It was something about Tony's touch that made her pussy ache to feel him inside her.

"So what are your plans on your day off?" She asked and wished she could've spent the entire day with him.

"Hmmm." Tony stroked his goatee and pretended to be in deep thought. "Oh now I remember. I'm going to get my truck washed, stop by the mall to pick up an order. For the most part, I'm just gonna relax at home until I get to see you at dinner."

"Don't say that to try and make me feel better," she said and walked off.

Tony followed behind Carla who was now standing inside of her closet. "No. Real talk. I don't have much of anything planned today...Really. I am literally going to stick around until our dinner date," he pleaded.

Carla stopped searching through the rack of clothing and turned around to face Tony. It was the sincerity in his voice that grabbed her attention. His plea sounded like that of a little boy trying to prove his innocence. "I really didn't mean anything by my statement, I was kidding. Don't take it so seriously."

Tony became embarrassed. He felt like he made himself appear desperate for Carla's validation of his explanation. He covered his face with his hands and walked out of the closet. *What was I thinking? I hope she doesn't think that I'm trying too hard.*

"What's wrong? Was it something I said?" Carla yelled.

"No, it's not you, it's me." He yelled back.

Did I miss something, she wondered. Giving it no further thought, Carla shrugged her shoulders and continued her search for something comfortable to wear. She wanted to keep her look professional but still sexy. Carla walked out of the closet with a pair of wide legged, dark blue jean pants and a flower print, sleeveless tunic.

Carla hauled the tunic over her head and pulled the pants up and over her round apple bottom. Tony watched like he was viewing a peep show. He admired her body and the way her jeans hugged her in all the right places. Carla had immaculate taste in fashion and he had to give her props on her fashionable taste. She even appeared immaculate in her nude state. There was always something about her that stood out to him. Carla took no notice of the way Tony observed her and ran to look at herself in the mirror.

"It doesn't take much for you to look beautiful." Tony stated and brought her to his attention.

Carla turned to look at him and smile. She was oblivious to the fact that he had been sitting there the whole time. When is she going to quit lying to herself about not wanting with him what he wanted with her?

"I better going." She grabbed her handbag from the closet door and slipped her feet into a pair of violet colored patent leather pumps that matched the print on her shirt, and headed towards the front door. Tony followed suit and Carla turned the key to lock the door.

Carla entered the doors of the firm and stumbled upon the CEO of the company. "John! It's good to see you." She was surprised to see John in the office in the middle of the day, especially on a Friday.

"Hey Carla, how's it going? You're just the person I wanted to see." John looked like one of those Italian mafia godfathers that you would see on the A&E sitcom, *The Sopranos*. He always adorned himself in a slick tailor made suit with shiny cufflinks and sported an expensive Rolex watch.

When Carla first interviewed for the associate position with the firm two years ago, she wondered if John was somehow involved with the mafia in his past life. He always had someone working for him; even when it didn't pertain to the practice. It was obvious that John was in charge and living large. Carla could not remember when he was not being chauffeured to and from the airport to his many "business meetings". There was no doubt that the firm made money, but the many so called "business trips" that John took, seemed suspicious. But she did not care to make it her business to find out. As long as her five figure paycheck was directly deposited in her bank account on time, she had no concerns.

"Oh really? What about?" She grew nervous. John hardly requested to see her. Everything was conveyed via email if he needed to inform her of anything. Carla was one of his best attorneys so she was curious to find out what he had on his mind.

"I heard you kicked some arrogant prosecutor's ass yesterday," John said with a bear laugh.

"I wouldn't necessarily put it that way."

"Don't be so modest, Carla. You did one hell of a job. That was a tough case. I am proud of you," he told her and gave her a pat on the back. His Italian accent was becoming noticeable. "We should celebrate over lunch. Let me know when you're schedule is clear."

"Oh wow! Thanks John."

"You managed to pull it off by yourself and that is something to be recognized for. Congratulations." John shook her hand and walked off towards the elevator.

Carla was amazed that John gave her such recognition. He had congratulated her a few times in the past, but not once did he take time out from his busy schedule to invite her to lunch. As a matter of fact, she doubts that he treated any of his junior or senior partners to lunch. If word got out, Carla knew that a lot of hating and gossiping would take place, but she could care less. The fact that he noticed her hard work gave Carla courage to approach him about making junior partner in the months to come. Senior partner is what she hoped but she figured she would crawl before she walked. *I just have to play my cards right*, she thought.

As Carla turned to convene to her office, she looked over at Sarah's desk and noticed that Sarah was eves dropping on her conversation with John. She knew this much because she saw the jealousy in Sarah's eyes. Sarah tried to look away; but instead, she moved away from her desk and walked off in the opposite direction. Carla continued to her office and shook her head.

When Carla reached the doorway to her office, she threw her handbag in the chair by the door and walked towards the break room. She walked over to the water cooler, grabbed a plastic cup from the stack that was placed on top of the bottled water, and leaned over to dispense water into her cup. When she stood up and brought the half filled cup of water to her mouth, she immediately spewed the water out of her mouth and onto the floor. The reaction resulted from the feel of someone from behind sliding their hand up between her thighs.

"WHAT THE FUCK!..." Carla wiped her mouth and quickly turned around to face her harasser. Her eyes widened when she saw that it was Sarah.

"Are you out of your fucking mind?" Carla had an instant reflex and slapped the shit out of Sarah, causing her face to lose its color and made her head swing a 180 degree turn. If she slapped her any harder, Sarah's head would've done a full 360 degree turn. Sarah's cheek turned fire red and without a word, she held her cheek with her left hand. Sarah was no lesbian, but she had an appreciation for women, especially Carla. Sarah was so fascinated by Carla's beauty and body that she would sometimes secretly masturbate in the bathroom to naked fantasies of Carla.

"How dare you violate me like that?" Carla clenched her jaws and pointed her finger in Sarah's face, and then mushed her in the head. Carla was not a fucking lesbian and the fact that Sarah overstepped her boundary, pissed her off. "You are one sick bitch and you better be lucky we're not out in the streets where I would've stomped your ass for making that fouls ass move. I ought to just kick your ass anyway but you're not worth me losing my job."

"I...I...I'm sorry Carla." Sarah ran out of the break room. She was surprised at herself for the move she'd just made. She had no idea of what came over her. She was embarrassed and didn't know how she would face Carla again. The many fantasies she's had of one day catching Carla alone in the break room so that she could fondle her and lick her dry seemed to have gotten the best of her.

Carla was disgusted and needed to clear her mind. She stormed off to her office and slammed the door. She slammed it so hard that the law degrees she had hanging on the walls nearly fell to the floor. Carla paced back and forth for a few seconds and tried to collect her thoughts, but it was hard to think through her anger, so she decided that she had to get out of there. Carla grabbed her handbag from the chair and ran out to the parking lot, giving Sarah the evil eye when she passed her desk.

Sitting in her truck, Carla needed to do something to ease her mind. She pulled out her cellular phone and dialed her hairstylist's number. She needed a fresh do for her dinner date with Tony and now would be the best time to get her hair done.

"Hey Diane. You think you can squeeze me in today?"

"Are you okay? You sound a little agitated."

"Yeah I'm cool. Nothing I can't handle. Just had a minor run-in with someone, that's all."

"Oh, okay. Just wanted to make sure you are okay. Well, my two o'clock just canceled so you're in luck. If you come on over now, I can get you in the chair."

"I'm on my way." Carla hung up and sped off towards the hair salon.

After listening to a few upbeat songs from Mariah Carey's new album, Carla swept the incident with Sarah to the back of her mind and knew that if she violated her again, there is an ass whooping with her name written all over it, job or no job.

Pulling up to A Touch of Class hair salon, Carla parked in front of the building and climbed out of her truck. The second her feet landed on the freshly paved concrete, her cell phone vibrated on her hip. She removed it from the holster and answered.

"Hello."

"Whassup...Whassup...Whassuuppp!?" Tamika screamed through the phone imitating Martin from the sitcom, *Martin*.

Carla laughed at Tamika being silly. "Hey fool!"

"Watchya doing?"

"What is up with you today?"

"I'm just being silly. I am happy that it's FRIDAY! They are about to drive me crazy up in this place. I swear, if another file is thrown on my desk, I am going to scream," Tamika said.

"Sounds like you need a happy hour ASAP," Carla teased.

"Now you're speaking my language. So what's going on with you?" Tamika asked.

"I just pulled up at Diane's."

"You're earlier than usual. I thought you were at the office today."

"I was but I left early. After the day I had yesterday, I deserve to take a load off."

"Which reminds me, how did it go yesterday? I meant to call you, but I got swamped and it slipped my mind."

"It went great! It actually turned out better than I expected."

Tamika interjected. "Did your client get off?" Her voice was filled with excitement.

"Not exactly but he got a way lesser sentence than what he was up against. You should've seen the look on the prosecutor's face when the jury read the verdict."

"And again, LADIES and GENTLEMEN, Carla Milford scores," Tamika said in a voice mimicking that of a sport commentator.

Carla laughed. "Thank you very much," she said in her Elvis Presley impersonation voice.

"I'm so proud of you. Congratulations. You know I'm coming to you if I ever catch a charge," Tamika joked.

"Your ass don't need to be catching no charge, but I got your back."

"Haha. I'm just saying. You never know when a bitch might make me snap."

"Yeah, we all know you have a few screws missing upstairs."

"Whatever. So what you have planned for later?"

"I'm going to dinner with Tony."

"Oh. So you changed your mind? Now it's all coming together. Is that the reason you're a day early for your hair appointment? I see what time it is," Tamika teased.

"No, my decision stands. There's nothing wrong with having dinner with a homie lover friend. And I am in need of a wash, if you should know. Anyhow, shouldn't you be working on those thousands of files that are on your desk?"

"So you have jokes?" They both laughed.

"I'm walking into the shop now so I'll call you later."

Carla hung up and returned the device in the holster. She pulled open the door and the smell of spritz mixed with oil sheen and the hot curling irons tackled her nose.

"Good, you're on time," Diane said when she saw Carla walk through the door.

Diane has been Carla's stylist since her freshman year in college. She was in her mid thirties, but looked like she was still in her twenties. She has a nineteen year old son that people have often mistaken her of being his sister. Her medium brown complexion and bone straight hair that came down to the center of her back, gave her a similar look to that of the mogul bombshell, Kimora Lee Simmons. Diane looked Korean but denies having any Korean blood in her DNA. The white skinny jeans and purple tank top that she wore, made her look youthful.

"Go to the shampoo bowl," Diane instructed Carla.

Carla was glad that she made it when she did because Diane had three people under the dryer, one lady in her chair that was waiting for a relaxer and another lady that was waiting for her new hair color to be processed.

"You look younger every time I see you," Carla told her as she adjusted her head on the neck of the sink.

"Look who's talking. You look the same as you did when you first came into my shop eight years ago."

"Thank God your two o'clock canceled because had I been any later, I would not be getting out of here no time soon. And I am not trying to be up in here all day with you. You have quite a full house in here today."

"It's like this on most Fridays. Didn't you have work today?" Diane asked as she gave Carla's hair the first dose of shampoo.

"I had a half day today."

"I knew it was something because I was shocked when you called me. I'm use to seeing you here on Saturday mornings at 7 a.m. sharp," Diane stated.

Diane rubbed conditioner into Carla's hair and placed a plastic cap over her hair. "Sit under the dryer by the plant."

Carla sat under the dryer with a magazine in her hand and in between breaks from reading, she watched as Diane went to work on her client's hair. Diane worked her hands and hurried to get two of the women dolled up and sent them on their merry way.

"How are you going to style your hair today?" Diane asked Carla when she sat in her chair.

"I don't know. I'm in the mood for something different. Put your skills to work and hook me up."

Diane worked her magic and once again, Carla was a satisfied customer. When Diane spun her stylist chair around, Carla was pleased with the outcome when she looked in the mirror. Diane had her looking like Nia Long when she made a guest appearance on the *Monique show*.

"I love it!"Carla exclaimed. Her lavish loose curls reached the top of her shoulders and they danced each time she turned her head from left to right. Carla admired herself in the mirror and there was no doubt that she was definitely a diva. She looked forward to showing off her new look to Tony.

"Thank you, Diane. You always come through for me. You did your thing with these curls." Carla reached into her bag and removed a fifty dollar bill from her wallet and handed it to Diane. "See you in two weeks."

"Okay. Knock 'em dead girl," Diane yelled after Carla, who was on her way out the door.

The moment Carla entered her front door, anxiety kicked in. She raced to her closet and removed the silk dress that she purchased from Neiman Marcus. Carla laid it on her bed and searched for a pair of shoes that would go perfectly with the dress. In the midst of her search, Carla found a pair of black peep toe stilettos that she'd bought last winter.

"I almost forgot that I had these." With the million and one pairs of shoes she owned, it wouldn't be hard to forget owning a pair or two. She pulled the shoe box from the shelf and removed the lid.

Love Finally

They still looked brand new. After all, she only wore them twice and to imagine that she spent $500.00 on them.

To Carla, money wasn't really an object. She was her only responsibility and she didn't mind paying the cost to look like the diva she was. Besides, she deserved the best and she worked harder than most people to earn every penny she owned. Her bank account was sitting well on five figures, but she was no bimbo and learned to be smart about her finances. Carla had money stashed away in a *CD* account because God forbid that anything should happen to her, she would at least know that there was something available for her to fall back on.

Stepping inside the shower, Carla lathered her body with the sweet scented shower gel and traced the outline of her own body with her palms. She let the warm water rinse her clean and the feel of the water beating against her skin made her pussy feel like it was on fire. Carla cupped her vagina with her hand and smoothly inserted her finger to cool the heat. She moved her finger in and out until she brought herself to a roaring climax. It was nothing compared to the way Tony made her feel, but it was enough to hold her until she could be with Tony again.

Walking into her bedroom, Carla looked at the time. It was still early, so there was no need to rush. She dropped the towel to the floor and stood in front of her floor length mirror. She was feeling herself and those bouncy curls made her feel herself more because they gave her an exotic look.

"I can get use to this look," she said and fluffed her hair. Carla stepped away from the mirror and walked towards the drawer where she kept her panties. Her first thought was not wearing any, but she decided against it and slipped on a nude colored thong. Displaying panty lines were a thing of the past and for that reason, thongs became her next best friend. After hooking the matching bra together, Carla walked back into the bathroom to apply her makeup. She created a smoky look with her eyes using her black l liquid eyeliner.

Carla pulled on her dress and loved the way the silk material felt against her skin. The way her back was exposed from the low V-cut, was a sight to keep other women staring and make men wonder. The colors in the dress complimented her caramel complexion and the dress made her look like a Venus goddess. Completing her look with the pair of stiletto heels, Carla heedfully slipped her feet into them; and then walked around her bedroom to get a comfortable feel for the height of the five inch heels. She looked elegant and couldn't wait to face her date.

After a few spins here and there to make sure that she looked her best, Carla heard knocks at the door. Forgetting that she was wearing five inch heels, Carla ran to open the door and nearly broke her neck in the process.

"Wow! That dress is magnificent," Tony praised her when he laid eyes on her. He walked inside and took her by the hands. "Absolutely flawless," he continued and looked her over from head to toe. "I really like what you did to your hair," he added.

Carla blushed and was pleased to see that he noticed her new look. *Yup, he's definitely a keeper*, she thought to herself. It was rare for men to pay attention to some of the minor changes that women made to their outer appearance. They were either too busy thinking about being fucked or they had another woman on their brain. Tony whirled Carla around to get a good view of her from front to back. Carla admired Tony as well. He sported a white Armani shirt and a matching blazer with a pair of blue jeans and a pair of white Templin on his feet.

"Mmph. How did I ever get so damn lucky to have such a fine woman in my possession?" he asked after he let her hand loose.

"Let's not forget that we have some place to be." She said in a low yet seductive voice.

"Oh...yes. But before we go, I have something for you."

Tony reached into his blazer pocket and removed a large jewelry box with the word, TIFFANY, engraved. Carla gasped and her eyes widened at the box. Tony handed her the box and she took it in her hands.

"Oh my," she gasped. "What on earth is this?"

"Open it and find out."

Carla removed the lid and dazzled at the sight of the big round pearls. They were beautiful. She looked up and turned to face Tony. "Wow! They are amazing. I like them a lot."

Tony stood in front of her and removed the pearl necklace from the box and then placed it around Carla's neck. She traced her hands over it and thanked him.

Carla stood at the entrance of the building and waited for Tony to pull his car around. Tony climbed out of the driver's side and the custom made grill and shiny rims beamed at her through the headlights. Tony opened the door and escorted her in. He climbed into the driver's seat and they drove off, headed to their destination.

As they continued to travel in the downtown Atlanta area, Carla felt like a celebrity when they would stop at the stoplights, only to have other drivers and their passengers break their necks to look through the tinted windows. Carla smiled and sopped up all of the attention she was receiving. Tony saw the joy in her eyes, which he assumed was they were headed on their first date, and placed his right hand on her left thigh. Carla put her hands over his and was tempted to hike up her dress and guide him to the heated opening of her tunnel. Instead, she let off a devilish grin and thought about all the freaky, oh so freaky things she would do to Tony after their date. But for now, she just stroked his hand up and down her thigh, loving every bit of his soft hands and gentle touch.

Pulling up to Morton's Steak House, Tony drove up to the valet area and handed the keys to a young Latino fellow as he stepped out of the car. "Be careful with her," Tony warned and tipped him fifty dollars.

"I will." The young man grinned and shoved the fifty dollar bill in his pocket. Tony smiled, knowing that the guy was grateful. He watched as the young man climbed in and drove off to park.

"Shall we?" Tony took Carla's arm into his and led her into the restaurant. As they walked down the entryway, Carla beamed from ear to ear. She was being treated like royalty and for once, she was being treated instead of treating. They approached the wide opened doors and a young lady bowed as they approached her.

"Welcome to Morton's," she greeted them in her French accent.

They never did this shit the last time I dined here, Carla thought. *Morton's really stepped their game up. I feel like I'm in a fucking fairytale.* Carla continued to smile and they walked towards the hostess, who without saying a word, smiled at them and led them to a secluded area of the restaurant. Other guests stared as they walked passed their tables and even older men who were dining with their wives, glared at Carla in awe. With all the stares she got, Carla was satisfied that her dress was the right choice.

They were now seated in a VIP booth and Carla raised an eyebrow. "I never reserved seats in VIP. Do you know how much this thing costs? It is too rich for my blood. Maybe she made a mistake." Carla stood up from her seat, ran her hands along the sides of her dress to straighten it out and attempted to go and search for the hostess. Before she could put one foot in front of the other, Tony grabbed her arm.

"Carla, wait." She turned around to face Tony and looked as if to say, *"You better not ever in your right mind grab me like that again."*

Tony read her expression and released his hold on her. "I'm sorry. I didn't mean to grab you like that, but I needed to stop you before you stormed off. It's okay, Carla. Sit down." Following his directions, Carla sat down immediately.

"But Tony..."

Love Finally

He cut her off. "Don't worry, I did this." His voice was smooth and calm.

Carla looked confused. "What do you mean?"

"See," he continued, "I contacted the owner of the place, who is also an old friend of mine, and I told him that I had reservations to dine here tonight with a beautiful woman. He offered us VIP seating, free of charge as well as the meal. Besides, he owes me a favor. He and I met last year when he dined at the Waffle joint and I gave him the connection with one of the city's best chef. So I would say he owes me."

Carla's confused looked turned into a stunned one. "Wow! I...I...I'm impressed. I mean, that was very generous of your friend." She couldn't imagine that Tony had this type of connection.

Tony took her hand and interlocked his fingers with hers. "I looked forward to this night, and I wanted our first date together to be special and memorable. If we're lucky, we could probably recap this memory with our grandchildren," He said with a wink.

Carla started to feel warm and bubbly inside. *Is he implying what I think he is,* she wondered. Carla blushed. Throughout the ten years that she dated her ex, not once did he mention the idea of spending the rest of his life with her. He was comfortable with shacking up and Carla often blamed herself for allowing it. *Love can really make you blind,* she mused. As crazy as it sounds, she was now thankful that he left her for another woman and could beat herself up for the way she became depressed about it.

The VIP area was decked out with ice sculptures and flower arrangements encircled them, three crystal chandeliers hung above their heads, the seats were made of a soft, white velvet material, and the tables had mirrored glass and platinum metal along the edges. They even had state-of-the-art audio and visual equipment with Wi-Fi Technology. She was feeling about her date.

After endless conversation and finishing their hundred dollar filet mignon, double cut porterhouse steak with asparagus and mashed potatoes that they washed down with a glass of the finest merlot, Tony made a request to have Teddy Pendergrass', *"Turn off the lights,"* lyrics play through the hi-tech speakers that surrounded them.

"May I?" Tony pulled Carla to her feet and they stood face to face with each other.

"You have really out done yourself," she whispered in his ear and then pulled him close as they waltzed into the wee hours of the night. Carla relished the moment and when they were finished dancing the night away, Carla and Tony made their exit and waited for the valet to return with their car. She had the night of her life, and couldn't wait to get home so she could rock Tony's world for showing her a great time.

Chapter 7

"It has been reported by federal agents that a seven year old girl went missing in the..." The news reporter's voice echoed through the speakers of the fifty-two inch flat screen plasma that was mounted on her bedroom wall and woke her. Carla rolled over and abruptly opened her eyes. Tony had left her condo at six O'clock in the morning to get prepared for a mandatory staff meeting at the restaurant and he apparently forgot to power the thing off. Squinting her eyes, Carla realized that she was alone and turned flat onto her stomach. She buried her face into the pillow and closed her eyes, attempting to go back to sleep. Her night with Tony was unbelievable and Carla reminisced at the moment she previously shared with her lover. It was difficult to put herself in a zone with the loud voices on the TV interrupting her thoughts, so she reached for the remote and lowered the volume, but she found herself tossing and turning for at least five minutes.

"Ugh," Carla let out a sigh and sat up on the edge of her bed. It was 10:00 a.m. on a Saturday morning and she hoped to have slept in 'til noon. "Since I'm up, I might as well put this time to good use," she spoke into the air. Carla reached for her house phone and dialed her mother's number. She planned to treat her to lunch and spend quality time just like she'd promised herself she would.

"Hello dear," Ellen's cheerful voice sung through the receiver. Ellen lived alone since the passing of her late husband and you would think that her life came to an end when she restricted herself to staying indoors, only to get out when she ran her errands.

"Mother, you sound mighty excited." For the first time in a long time, Ellen sounded like her old self again, the way she would always sound when Carl was around, before he died. Carla smiled and reflected on the happy times she shared with her mother and father as a little girl. Although they didn't discuss it much, Carla knew how much Ellen missed Carl.

"Why wouldn't I be excited? I mean; after all, it's rare that you even called me on a Saturday morning, especially at this hour. I'm excited to hear my only daughter's voice."

"Well, what are you doing?"

"Oh, I'm just sitting here watching the *Golden Girls*...hahaha...I tell you, that Sophia is something else," Ellen laughed.

"You really enjoy watching that show, don't you?"

"It's entertaining."

"What do you think about me treating you to lunch?"

"That would be great!" Ellen re-directed her attention to Carla.

"Okay. Get dressed and I will be there in an hour." She ended their call and Carla rushed to take a quick shower.

After rummaging through her closet, Carla picked out a purple sundress that was mixed with hot pink. When she slipped it on, the knee length dress made her look airy and she loved it. She fluffed her curls and slid her feet into a pair of purple sandals and made her way downstairs to the parking lot. When she turned the key into the ignition, Carla revved the engine and listened to it roar like a lion in the jungle. But before she drove out of the lot, Carla pulled out her cell phone to call her mother and told her that she was on her way. She ended the call and injected a Brian McKnight album into the disc player and drove off into the direction of I-85.

As she cruised to the smooth sounds of Brian with the sunroof slid back and the wind blowing through her hair, Carla thought about how much she wished her dad was still around. *If only he could see me now,* she thought. *He would've been so proud to see how much I've thrived.* She also thought about visiting his grave site, but decided against it when she remembered the despair she felt the last time she visited.

Carla pulled up in Ellen's driveway and an instant rush of childhood memories flooded her mind: from her first scar to the first day she met Tamika at the bus stop. Carla parked her Range behind Ellen's black Maserati Quattroporte S model and took notice of her mother's well manicured yard and realized that her old neighborhood hadn't changed much since she left for college. As a matter of fact, a guilt trip came over Carla because it was actually her first time visiting since then. The huge estate mansions, including Ellen's, that were lined on every block in the suburb Sugarloaf area, looked like multi Gould castles at the Hempstead house, located in Sands point, New York.

Carla hopped out of her truck and walked up the walkway to her mother's front door. She rang the doorbell and the door swung open. Ellen stood in the doorway and rushed to give Carla a big hug that nearly sent Carla landing flat on her bodacious ass. "Hi baby!" Ellen squealed and then pulled herself back to check her daughter out from head to toe. "I'm so glad to see you. Come in come in." Ellen walked inside and Carla followed behind her.

"You look like a baby doll in that dress," Ellen yelled over her shoulder to Carla. "Those colors really look good on you." Without looking back, Ellen continued to talk to Carla as she walked up her semi-circled stairway.

"I'll be ready in just a minute, I just need to apply my moisturizer," Ellen shouted as she disappeared upstairs. It made no sense for Carla to respond, because she doubts that Ellen could even hear her from the third floor of the house. Carla wondered why her mother chose to stay in the eight bedroom, six bathroom residence all by her lonesome. She reminded herself that it was probably the closest Ellen could remain to Carl, with all their happy memories, and with that reminder, she decided not to question the issue any further.

As she waited for Ellen to return, Carla scanned the family portraits that hung on the walls in the family room and she came across one that she remembered like it was yesterday. It was a photo of when her father handed her her first set of car keys at her high school graduation party. Carla remembered how happy she was when she received the set of keys to her very own, brand new Acura Legend. That was twelve years ago and here she was, a twenty eight year old attorney who graduated at the top of her class, with a paid off SUV and her condo mortgage paid up for twelve months in advance. She ran her hand over the picture and fought back tears as she oh so wished that her father were still alive.

"I'm ready dear." Ellen yelled from the front door. Carla released the photo and walked towards her mother.

"Do you have everything?"

"Yes, I made sure of it."

They walked outside and climbed into Carla's SUV. "Your car still looks good. It even smells new," Ellen commented while buckling her seat belt. "So, where are you taking me?"

Knowing how much her mother enjoyed seafood, Carla elected to take her to Strips Steak and Sushi restaurant in the Midtown Atlanta area. She doubts that Ellen has ever eaten there before; being that it is a setting for a younger crowd.

"We're going to go to a restaurant in Atlantic Station." Carla told her. Ellen trusted her daughters choice and nodded her head in agreement before sitting back to enjoy the ride.

They reached Atlantic Station, and Carla drove into to the parking garage. The place was packed, which forced her to circle the levels a few times before she spotted a vacant space on the ground floor. She quickly pulled into the space when she noticed two young girls, probably in their late teens, trying to pull their outdated Ford Explorer into the space that she searched hard to find. When Carla beat the young teens to it, the driver of the Explorer rolled her eyes and sped off. Carla could care less because she was happy that Ellen didn't have to walk far from the garage to the restaurant.

They'd taken the elevator to the first floor and walked across the street in the direction of the restaurant. It wasn't unusual for Atlantic Station to be busy on a beautiful Saturday such as this. Besides the restaurant, there were clothing stores like H&M, Banana Republic, Dillards, etc...just to name a few. There were also other restaurants like Fox sports grill, The Cheesecake Factory, and many others that you can think of. They even have a movie theatre, and grocery shopping stores.

Whatever you needed, you were guaranteed to find it at Atlantic Station; it was a small city all in itself. As they continued to walk to the restaurant, Carla checked out the people as they walked up and down the sidewalks, going in and out of stores carrying there many shopping bags, looking like they have not a care in the world.

They walked into Strips and the booming hip hop music from the overhead stereo pierced their ears. Carla was use to the atmosphere and already knew what to expect. She looked over at Ellen to see her expression and Carla could tell that her mother was not use to music of this caliber. Without putting up a fuss, Ellen just asked Carla how could anyone eat and think over such loud noise. Carla smiled and walked up to the hostess with Ellen in tow.

"Welcome to Strips. Will it be just the two of you today?" she asked.

Carla nodded her head and the hostess led them to a round table that could possibly seat four people. It wasn't very crowded inside, which was shocking, considering the amount of people that Carla saw shopping outside. They took their seats and the hostess laid two lunch menus in front of them. "Your waitress will be with you in just a moment," she informed them before walking off to greet the couple who were patiently waiting to be seated.

"Apart from the music, this is a nice place," Ellen told Carla as she removed the silverware from the cloth napkin and placed the napkin on her lap.

"I'm glad you like it," Carla replied and did the same.

Within minutes, a young girl approached their table. Carla took a good look at her and the girl had a youthful appearance. Carla guessed that she was probably a college student who was working to maintain her college career. Her bronze colored hair was swept up in a curly ponytail with bangs lined right above her eyebrows and she looked no older than twenty two. She looked cute enough to model for one of those *Seventeen* magazine covers.

"Hi, I'm Ashley and I will be taking care of you both during the remainder of your stay. May I start you off with something to drink?" she asked in a calm, polite tone. Carla and Ellen both ordered a glass of sweet tea and Ashley walked off to get their drinks. They continued to chat and Carla filled her mother in on what happened with Oliver's case and the whole shebang with Charles in the courtroom.

Ashley returned with their drinks and they immediately placed their entrée and appetizer orders. Ellen ordered the jumbo coconut shrimp with asparagus and mashed potatoes for her entrée and a crab cake with caesar salad for her appetizer. Carla ordered the lobster tail sushi roll for an appetizer and pineapple chicken with rice and broccoli for her entrée. While waiting for Ashley to later return with their meals, Carla saw a familiar face walking through the front entrance with a friend in tow. It wasn't long before the familiar face noticed her just the same.

"Carla?" he called out as he walked up to her table. His once deep voice now had a high feminine pitch.

"Hey Gerren, it's nice to see you." Carla stood up to give Gerren a hug then quickly pulled back from him.

Gerren and Carla met each other in their debate class during her sophomore year in college. He looked a whole lot different now than he did back then. Carla was surprised to see Gerren's former close cut look transformed into a head full of shoulder length, wavy tresses that flowed better than hers. His eye brows were neatly arched and not one hair was out of place. It was obvious that Gerren was wearing a weave, but if Carla hadn't known better, she would've sworn that it was his natural grown hair.

Love Finally

The Gerren who use to rock business casual slacks and buttoned down designer shirts, was standing in front of her dressed in a pink ruffled shirt and a pair of hip hugger D&G jeans with what seem like pink heels that were four inches high. Carla was shocked at his new look and tried to suppress her expression. Gerren looked like he was even growing breasts. This was all too much for Carla to take in all at once.

"So how you been girl?" he asked and continued to ask a dozen more questions about her life at current. During their mini question and answer session, Ellen looked baffled through all of this. She couldn't come to terms with the idea that Carla actually acquainted herself with what she liked to refer to as, "cross-dressers," like Gerren.

"Where are my manners?" Carla quickly caught herself when she noticed Ellen's disgusted stares. "Gerren, this is my mother, Ellen, and mom this is an old college friend of mine, Gerren."

"Nice to meet you Ellen," Gerren said and extended his hand.

"Likewise." Ellen faked a smile and reluctantly shook Gerren's hand.

"So who's your friend?" Carla asked of the medium built Caucasian man that stood next to Gerren. She couldn't imagine what ever happened to make Gerren desire poking another man in the ass.

It wasn't like Gerren was ugly; in fact, he was a handsome man that slightly resembled Denzel Washington. Carla did always wonder what was up with Gerren when they were in college, because some late nights when they were up studying in her room, she would walk around in front of him with short shorts and a tank top that would show the imprint of her hard nipples and not once did he try to make a move on her. She never recalled him having a girlfriend and suddenly, it was all starting to make sense. She just never guessed that he would be gay.

"I'm sorry, we got so wrapped up in our conversation and my manners just flew out the window just that fast," Gerren responded with a laugh. "Carla, this is my fiancé Jeff. He and I have been dating for four years now," he continued. Carla quickly did the math in her head and then it struck her. *Oh my gosh! Gerren has been gay this whole time. So all those masculine appearances that he displayed in college was nothing but a front,* she mused.

"It's a pleasure to meet you Jeff." Carla said with a smile. She didn't even attempt to shake his hand. She wasn't a homophobic or anything, but she felt betrayed by Gerren.

"By the way, I'm loving that dress on you. You look good as always. You better work it girl," Gerren said and snapped his fingers. Carla couldn't believe this feminine side of Gerren, it was all too weird for her.

"Thanks," she replied.

Ellen continued to look at Gerren in a confused manner and wondered how on earth he was ever able to walk in those tight jeans. She noticed Ashley along with an obvious colleague walking towards their table with their food and she immediately let out a sigh of relief under her breath. Carla too was relieved because she was becoming embarrassed by Ellen's stares and she hoped Gerren and his fiancé weren't feeling uncomfortable.

"Well, we better get going," Gerren said after their food arrived. "I'll be seeing you girl. You know Atlanta is a small city. And keep doing what you doing honey because you look divalicious. It was nice meeting you Ellen." Gerren did one of those Miss America's wave and started to walk off with Jeff following right behind him.

"He's interesting," Ellen made mention of Gerren once he was no longer in their sight. She then took a fork full of food and shoved it down her throat.

"He's actually a very nice and intelligent guy. You would have to get to know him to find that out though. But trust me, when I met him in college, I met him as a man. Can you believe that he was the salutatorian for our graduating class at Georgia State?" Carla took a swig of her sweet tea.

"Was he really?"

"Mmmhmm," Carla answered and realized that Ellen was enjoying this gossip.

"This shrimp is excellent," Ellen stated after sticking another forkful in her mouth.

"Their food is incredible isn't it?" Carla asked after wiping her mouth with the cloth napkin. After fifteen minutes or so, both Carla and Ellen gobbled up their meals and Ellen wondered about what Carla would have her do next.

"Dessert ladies?" Ashley asked when she made her last round at their table.

"We wouldn't dare," Carla commented. "I would burst wide open if I took another bite of anything," Carla said and then laughed. "You can bring us the check."

Ashley placed the ticket on the table and hurried off to serve other guests. Carla then laid the cash on the table and stood up from the chair and table to walk out of the restaurant.

"What would you like to do next?" Carla quizzed her mother once they reached outside. She thought about browsing the many clothing stores but decided against it because she wanted to do something more personal with Ellen. It had been a while since they spent any mother-daughter time with each other, so Carla wanted this moment to be memorable.

"I was wondering the same thing," Ellen answered. "You know I don't get out much so I would be the last person to ask."

"I have an idea," Carla said sounding excited like a five year old on Christmas. "I know how much you love paintings so why don't we go to an art exhibit?" she asked as her eyes lit up.

"That sounds like an excellent idea," Ellen responded sounding equally excited as Carla.

They walked towards the parking garage and once Carla pressed down on her keyless remote to unlock the doors, they hopped in. Carla slowly pulled out of the garage and plugged in the address for the museum into her GPS system and followed the turn by turn directions that were given by the computer operated voice.

"Are you enjoying yourself mom?" Carla asked as she came to a stop light. She turned to look at Ellen and Carla admired how beautiful her mother still was even at the tender age of fifty five. Ellen's caramel complexion sparkled when the sunlight beamed on her through the windshield. Her cropped hairstyle and diamond studded earrings made her face look like she fell from grace. She was wrinkle free and her eyes twinkled with every blink. Carla wondered if she would be just as beautiful as Ellen when she reached her age.

"I sure am. There's nothing better than spending time with my gem," she spoke of Carla.

A huge smile spread across Carla's face. Despite Ellen's constant nagging at times about Carla settling down with a man, she loved the fact that she was still mommy's little girl. She thought about telling Ellen about Tony, but she feared that it would upset her (knowing how she felt about Carla dating outside her rank), and Carla would hate to ruin the moment so she dismissed the thought and said, "I love you momma."

"I love you too Carla," Ellen replied as she turned to face her daughter.

They continued to drive through the city and an unexpected down pour of rain began to beat against Carla's windshield. The automated wipers swished on instantly and Carla decelerated her speed.

SCREECH...

Love Finally

Carla slammed her brakes and her Range Rover skid when an apple red, ford mustang cut in front of her and nearly sent her spinning into a light pole.

"OH MY GOD!," Ellen yelled when the truck spun out of control but then came to a complete stop, two feet away from the light pole. She saw her life flash before her eyes. "What is wrong with that driver?" Ellen asked angrily and placed her hand over her racing heart.

"Are you okay momma?" Carla asked franticly. Her heart beat felt like it was running one hundred miles per second. She tried to understand what just took place and took a deep breath. She was happy that no one was hurt and that no damage was done.

"I'm fine baby," Ellen told her with her hand still positioned over her chest. They sat for a second as other drivers drove by and blew their horns as if to say, "get your ass out of the way", but Carla ignored them and regained her composure. Once they calmed down, Carla put the gear in drive and slowly pulled off onto the road to continue her journey to the art exhibit. When they finally reached their destination, the rain was now a drizzle and Carla parked in front of the building. They ran from the SUV to the ticket booth to prevent the light drizzle from wetting their hair. It's something about a black woman not wanting their hair to get wet at no cost unless it was being washed to be styled afterwards.

"Two admission tickets please," Carla requested once they reached the booth. Carla slid forty dollars into the slot and the woman behind the window exchanged the cash for two tickets. Carla then grabbed them and dashed towards the entrance with Ellen by her side.

When they entered the building, they were instantly awed by a Mona Lisa painting that greeted them. It was the first time they had ever seen such painting of this caliber. It was a whole level different from what they were used to seeing in books and magazines. This painting had a unique appeal and almost seemed like a real person.

"Isn't it just beautiful?" Ellen asked. "The detail is amazing!" she wowed.

"I agree, this is an amazing piece," Carla agreed and they continued to browse the museum to view the other paintings. After walking for a couple of hours, exhaustion kicked in. They had no clue that the museum had three levels plus a basement level. They finally decided to leave and Carla heard Ellen say that she felt enlightened. Carla was pleased by that statement because all she ever wanted is to see her mother happy like she deserved to be. When they exited to the parking lot, the rain had come to a complete stop and the sun was trying to make its way back out. Ellen and Carla climbed into the truck and drove off into the direction of Ellen's home.

Pulling into Ellen's driveway once again, she kissed Carla on her cheek and bragged about the wonderful time she had before hopping out of the SUV. "I hope we can do this again soon. I had a really great time," Ellen confessed as she stuck her head through the passenger window.

"I will try to make it happen," Carla promised and on that note, Ellen turned to walk down the walkway that led to her front door. Carla watched to make sure her mother entered her abode safely before backing out.

On the quiet drive to her condo, it occurred to Carla that Tony hadn't called her since he'd left her house that morning. She knew that he was done with his shift by now so she pulled out her cell phone and called him on speed dial. With the four attempts that she made, she received his automated voice system every time.

Carla found it to be strange and instantly started to build ill thoughts in her mind. She couldn't help her negative assumptions. She'd been hurt and betrayed by her former love interest and the fear of having it happen to her again by another man, haunted her. "Whenever a man develops a sudden change in his routine, it means they're up to no good," Carla spoke to herself and then sighed. "That was the first sign "what's-his-name" showed," she continued. "And lo and behold, if I hadn't been so naive and took heed, I would have dropped his ass like a hot potato and save myself the heartbreak when I found out that he got some other bitch pregnant," she said through clenched teeth. She pounded her fist on the steering wheel.

"Why didn't I realize that this was all too good to be true?"

She was tempted to drive by the restaurant to see if there was a chance that Tony would still be there so that she could cuss him out and tell him what she thought of him and where he could stick it. Just thinking about the fact that he possibly had another woman, made her heart ache. But why was she feeling this way and why would she go through all of that if she didn't want him to be her man? *I'm tripping.* Why was she jumping to conclusions so fast? So, she hasn't spoken to him all day, does that really mean he's up to no good? Was it really that serious?

She convinced herself that she was being absurd and tightly gripped the steering wheel and continued her drive with a thousand and one questions racing through her mind. Was she falling for this man more than she knew?

When Carla approached her front door, she noticed that there was an envelope taped to it. *Hmmmm,* she wondered. *What the hell is this? The only thing I'm use to seeing attached to this door are work related packages from UPS or Fed Ex.*

Carla continued to stare at the envelope a little while longer before snatching it and ripping it open. The only thing written on it was her name in big bold letters. *Is this some type of joke? Could this have something to do with Tony not answering his phone?*

Carla thought of a million reasons as to why an envelope was taped to her door. The suspense was killing her. She quickly removed the envelope and held it in her hands. Her heart pumped a million beats. Carla felt her blood beginning to rush to her head as a nervous feeling came over her. Her hands trembled as she finally opened the envelope.

There was a note inside. Not knowing what to expect it to say, Carla took a deep breath and removed the thin piece of paper and began to read:

Carla, pack your bags and meet me at Hartsfield Airport at 8:00 p.m. go to the Delta Airlines terminal and I will be waiting. Our flight leaves at 9:30 so don't be late.

Love, Tony

Carla read the note again and tried to make sense of it. "That's it? Just meet him at the airport? Where are we going? What is the meaning of this?" Carla quickly turned the key into the lock and ran inside her condo. She attempted to call Tony's cell phone again, this time she blocked her number, but she received the same result as before.

Chapter 8

The moment she drove onto the highway, there was an accident involving a tractor trailer and a sedan, which kept traffic at a standstill and caused a minor delay for Carla. After the course was clear, she bobbed and weaved through the congestion of cars on the interstate and prayed that she would make it to the airport on time. Carla finally reached her exit. She let out a sigh of relief and was thankful that she didn't get pulled over for speeding and her reckless lane changes. A nervous feeling came over her again as she drove closer to her destination.

She parked in the long term parking deck and grabbed the mini suitcase from the back seat. She dashed towards the terminal in search of Tony. She checked the time on her watch. 7:45 p.m. When she couldn't locate him, she grew frustrated. *He said delta. Where the hell is he? This better not be a ploy. Oooh, Tony is gonna feel my wrath.* She looked through the crowds of people to see if she could point him out. No luck. Carla shifted her weight from one leg to the next and threw her hands on her hips. It was now eight and she felt suckered. Her head dropped. *Why am I allowing this man to give me the run around?* Carla reached for the pull handle on her suitcase to make a departure. Just when she attempted to walk off, she suddenly felt someone walk up behind her and kissed her neck.

"Leaving so soon?" Tony had been watching her the entire time. He was careful not to make himself visible for her to see him.

Carla swung her body around and was now facing Tony. He was neatly dressed in a white, short sleeve buttoned up shirt and a pair of khaki pants. His face lit up from her presence and Carla was now beyond vexed. She wanted to punch him the moment he got close to her. Trying to surprise her was one thing, but having her worried was another. She clasped her chest.

"Don't scare me like that." She gave a puzzled look. "You had me worried. What the hell is going on? Where are we going?"

Tony handed her a ticket. "Let's get checked in." He led her to join the line with other waiting fliers.

Carla parked her suitcase in front of her and took a moment to review the ticket. "This says we're going to Vegas." She lightly punched Tony in his arm and her face lit up. Tony looked at her and smiled.

"Are you surprised?"

"Are you kidding me? You sure have a way of surprising me. You nearly gave me a heart attack after failed attempts of getting in touch with you."

"I'm sorry but it would've ruined everything. I don't know how to lie well, so as much as I wanted to answer your numerous calls, I couldn't. Part of the plan was to keep you in suspense."

"Try your best not to scare me like this again. I thought that maybe you'd had enough and ran off with someone else and God knows what else."

"Don't depend on that ever happening." He brushed strands of hair from her face and kissed her cheek. His words comforted her and she wanted to believe him. She prayed and hoped that he meant every word because she would dread losing him. Or so she thought. They checked their bags and then made their way to the security check point.

"Prepare for landing," she heard the pilot announce through the intercom. Carla opened her eyes and looked at Tony who seemed wide awake, and then she looked out through the window. Her eyes widened when she saw a bright, flashing red sign that read: *WELCOME TO LAS VEGAS*. Carla gasped and Tony smiled at her childlike excitement. He knew that she would enjoy the surprise.

Carla bounced around in her seat like an ADHD patient who forgot to take their Ritalin medication.

"Oh my! Are we really in Vegas?" she turned to ask Tony.

"The one and only Sin City."

"This is truly a surprise...and to imagine how I almost overreacted back at the airport."

"Let's not worry about that, we are here now so let's go and enjoy ourselves," he told her.

When they exit the airport, there was a black limo waiting for them. The limo driver loaded their bags and held the door open to escort them in.

"Have you ever been to Vegas before?" Carla asked once they got settled in the back seat of the stretched Lincoln.

"No, but I always told myself that I would visit," Tony answered.

"How did you manage to pull this thing off in one day?"

"Actually, I've been planning this for some time now, but I had to find the perfect time to surprise you."

"I really hope you didn't have to go out of your way."

"Let me make myself clear here. Look at me. You mean a lot to me. I know that you probably aren't ready for a settling relationship right now, but I'm willing to wait on you. I someday plan to make you my wife. It's never a problem for me to plan something for you. Carla, I don't think you understand just how much I am falling in love with you," he continued. "You bring me a world of joy that no one ever came close to. I have been searching for love for quite some time now and whether you believe it or not, I know that I found it in you. You make me feel things that I've never felt for another woman. You brought new meaning to my life," he confessed.

Did he just say that he's in love with me? She ruminated. His words hit her like a ton of bricks. Why was it so easy for him to express his feelings for her, but she kept hers hidden? Butterflies filled her stomach and the truth of his words stung her like a bee. She wanted to tell him how much she loved him just the same, but the words wouldn't leave her lips. She feared putting her heart on the line knowing that she had to protect it from being shattered. Carla didn't think that she would be able to survive another heart break, so she stuck her tongue down Tony's throat to express what her mouth couldn't say. Little did Tony know, but Carla felt the same way about him. She too wanted to experience unconditional love with a man but every time she thought she found love, she kept coming up empty handed and disappointed. It was then that she realized that she was not the only one looking for love. Should she give in and give him a chance?

"How long are we staying?" Carla probed after breaking free from their tongue action. She was excited to know that she had love at arm's length, and was anxious about venturing the new city.

"This time we'll be here just for the weekend."

She liked the sound of that because that meant they will be visiting again. She rested her head on Tony's chest and enjoyed the remainder of their ride to the hotel. The limo pulled up to the Four Seasons and Carla watched as other tourists and residents strolled down the crowded sidewalk.

The night life in Vegas was totally different to that in Atlanta. There were people of all ages roaming on the busy streets and bright lights were everywhere. She even snickered at some of the ridiculous outfits that some passersby wore. The limo driver opened the door to let them out and once she was standing outside of the car, Carla marveled at the many high rise buildings that stood before her. She has never seen so many hotels on one street alone. She spotted the Palms hotel and other famous ones as she continued to scope out the scenery. Not long after the limo arrived, a bellhop wearing a four season's uniform shirt walked up to the car and removed their bags from the trunk and loaded them onto his empty cart.

"Welcome to the Four Seasons," he greeted. "I'm Brian, and I will be taking your luggage to your room." Brian was tall, about six feet two inches in height and weighed no more than one-hundred and seventy pounds. He had disheveled blonde hair and striking blue eyes.

"Thank you," Carla said with a smile as she waited for Tony to join her. She saw him tip the driver with a hundred dollar bill and pounded fists with him before he turned to walk in her direction. The driver took off in the limo and they followed the bellhop inside the lobby area of the hotel. The lobby was filled with people who were either waiting to check in or just hanging out conversing with friends. Tony walked up to the receptionist desk and presented her with his American Express credit card in exchange for a key card to enter his room. After he was checked in and with his room key in hand, Carla and Tony followed the bellhop to a bank of elevators.

"Is this your first time visiting Vegas?" Brian asked them.

"Yeah, it is," Tony responded.

"Oh cool. You guys are really gonna enjoy it here. There's so much to do and see," he continued. "Trust me dude, you'll hardly get much sleep with all the continuous activities."

"Thanks for the heads up," Tony said.

The elevator doors finally opened up and they boarded the small space along with tons of other guests. They came off on the sixth floor and walked down a hallway that would eventually lead to their room.

On the walk down the long hallway, a Barbie look-alike pushing an older man in a wheelchair, walked towards them in the opposite direction. The woman stood about five feet seven inches, her complexion was golden brown like that of a baked yellow cake, and Carla knew that the woman had a tan. Her blonde hair was bone straight and it flowed down her back. She wore a tropical print, spaghetti strapped dress that moved freely around her ankles with each step she took. Her breasts stood at attention and led Carla to believe that they were implants. The woman was gorgeous. Carla surmised that this beautiful woman and the old man that she pushed in the wheelchair made an odd match. Carla searched for a wedding ring, but none was displayed. The man's head was slumped forward and he wore an oxygen mask with the tank attached to the back of the wheelchair. *I wonder how much money she's banking from him,* Carla thought as she took in this theatrical sight. It almost reminded her of Anna Nicole Smith and her elderly husband, J. Howard Marshall. The woman walked closer to Carla and shooted her nose up in the air as if she read Carla's thoughts. The woman carried a dog in the straw bag that hung of her shoulders and it barked when it saw Carla, who then picked up her pace to catch up with Brian and Tony.

She continued down the hall and passed other couples walking up and down the hallway and then Brian stopped in front of their room door.

"Here we are, room 6-J."

Tony slid the card key into the designated slot and when the light turned green, he pushed the door open. Brian took the bags from the cart and walked them inside the room. Tony tipped him sixty dollars and Brian took off.

"This is beautiful," Carla squealed and kicked off her shoes faster than an Olympic sprinter. The embedded ceiling lights brightly lit the room and the king sized bed was adorned with an oriental sheet set and matching comforter, made of silk. The plush carpet felt soft under her feet and she went on to examine the bathroom.

The marble counter top and complimenting shower walls were a luxurious look within themselves. The glass encased shower stall had three shower heads and Carla couldn't wait to enjoy them with Tony. The vanity mirror gave the place a finished touch and she made sure that she would put it to good use, by checking herself out every chance she got.

Love Finally

Carla rushed back out into the bedroom and saw Tony sitting on the edge of the bed. He was looking oh too fine and she couldn't resist him. They were in the infamous "Sin City" and she was in the mood to commit some sinful acts.

She lowered her stare to Tony's crotch and a bulge formed through his pants. This made Carla extremely excited so she parted his legs and stood in between them and then leaned in to kiss his lips. Tony held her face between his hands and kept her lips pressed against his. Carla pulled away and kneeled down in front of him. She wanted to give Tony the pleasure that she knew no other woman would be able to give him. She unbuttoned his khakis and Tony grabbed her hand to stop her.

"You don't have to do this," he told her.

"But I want to," she said with a pout that he couldn't help but to oblige her. Carla released her hand from his grip and continued what she started.

After successfully unbuttoning his pants and sliding them down his legs, Tony's aroused flesh saluted her like a soldier at war. Carla admired how thick and beautiful it was before she slowly rubbed her hand up and down his shaft and then licked the pre-cum that oozed from the head of his penis. Soft moans escaped Tony's mouth and she took all nine inches of him into her mouth until it touched her tonsils. Carla nearly gagged, but she continued to massage his dick with her mouth until she felt his muscles flexing. Tony moaned from the pressure she exerted against his sensitive part and within a matter of seconds, his moans grew louder and by the way he screamed her name, she was sure that the entire floor would know who she was once she got finished. Carla looked up at him to see his eyes rolling to the back of his head. She contracted her cheek muscles against his stiff member and gave him an unforgettable deep throat action.

She removed her mouth from his member and then suctioned his balls like a vacuum cleaner, juggling them on her tongue and sucking them like a cherry flavored blow pop. Her mouth traveled back up to his dick and she took in as much as she could.

Tony's legs trembled and fell weak from the sensation and before she knew it, a gush of his juices exploded in her mouth. The warm fluid trickled down her throat and Carla wiped her mouth with the back of her hand.

Tony pulled her up from the floor and told her to get on all fours. Carla hiked her ass in the air and Tony hauled Carla's dress over her ass and pulled her panties down her legs and off her feet. He wanted to give her a dose of what she just gave him. He massaged her with his tongue by running it up and down against her clit. He then made figure eights around her clit before driving his tongue into her wet mound. Carla held onto the comforter for dear life as Tony sucked and ate her like his life depended on it. He brought her to a climax and her juices erupted onto his lips and tongue. Tony devoured her until she was weak.

He then stood up and entered her from behind, having her in the doggy style position. Carla wanted to throw her ass back at him, but he felt so good inside her and she wanted him to have his way, she was his slave for the moment. She could feel his muscles flexing and his dick pulsating inside her as he pumped his love stick in and out of her womanhood. She closed her eyes to capture a photographic memory of this moment and enjoyed the strokes that he delivered.

After recuperating from the mind blowing sex they just shared, Carla realized that being with Tony was where she finally belonged and should've been a long time ago. She's never felt pleasure so sweet and satisfying. She wasn't a hater or anything, but Carla realized that "what's-his-face" couldn't please her like Tony could.

In the ten years that she wasted with "what's-his-name", Carla was missing out on what she was now finding out to be a breath taking sexual experience. Half of her life had passed her by, but Tony was there to help her capture all that she missed out on.

She jumped up from the bed and rushed to the shower to enjoy the three head experience. If Tony hadn't given her the delightful satisfaction that she just experienced, she knew that she would've masturbated to the forceful ejection of the warm water from the shower heads, like she often did at home. The only difference is that she only had one shower head at home and figured that three heads would be more satisfying than one. She smiled at the thought, but quickly reminded herself that she and Tony planned to enjoy an adventurous outing in the busy nightlife. Carla hurried to take a quicker shower than normal. She skipped back into the bedroom and Tony got up from the bed and walked to the bathroom to wash the secretions that he just saturated himself in from his body.

Carla pulled out a pair of jeans with a cream colored, sheer shirt out of her bag and quickly pulled them on. She pinned her curls up and applied her Chanel lip gloss. Her flawless skin was beautiful without makeup, so she chose not to apply any. Tony returned into the room with a hotel towel draped around his torso. The sight of his veins protruding from his arms and chest made Carla want to jump in his arms and take him for another orgasmic round. Tony pulled the towel from his body and her eyes traveled to his penis and she reflected on how just moments ago she sucked the old life out his erect cock and gave it new life with the passion of her mouth. She continued to watch as Tony dressed himself in a pair of Rock and Republic Henlee jeans and a Royal Underground woven stone shirt. He had expensive taste and Carla admired him.

"Ready to roll?" he asked her after giving his close cut hair one last stroke with the wooden brush.

"Yup."

Tony sprayed a fragrance and they headed out the door. The sweet smell dispersed throughout the hallway and if Carla should get lost, all she had to do was follow the smell of the fragrance to lead her to him. They took the elevator to the lobby and Tony noticed a bar area on the other side of the room. They walked in the direction of bar so that they could share a few cocktails before venturing the busy strip. They took a seat on the swiveled stools and the stocky, curly haired bartender instantly walked over to them.

"Hi folks. What can I get ya?" he asked.

"Hennessy on the rocks," Tony ordered.

"I'll have an amaretto sour," Carla told him.

Within seconds, he returned with their drinks and Carla noticed the same blonde haired woman that she saw earlier in the hallway walking towards them. She wasn't pushing the old man nor did she have her mutt with her. Carla figured she probably left them in the hotel room so that she could prowl for a young tenderoni. She'd changed out of her tropical print dress and replaced it with a barely there top that her breast were spilling out of, with a short jean skirt and black knee high boots. She was dressed as if she were going to turn tricks.

Carla took a sip of her liquor and the woman took a seat on the swiveled stool beside Tony and lit a parliament cancer stick. Carla wondered what this woman had her intentions set on because being a woman herself, she knew a home wrecker when she saw one and this blonde bitch looked like the type who will stop at nothing to have another woman's man land in her bed. Carla played it by ear and watched to see what this woman's next move would be. The bartender spotted the woman next to Tony and rushed over to take her order.

"I'll have what he's having," she mentioned and Carla could feel her blood boiling. The bartender returned with a Hennessey on the rocks for the woman.

"Is this all on one check?" he asked.

"HELL NO," Carla spoke up. We don't know this bitch and if she knows what's good for her she will get up from beside my man. She was so upset and didn't realize that she'd called him her man.

The bartender looked confused and quickly walked away from what he feared might happen next.

"Oh honey," the woman blew an O of smoke through her thin lips and then turned to address Carla. "The name is Katie, not bitch."

Carla was becoming infuriated and stood up from her stool. Tony quickly stopped her in her tracks and told her to sit back down. "Are you protecting this slut?" she yelled irately.

"That's right, sit down like a good little girl," the woman instigated.

"That's it," Carla fumed. "I am going to kick this whore's ass." Carla stood up and this time she broke away from Tony and walked over to where Katie was sitting. She pointed her finger in Katie's face and the venom started to roll off of her tongue. "Look you Anna Nicole wanna be trailer park trash…"

"All right, break it up. We're all adults here." Tony stood in between the two women to prevent a violent altercation. "Look lady," he turned to face Katie. "I don't know what you were thinking, but you owe my date an apology. Your behavior was rude and very unladylike."

"Tell that to your ghetto tramp," Katie retorted and pulled a twenty dollar bill from her bosom and placed it on the bar counter before she stood up and walked away.

"I'll show your ass ghetto," Carla yelled after Katie and sucked air through her teeth. "I swear that ho needs a good ass whooping." This was not typical behavior for Carla, but she was in a foreign city and this crusty woman pushed her buttons. She was allowed to show her ass in Vegas. Whatever happened there will stay there. She refused to let some random woman disrespect her like that.

"Don't even let her get the best of you babe. She's just jealous because you look better than her," Tony said to calm Carla.

"So I'm your man now? I heard you tell her to 'get up from beside your man'."

"Did I say that? I…it came out wrong. I mean…"

"Shh. It's okay. I was only kidding. I understand. I don't want you to feel pressured into anything. I'm waiting, remember? It was cute to hear it from your mouth though." He wrapped his arms around her waist and nibbled on her earlobe.

"You know that's my spot right?" Carla toyed.

"Let's get out of here and enjoy some fresh air," Tony said after he placed a fifty dollar bill on the bar counter.

They walked back into the lobby so that they could exit the hotel. There were twice as many people swarming the area than what Carla saw when she first walked in. *This place does good business*, she thought as they walked out onto the sidewalk.

The sidewalks were filled with people from different walks of life. Carla couldn't imagine the amount of people that were out and about. *And they say New York is the city that never sleeps...ha, that is an overstatement,* she thought as she continued to absorb the action that stood before her. She's heard about some of the scandalous things that took place in the Sin City, but she had to experience the place for herself to understand the hoopla.

They planned to take in a couple of stage show performances before retiring to their hotel room. There was a display about a comedy show that would be starting in forty five minutes, so they agreed to watch that show first.

On the way to the showcase, Tony decided to stop into a nearby convenient store. After browsing the isles to select a bag of chips and a pack of gum, they made their way to the cashier and suddenly, a gang of masked men bolted through the doors and waves their guns in the air. "Nobody moves," The one who appeared to be the leader yelled. Tony panicked and despite what the gunman said, his first reaction was to grab Carla and bring her to the floor for cover. Besides the cashier, they were the only ones in the store and the possibility of them being killed was a strong one. Tony's sudden move startled one of the gunmen because the moment he saw Tony turn to grab Carla, he aimed and fired three times. Pow, pow, pow.

"NOOOO..." Carla screamed when she heard the loud ricochets. She instantly fell and covered her ears and buried her face into the floor. She wanted so much to check on Tony to see if he was okay but she feared that they might aim at her next. She listened to hear if Tony would make a sound to let her know that he was still alive, but she heard nothing. Her heart beat picked up speed and she wanted this moment to go away; she wished they had never come to this city. *Please, Lord, keep him alive*, she prayed silently.

With her eyes closed, Carla couldn't get the image of the gunman aiming at Tony out of her head and tears started to pour down her face. She folded her lips to suppress her sobs from being heard and wished that it was all a dream. She heard one of the gunmen ordering the cashier to empty the register and threatened that if he alerted the cops, he would blow his brains out. Seeing how the man shot at Tony without remorse, Carla knew that he meant every word he said. She hoped the cashier complied because it wouldn't be worth it to lose his life over a couple of measly dollars and not only that, but she couldn't stand the thought of bearing witness of someone's death. It was painful enough that she couldn't reach out and be at her man's side, and this moment made Carla realize that she really loved Tony and she didn't know what she would do if he didn't survive.

After what seemed like a frozen moment in time, Carla heard when the gunmen ran out of the store and she forced herself up from where she knelt and rushed over to Tony. He was bleeding, but it wasn't as bad as she'd thought. She kneeled over him and started screaming his name. "Stay with me baby, don't you give out on me Tony, dammit," she grabbed his shirt and started shaking him. Tears streamed harder down her face. "Tony I can't lose you now, I need you more than ever. Say something baby, talk to me so that I know you're alive." Tony lifted his arm and placed it on hers. Carla laughed through her tears and shouted to the cashier to call the police. Tony was going to make it and that's all that mattered at the moment. He attempted to speak but she told him he didn't have to and assured him that help was on the way.

The police and paramedics finally arrived and they rushed Tony onto the stretcher, placed an oxygen mask over his face and rolled him into the back of the ambulance. Carla stayed right by his side through it all and left the cashier behind to give his statements to the police.

It had been twenty four hours since the incident. Carla stayed by Tony's bed side the entire time and by now, she felt starved. Her stomach growled and she decided to step away from Tony for a second so that she could go to the cafeteria to grab a bite. Despite the fact that she hadn't showered in a day, Carla still looked beautiful; although, she felt like crap. She took a seat at a vacant table after she purchased a soup and salad. She hurriedly drank the broth before it got cold and she reflected on the incident that took place in the convenient store. She thought back on the clerk and prayed that he was okay. Carla tried to figure out how her life took a sudden detour from enjoying a romantic weekend in Vegas with the man she has grown to love, to almost losing him to gunfire. Tears stung her eyes but she kept it from emerging and took a forkful of salad in her mouth. She made up her mind to tell Tony that she was ready to be official.

When she returned to Tony's room, the doctor entered shortly after and informed her that he would be discharging Tony that afternoon. He also went on to tell her that Tony was very lucky that the bullet didn't pierce any major arteries when he was shot. He informed her that Tony was only grazed by the bullet so no major injuries took place and his healing process would not take very long. Carla thanked the doctor and watched as he made his exit.

Carla stood beside Tony and grabbed a hold of his hand. Tony opened his eyes and looked at her and mustered up a smile through his pain. Carla stroked his forehead and then planted a kiss on it and told him not to say anything when she noticed he was trying to speak. "It's okay baby," she told him and stroked his head. "I love you Tony." She finally allowed the words to leave her lips and she felt good about it because she truly loved him. She leaned in and kissed him on the lips and waited for the nurse to come to check his vitals and discharge him so that they could return to their hotel room.

They entered the room and Carla was relieved that she was finally out of the hospital. She ushered Tony onto the bed and ran to take a quick shower. Their two day weekend was coming to an end, but Carla was grateful to have her man by her side.

She returned to the room with a towel accentuating her body and was surprised to see Tony propped up on a stack of pillows, watching sports center. Carla expected that he would be resting, but smiled to see that he was slowly returning to his old self. Even in his injured state, he was turning her on. Carla dropped her towel and Tony instantly gave her his undivided attention. She wanted to cheer him up a bit and make the remainder of their stay worthwhile, so she planned on strip dancing for him.

She hurried to her overnight bag and slipped on a pair of heels and danced around an imaginary pole like she was really at a strip club. Without music, she was still able to maintain a steady rhythm and Tony took great pleasure in her performance as he was becoming aroused. Carla did moves that she never thought she could and wondered if she was really a stripper in her past life. It all came too naturally and she was even enjoying it.

She was getting caught up in her little act and before she knew it, she was finger fucking herself and Tony watched as she climaxed all over her fingers. With her pussy still filled with heat, Carla climbed on top of Tony, unzipped his pants to free his captive member, and slid her wet pussy back and forth over the head of his rocketing dick. She flickered her tongue behind his ear.

"Oh Gosh!" Tony yelled. He craved to be inside her, so he quickly pulled her down onto his piece and within seconds of entering her, he spurt his juices all over her vaginal walls and Carla was in heaven. She could never get enough of his dick action and she was glad that his dick belonged to her.

The rings from the hotel phone frightened her and Carla jumped up from Tony's chest. She realized that she had fallen asleep after their orgasmic encounter and Tony's member was now soft and hung out of the opened zip area of his jeans. Carla answered the phone.

"Hello."

"This is the receptionist from downstairs and I was wondering if you would be interested in having room service today?" the lady asked through the receiver. Carla quickly placed her order and hung up the phone. She climbed out of the bed to pull on some clothes to cover her naked body.

"Who was that?" Tony managed to ask with his eyes still closed.

"That was room service. I ordered us some food so they should be up shortly. I know you must be starved," she said to Tony.

"Did the limo service call? They're supposed to pick us up at six O'clock this evening."

"Not yet. Well it's only 1:15 p.m., so give them another hour or so to call and confirm and if we don't hear from them, we'll give them a call," she assured him.

Tony smiled and loved how she always knew how to handle every situation. He finally opened his eyes and sat up in the bed. He seemed to be doing a whole lot better and Carla was thankful. She couldn't wait to return to Atlanta where she could return to her normal life. These two days in Vegas had been more than she bargained for and she wished to never encounter another episode like the one from the convenient store. She knew it would take a while before she could bury the memory of what she saw, but for now, she wanted to erase it from her mind altogether.

There was a slight knock at the door and Carla ran to open it. "Room service," she heard a woman say before she could pull the door open. The woman rolled a cart loaded with food on three silver serving trays. The aroma tickled Carla's nostrils and she couldn't wait to dig in. Everything looked so delicious. She could feel the saliva building up in her mouth like a hungry wolf. The woman made her exit after Carla tipped her and then she stuffed her face and Tony did the same.

They ate until they could barely move. The hotel phone rang once more and this time it was the limo service calling to confirm their 6:00 p.m. appointment to be picked up and shuttled to the airport. Carla wrote down the details that the man told her through the receiver and Tony jumped out of the bed and ran to the bathroom to take a shower. Carla wished she hadn't taken a shower earlier so that she could join him. *What the hell*, she thought. *It wouldn't hurt to take another shower.* She peeled off her mini black dress and dashed towards the bathroom to join Tony, where they delved in more passionate love making.

Moments later, the limo service arrived and they made their way to the elevator with their bags in hand. Once they reached the lobby, Carla was surprised to see how scanty it was. She figured that just like her, other visitors had to return to their normal lives. They finally walked outside to the waiting limo where she saw Brian waiting for arriving guests and she shot him a smile. Brian recognized her and waved.

"I hope you all come again," he yelled.

"We'll have to think about it," she yelled back. Brian didn't understand what she meant but he gave her a smile anyway and Carla hopped into the back of the stretch limo with Tony in tow, anticipating their landing in Atlanta, Georgia.

Chapter 9

The alarm buzzed and Carla jumped up to the annoying sound. She quickly shut the thing off and rolled over in bed. She was exhausted from her crazy weekend in Vegas. She managed to drift back to sleep for the next thirty minutes, but jumped up again when she remembered that she was due in the office.

She leaped out of bed like that bouncing tiger from the *Winnie the Pooh* cartoon and raced into the shower. With water still dripping from her body, Carla brushed her teeth and then swished around a cup of Listerine in her mouth.

Her next move was in her closet and they way she glided across the carpet would force one to think that she was on skates. Besides practicing law, there was one other thing that she knew how to do best, and that was to hammer a nail on the head under crunch time.

This morning was definitely crunch time for Carla because she was running super late for work and on top of that, she was to meet with a client first thing when she arrived. She hated to show up late to her appointments because it (A) made her look unprofessional, (B) made her seem unprepared and (C) made it seem like her client was paying her to waste time when that was nothing close to the truth.

Carla peeled off a purple, wool skirt and a sheer purple shirt from the hanger and got dressed in record time. She buckled a pair of black, suede Louboutin T-strap pumps on her feet, teased her curls to give her a spunky look, since she noticed that her hair was in dire need of a makeover. She made a mental note to call Diane ASAP and made a run for the front door.

Carla walked or more like rushed into the building and was pleased that she didn't see her client in the lobby waiting for her. She would like to believe that she reached the office before her client.

She looked over at Sarah who was sitting at her desk, pretending to be busy with paper work, and the sight of her struck a nerve because it brought her back to their encounter in the break room. Carla paid her no attention and continued her walk down the hallway to her office and shut the door behind her once she was entirely inside.

There was a message indicator on her phone so she quickly pressed the play button to listen. "Carla, it's Mrs. Hinton. I cannot make it to our scheduled appointment today. My husband is threatening to kill me and I have to leave the country. I will contact you soon..." *beep*. After hearing the fear in Mrs. Hinton voice, Carla placed her hand over her chest in shock and decided to save the message just in case there is a possibility that it may be beneficial in the future.

Mrs. Hinton was released from prison a month ago after allegedly trying to stab her husband. She heard so much about Carla's capabilities and trusted her to handle her case to prove her innocence. Carla made a promise to Mrs. Hinton that she would do just that and today they were supposed to meet up to discuss the details so that she could conjure enough information to prepare her motion.

Carla plopped down on her leather chair and played Mrs. Hinton's message over and over in her head. She prayed that Mrs. Hinton would be in safe hiding, but she knew that there were other cases to work on so she spun her chair around and grabbed a handful of files from the cabinet.

Buzz.

"Carla, there's a young man out front who is requesting to see you. He said Mrs. Thompson referred him." The buzz from the intercom along with Sarah's unexpected voice caught her off guard.

"Did he call to set up an appointment?"

"No, but he claims to really need your help."

Carla sighed. She didn't mind getting referred clients; it only meant more business for her as well as more money in her bank account, but she preferred to work strictly by appointments because it would give her something to work from. Then again, Mrs. Thompson is a good person so Carla new that it would be a case worth defending.

"Did he give you a name?" she asked Sarah.

"Yeah, it's Sergio."

"Send him in Sarah."

There was a knock at the door. "Come in," Carla answered to the knock and stood up to greet her potential client. When the door swung opened, she was surprised to see a handsome young man standing before her. He looked a little rough around the edges, but was still attractive just the same.

She stepped forward. "Carla Milford. Nice to meet you."

Sergio examined her and didn't recognize a wedding ring on her finger. "It's a pleasure, Ms. Milford," Sergio said in a nonchalant tone and returned the handshake. "My godmother told me so much about you and what you did for her son, Oliver."

"Did she? Oh, for future reference, calling me Carla is fine."

"I'll remember that." He admired her silhouette but noticed that she didn't seem the bit interested in him.

She quickly pulled her hand away from Sergio, who quickly took a seat, and then she walked around her desk to sit in her chair. She pulled out a note pad and pen and immediately began with a series of questions. It was a normal procedure to fork up information from her clients to build a case. "So what brings you here today?" she asked. He admired her professionalism.

"Well, I got myself into some trouble and I need you to defend my case. I don't care about the cost, because as far as I am concerned, my freedom is more important. I also heard that you are the best at what you do so I will take Mrs. Thompson's word for it when she told me that you are the go to person. It's hard to find a lawyer who really cares about their client and not so much about the money. A friend of mine once said that a lawyer fed him a bunch of sweet nothings, only to have my homie serve ten years behind bars and the lawyer made off with a nice payment of one hundred and fifty thousand dollars. Said the lawyer was nowhere to be found when he tried to contact him to discuss an appeal."

I'm gonna get Mrs. Thompson for this. Carla rolled her eyes in the back of her head and tapped her pen against the note pad and wished that he would cut the small talk and get on with it. She was not once to discuss how other lawyers went about handling their business. She was only concerned about hers. Of course she knew that he was in some sort of trouble or else he wouldn't be seeking her help. She is a fucking lawyer for crying out loud. She didn't get paid by the hour to listen to him vent. All she wanted was the essential details to build his case and then she would send his ass on his merry way out of her office. She was tired as hell and was ready for the day to be over with. She silently counted to ten and remained calm.

"Well, I do have more clients to attend to today, so if we can get down to business, I'm all ears. What kind of trouble did you get yourself into?" she asked and put the pen to paper to take copious notes.

Carla gave him the "get on with it or get out" look. Sergio clearly got the message from her facial expression, so he took a deep breath and started to explain himself.

"In order for you to understand what I did, I have to fill you in on my background and I want to be completely honest. After college, I entered as a free agent in the NFL," he continued. "I was later picked up by the Buffalo Bills and that career was short lived after I got injured. I took on a job as an accountant at a major firm and things were beginning to look up for me. I got married a year later and had a set of twin boys. A few years later, the firm downsized and did some layoffs, but I was fortunate enough for them to keep me on staff. I guess with this whole recession deal, my wife got laid off and things went downhill from there. Money got tight and the struggle to keep my marriage afloat began…next thing I know, I was being served with divorce papers. The thought of losing my kids drove me insane and I later ran into an old friend who knew a man that could help me out financially so I jumped on the bandwagon. It was an offer I couldn't refuse at that moment. The job was for me to deliver some goods and I had to go across state lines. I begged my wife to let the boys take the ride with me but she refused and I didn't care so I took them anyway. The minute I entered South Carolina, a cop pulled me for speeding. He ran my tag and told me someone reported me for kidnapping. I almost lost my mind…I couldn't believe that she would do that to me. They searched my car and found the three kilos of coke. Next thing I know, my kids were being placed in the back of a squad car and I was being detained in another. They charged me with kidnapping, trafficking, child abuse and drug possession."

"Wow! That's quite some trouble," she managed to say. She could see the hurt in his eyes and she somehow felt sorry for him. After he explained everything, she noticed the blank expression on his face and wondered about the thoughts that might be flowing through his mind.

She studied his face and he possessed youth like facial features. He sported a beard and she thought it looked good on his almond complexion. His athletic body was intact and he smelled like fresh rainwater. She saw a man who was filled with pain and a broken heart. She never understood why she was always a sucker for the underdog.

This case would be a definite challenge for Carla and even though she normally didn't defend clients in his predicament, she thought long and hard about taking the case. If she won the case, it would be a definite step closer to being partner, but right now it wasn't about that. She heard the sincerity in Sergio's voice and she wanted to help him.

"When is your preliminary hearing?" she asked.

"In three weeks."

She nodded her head and jotted something down on her notepad. "I need you to understand that this is going to be a heavy case. You have everything going against you right now," she said, not meaning to sound harsh but she had to keep it a hundred percent with him. "I normally don't defend cases that involves kidnapping, but I've decided to represent you."

Sergio's eyes lit up from the fact that she was willing to help him. "I really appreciate your help."

"I have some homework to do so I need you to come back in two days. Have the receptionist up front schedule you an appointment. I want you to stay away from your kids until further notice and don't try anything stupid," she demanded. "Do you remember the arresting officer's name? I need to recover the footage from the time he pulled you over."

Sergio gave her all the information she needed and then they shook hands once more before he departed her office. She sat back in her chair and let out a sigh. She really needed to think this through. *Why the hell did I jump the gun so fast?* She wondered. "Am I really capable of defending this man? What have I gotten myself into?" she asked herself aloud. It was more than she bargained for. Carla felt overwhelmed. She pulled herself together and decided to head home.

She sat in her truck with her head leaned against the head rest in the driver's seat. She needed to talk to someone she trusted, so she pulled out her cell phone and dialed Tamika's number.

"Hey 'C!" Tamika's voice squealed through the other end, obviously knowing who was calling.

Carla had no idea that she would feel so refreshed to hear Tamika's voice. She needed to relax her mind. "'Mika, what are you doing right now?"

"I am at the office. I'm working on a client's account right now but I plan to leave here in like thirty...is everything okay?"

"I need to unwind. Long day. Can we meet for dinner after you're finished with everything?"

"Just name it and I'll be there."

"How about Chops Lobster Bar?"

"This better be good Carla. You know how expensive that damn place is?"

"It's not like you can't afford it Ms. big time executive marketing consultant. It's my treat."

"On that note, I will be there," Tamika said and then laughed.

Carla knew that she could depend on Tamika. Tamika always had her back since day one and she didn't expect anything different now.

"See you in a few," Carla told her and then hung up.

Traffic on the Interstate was bumper to bumper. Carla's exit was the next one ahead, but by the looks of things, it didn't look like she was going anywhere anytime soon. She put the gear in park, slid back the sunroof, and popped Usher's latest album in her CD deck and chilled until traffic would pick up again. She thought about Sergio and had a hard time shaking the image of his face out of her head. She wished the traffic would flow. After sitting on the highway for forty five minutes, Carla was relieved when the cars began to move. She put the gear back in drive and took the ramp at the next exit.

She pulled up to the restaurant and to her surprise, Tamika's car was already parked. Happily, Carla hopped out of her truck and dashed towards the black BMW that Tamika was sitting patiently in. She knocked on the window and that was Tamika's cue to get out and when she did, they greeted each other with a hug.

"How did you make it here so fast?" she asked Tamika. "I got held up in that messy traffic."

"I know better than to take the highway at this time, girl I took some back roads. I wouldn't dare get caught up in that mess," Tamika responded and they made their way to the entrance.

The crowd was light, which was a good thing because it meant faster service. "I can hear the clam chowder soup calling my name," Tamika whispered as they were waiting to be seated. "I am hungry with a capital H."

They were finally escorted to their seat and they immediately scanned the menu. The waitress returned with two glasses and a pitcher of water and without delay, they placed their order.

"So what's up with you?" Tamika asked.

Carla sighed as she almost forgot the reason for their meeting. Being in Tamika's company always helped her to forget her current troubles. "Where do I start? Well, Tony and I flew to Vegas this weekend…"

Tamika cut her off. "WHAT? Shut your mouth, Carla…Vegas? That's huge! How was it?"

Carla waved her off. "It was great minus the fact that he got shot."

Tamika furrowed her eyebrows with a look of confusion. "What do you mean?"

Carla told her everything that happened in the convenient store down to the hospital visit. She went on to tell her about the blonde bimbo at the hotel bar.

"She obviously didn't get the memo about getting your foot stuck up her ass for pulling some shit like that," Tamika commented.

"Obviously not."

Shortly after, they were being served with their meals. They put the discussion on hold so that they could stuff their faces. Halfway through her meal, Carla looked like she'd seen a ghost. *Okay, where are the fucking cameras because this has to be a joke,* she thought of what she witnessed. As she continued to watch, her heartbeat decelerated and she hoped it was just a big prank, but the more she took notice, the more she realized that it was all so real. Tamika noticed her perplexed look and instantly became concerned.

"What is it Carla? Are you okay? You look like you just saw a ghost or something."

Carla couldn't allow herself to swallow the food that she had in her mouth.

"Is there something wrong with the food?" Tamika asked. "Because if there is, you can always send it back and order something else," she continued, having no clue as to what was happening.

"That bastard," Carla said through gritted teeth. If she were in a cartoon, steam would be blowing from her head like a train exhaust.

"Who? I mean, what are you talking about? Okay Carla you're behavior is becoming a little scary."

"I'm talking about Tony."

"What about him? Did you see him or something?"

"Yeah, right behind you." Her blood boiled.

Tamika turned around to see what made Carla so suddenly upset and she too couldn't believe her eyes. They both had the looks on their faces as if they'd both seen a ghost. Tamika's mouth flung open at the scene before her. It was Tony alright, in the living flesh, but it wasn't his appearance that puzzled her, but the fact that he had another woman on his arm. And to think that just days ago, she comforted him on his hospital bed. And now here he was, wining and dining some Asian bitch. Carla felt her blood pressure raise ten levels.

"Who is that bitch?" Tamika turned to ask Carla.

"I want to know the same thing." Carla would hate to make a fool of herself in front of all those people in that high class restaurant and get kicked out for starting some shit, but she refused to have him play her like a fool. She paused and tried to think of the best way to go about the matter at hand without embarrassing herself in front of everyone.

"So are you going to confront him or should I do the honors?" Tamika asked and intercepted her thoughts. That was one thing Carla admired about Tamika, she was ready to handle business at all costs, not giving a damn about the consequences. Tamika was always the one, who would be ready to fight at the drop of a hat, and Carla was more reserved. But if push came to shove she knew how to kick some ass.

"Calm down 'Mika, I got this." Hell yeah she wanted to march up to him and demand some answers. She had an image to protect and you never know who was watching. She felt like such a fool after all the bragging she did about how good of a man he was and now to see him with another woman pained her to the depths of her stomach.

"I commend you for your tolerance level 'cause if that was Marcus, I would've been all over him like white on rice."

Carla didn't want to add more fuel to the fire, so she remained quiet as Tamika rambled on about the embarrassing things she would do to Marcus if she should find herself in Carla's current position.

Carla watched as the hostess escorted Tony and the woman to a booth on the other side of the room. She prayed that he didn't see her, or it would give him time to think of an excuse when she chose to address him of this matter.

She directed her focus on the woman that accompanied him and she somehow felt threatened. She had to admit that the woman, who seemed to be of an Asian decent, had prominent facial features that made her beauty exotic and striking. Her long, silky black hair was pulled back into a bun and her defined cheekbones gave her a heavenly appearance. Carla admired the silk Vera Wang beaded dress that she wore which made her look like she just stepped out of a movie screen.

She did notice that the woman carried a briefcase and she was beginning to wonder what the hell was really going on. She was really starting to wonder if she really knew this man. *Something just doesn't seem right*, she thought. *Could he be living a double life? Was everything he told me a lie? There are some skeletons that need to be revealed. And who the fuck is this woman?*

Carla continued to watch their every move and when Tony placed his arms around the woman, her anger climbed like the speed of mercury in a thermometer. She didn't want Tamika to see how upset she'd become. Without creating a scene, Carla excused herself from the table and told Tamika that she would be right back. She walked over to Tony and the woman. Their backs were facing her so she lightly tapped his shoulder. When Tony turned around and saw her, he became tongue tied.

"C...Carla. What a surprise. I didn't expect to see you here."

"Yeah. I know. Neither did I. Well, I saw when you came in, so I just wanted to come over and say hi." Before Tony could respond, she walked off.

Carla returned to the table and asked the passing waitress to bring her the tab. Carla paid the check and dashed out of the restaurant like the speed of light with Tamika right on her hells.

"Do you want to tell me what the hell just happened in there? I still don't understand. Why did you just sit there and watch your man have dinner with another woman?" Tamika asked with her hands on her hips. Carla knew that Tamika would not let it rest.

"I am not worried. Weren't you the one who said that there are plenty of other men out there? Listen, we need to get going before Marcus starts hunting you down."

"You are something else. You're taking this pretty well. I'm surprised that you didn't go off."

"Why? To give them the satisfaction of seeing me get worked up? Hell no. It's just like you said, at least I gave him a try. Never let a man see you sweat."

Tamika shook her head. "If you say so, but I know you too well to know that you are not going to let it go that easily. Who do you think you are fooling?"

No longer wanting to discuss the issue, Carla gave Tamika an excuse about having a sudden headache so she would rather discuss the issue at another time and that she promised to handle Tony, but in the mean time, she needed to get home and rest.

They hugged and hopped into their vehicles and drove off in separate directions. On the drive home, Carla blocked her number and dialed Tony's number but all she heard was, "You've reached Mr. Simmons, I'm not available so do your thing at the beep." *Beep.* She quickly hung up before anything could be recorded. *Bastard.*

She became emotional and started to feel like she was cursed when it came to finding a good man. She was such a nervous wreck that when the tears streamed, she couldn't control them. *What the hell is wrong with me? Why am I always the one to get hurt? This is it; I am through with these cheating, lying ass motherfuckers. From now on, I'm just going to worry about Carla.* She wiped her face and continued her drive in silence and reflected on what she saw back at the restaurant.

Carla's cell phone rang before she could even unlock her door. Praying that it wasn't Tony, Carla pulled the phone from her bag, glanced at the ID screen and pushed send.

"Hello," she answered and turned the key before pushing the front door opened.

"Are you going to be okay?" Tamika asked.

"Why won't I be?"

"Because I know you. I also know that when you really like a guy, you can be vulnerable. Don't start thinking crazy and go flatten any tires or key no cars," Tamika warned and then laughed. "But you know that I'm always here if you need me."

"I know. Thanks 'Mika. I just need to take a shower and get to bed and I'll be fine," Carla assured her.

"If you wanna do a drive-by, you know I'm down. And I know you know how to kick some ass. Remember our sophomore year in college when you fought that girl who spilled her drink on the white dress you planned to return to Macy's? That fight was hilarious and what made it better was when you pulled her weave out," Tamika laughed as she recaptured that moment.

"Leave it up to you to remember that night," Carla laughed. "It was pretty funny but the part that got me mad was that the skank didn't even apologize after I brought it to her attention that she'd ruined my dress. Shit, money was tight in college and that was my cell phone bill money. The idea of a drive-by does sound tempting."

They laughed and reminisced on the good 'ole days. After talking to Tamika, Carla felt much better and she convinced herself that tomorrow will be a better day. When she finally hung up, she took a long hot bath and climbed under her sheets with her naked body. She loved the way the crisp linen felt against her skin. Carla closed her eyes and wished that Tony was there to hold her, but before that could happen, she needed to get down to the bottom of what she witnessed. *Men. You can't live without them, but can't trust them either. Why do I even bother?* "Guess I'm back at square one," she whispered.

Love Finally

Chapter 10

It had been two days since the incident at the restaurant and Carla refused all of Tony's phone calls. He'd even have flowers delivered to her home and office, but that wasn't good enough and she wasn't ready to face him. She still needed more time to think things through. Was she going to take him back or call it quits? Well that was the war she fought within her head. She loved Tony dearly, but she couldn't allow him to walk all over her heart.

Today was the day that she'd told Sergio to meet with her so Carla pulled his file together and waited for his arrival. She booted up her computer and in the midst of her waiting, she decided to search a few databases to conjure more information. The more she knew, the better his chances would be in court.

Thirty minutes later, Sarah informed Carla that Sergio had arrived and she instructed for her to send him in. Carla hoped that she was making the right decision by representing him. Sergio stood in the doorway and his fragrance instantly tickled her nose. She beckoned for him to come in and have a seat. He did as instructed and she realized that he looked more handsome than the two days prior. Sergio had a fresh haircut and his black waved hair was sharply lined around the edges. The beard he once had was transformed into a neat goatee just the way she liked it and his eyes glowed like a halo. He resembled Hill Harper from that TV show, *CSI: NY*. The only difference was that Sergio was taller and his frame was more defined, due to his athletic background. Sergio's almond complexion was ever so smooth and his strong arms were attracting. He was dressed in a crisp black shirt; she believed it was a True Religion brand, with fitting jeans. She couldn't believe how well he'd cleaned himself up since their last visit. He was absolutely striking and oddly enough, her inner thigh became moist.

"It's good to see you again, Carla," Sergio said after taking a seat across from her desk.

"Likewise," she responded and got down to the details regarding his case. When they got finished two hours later, Sergio invited Carla to lunch. She was shocked by his offer and as tempting as it was, she quickly declined. It would've been nice to get out, but she wasn't over Tony.

"First of all, I am involved in a relationship. And secondly, anything that happens between us is strictly business. Please don't take me helping you the wrong way. I don't think that me having lunch with a client is a good look anyway," she said, wanting to make herself clear on the matter.

Oh no, he has to come harder than that. I am mainly taking his case for Mrs. Thompson's sake so I really hope he understands that.

"I didn't mean to offend you. I only figured that I would treat you to lunch to express my gratitude for all that you are doing for me. I mean, you could've easily refused me, but you were willing to give me a chance and that really means a lot to me. I wasn't trying to come on to you or anything of the sort," Sergio explained.

Carla felt somewhat embarrassed about jumping to conclusions, but she wanted to nip it in the bud before he developed any ideas and got the wrong conception. They locked eyes and a sudden feel of electricity shot through her body. The feeling was uncontrollable and she couldn't understand what was happening. Was she really attracted to this man? The only image that flashed across her mind was shoving all the papers off her desk so she could lay Sergio down and climb on top of him and ride him like a horse.

She cleared her throat. "Well, I have nothing further," she said and tried to keep herself from acting on her thoughts.

"Alright. When is our next meeting?"

"I will give you a call to notify you."

"Okay. I will be listening for that call," Sergio said then he turned to walk away.

Carla quickly shut the door once he was completely out of her office and leaned her back up against it. She let out a deep sigh. "Huuuugh. What is wrong with me? Am I out of my damn mind to think about wanting to fuck this guy? I am really losing it."

She walked back to her desk and dropped down in her chair. Her cell phone rang and when she picked it up to see who was calling, Tony's name flashed across the screen. Carla thought about answering, but quickly pressed the ignore button instead and leaned her head back in her chair. Before she knew it, the time had run off and it was now going on 7 p.m. Carla packed up her things and headed to her truck. On the ride home, Carla stopped into Blockbuster to rent *The Queens of Comedy.* She could use a good laugh, after all that has been happening, and those women, especially Monique, knew just how to do that.

She pulled into the parking lot of her complex and she immediately noticed a black Mercedes that was parked two cars down. She hoped it wasn't Tony because she was definitely not in the mood to deal with him. Carla fixed her hair in the rearview mirror and caught a glimpse of a human body walking towards her SUV. She paused for a while and stared at the figure to make sure that her mind wasn't playing tricks on her. "Oh shit," she blurted once the figure walked up to her window. She had a good mind to press the gas pedal to the floor and drive off, but instead, she pressed down on the button that was lodged in the armrest of the driver's door and the window rolled down automatically. She knew that it would only be a matter of time before Tony showed up at her condo anyway; she only hoped that now was not the time.

"What are you doing here?" she asked him through the window.

"What do you mean what am I doing here? Carla I tried calling you at work and you refused my calls, I called your cell and house phone but you won't answer. I was growing restless and figured that showing up here was my only option to talk to you. Why are you avoiding me? I am not leaving until I get an explanation."

She climbed out of truck and slammed the door shut. Carla stood toe to toe with Tony. "Do you hear yourself? Furthermore, you leave if I tell you to leave and frankly, I don't have to explain shit to you. Why don't you leave me alone and go harass your Asian bimbo?" she fussed. An elderly couple that lives on the eight floor walked by and Carla lowered her tone and waited for them to enter the building. She didn't want them to assume that something was wrong. When white folks see two black people arguing, they were quick to call the police and having the police come to her residence was the last thing she needed.

"Whoa, whoa, whoa...wait a minute." Tony threw up his hands in the air. "Asian bimbo? What the hell are you talking about, Carla?"

"Don't play stupid with me," she spat and pointed her finger in his face. "You know exactly what I'm talking about. That woman I saw you with at the restaurant, that's what." She ran off to prevent the tears from falling.

"Wait, Carla. It's not what you think," Tony yelled and followed after her.

"Oh really?" she stopped and turned to face him. "So you want to explain to me why you had your hands all over her?" Tony paused. "I didn't think so," she spat and continued towards the elevator.

Tony caught up with her and the elevator doors opened up. She hopped on and he was right on her tail. "Can we talk about this inside?" he asked once they were on the elevator.

"It's a free country, do whatever you like," she said with her arms folded.

Tony tried to make eye contact but she avoided him. "I would like to go inside, but I don't want to go if I'm not welcomed."

The elevator doors opened and Carla hopped off. Tony followed suit and they walked down the hallway until she reached her door. She turned the key into the keyhole and pushed the door open.

"You are welcomed," she said and stepped aside to make way for him to enter. She locked the door behind her, kicked off her heels, walked over to the sofa and slid her handbag off her shoulder. The bag fell onto the sofa and she took a seat. She shoved her keys into an outer pocket on her bag and turned to face Tony, who was already seated on the sofa next to her. "You said you wanted to talk, so I'm all ears."

Tony lifted her chin and she had no other option but to look him in the eyes. "Do you believe that I love you?" he asked. She believed that he did with all her heart, but what she saw that day just didn't add up.

"I would like to believe that you do, but I don't know what to believe after what I saw."

"Baby, I want you to listen to me," he continued, still holding her chin. "I would never do anything to hurt you or jeopardize what we have with each other. I told you that I plan on making you my wife and I mean every word of it." She nodded her head and listened to him continue to plea his love for her. She wanted to believe that he was telling the truth, but the fear of being heartbroken caused her to have her guard up. She had given him her trust before but she wasn't so sure if she could trust him the same way again. If he wanted things to work between them, then he would have to prove that he deserved her trust. Her trust was something he now had to earn.

"So why were you having dinner with that woman?" she probed.

"That woman's name is Trish and she is a jeweler. We were merely just discussing a business deal that's all."

"What kind of business could you possibly be "discussing" with a jeweler? Over dinner at that. And not to mention how you had your arms around her. I really don't like the sound of what you're saying or what I saw. So now you're making jewel deals? What the hell is going on here? What are you not telling me?"

"I can't get into that right now, but you're going to have to learn to trust me. I promise that I am not doing anything that you need to worry yourself over, so don't get all bent out of shape over it."

Carla snapped her head back. "You call it getting bent out of shape? I see my man with another bitch and you're telling me I'm getting bent out of shape? You can't answer any of my questions and you call it getting bent out of shape? If I were the one acting suspicious, what would you think? This conversation is obviously getting nowhere," she snapped and walked towards the door. "I think you should leave, Tony," she said and held the door open.

"You have it all wrong, Carla."

She stared into his eyes and her heart wanted to believe the truth that they revealed, but her head told her to kick his ass out and not fall for his lies. "I'm sorry Tony but you have to go."

Tony stood up from the couch and walked towards the door. He grabbed Carla and pressed his lips into hers. He tried to stick his tongue in her mouth but she refused and ordered him to leave.

"I'll show you that everything I am telling you is the truth. Please don't take your love away from me." With that said, Tony made his exit and disappeared down the empty hallway.

Chapter 11

It had been weeks since she'd spoken to Tony. He left countless messages on her office and cell phone, but she refused to return the call. She never expected that her relationship with Tony would come to this. She hoped that everything would take a turn and work out for the better between them. There was too much on her mind. She began to pack her belongings to head out of the office when her cell phone rang. Tamika's name flashed across the screen and Carla quickly answered. "Hello."

"You sound better. Did you talk to him and put his ass in check?" Tamika asked. She had been busy making plans for her upcoming wedding and she hadn't spoken to Carla since that night when they left the restaurant.

"We tried to talk about it but the whole thing turned into an argument and I told him to leave my house and I haven't spoken to him since."

"Did he try to call you?"

"Every hour of the day like clockwork, but I refuse to accept his calls."

"I mean are you ever going to speak to him again?"

"Maybe. I don't know. Eventually, I guess."

"Well, did he ever give you an explanation about being with that woman?"

"Yeah, he says that she is a jeweler and it had something to do with business but I think that they were too close for comfort if you ask me."

"I don't want to see you get hurt, Carla. Niggas think that they are so slick. They could be cheating on your ass and they will look you straight in the eye and tell you that the same bitch they're cheating with is a cousin or some other family member. I mean, do you believe him? To think about it, what the hell was he doing business over dinner with a jeweler? Unless she's more than that. I'm telling you, Carla, something could very well be up with him."

Carla knew that Tamika was not buying Tony's explanation and she was beginning to have doubts about whether or not she even believed him. She glued the phone to her ear and continued to listen to Tamika's logics.

"I thought about that too."

"Do you think he's involved in any illegal activities?"

"I doubt it. I think I would've noticed something by now. He says he's legit."

"Girl you better wake up and learn how to play like a detective and get some answers. These are things you should be concerned about because the next thing you know, some mob member will come looking for your ass."

Mob? Carla allowed Tamika's words to register in her mind and felt that her best friend made some valid points. Was Tamika overreacting? She knew that Tamika had her best interest at heart and if she never opened her big mouth in the first place, Tamika wouldn't be dogging Tony like she did.

Carla thought long and hard about what Tamika said. Should she really take things a step further and do some self investigation? Could Tamika's words be realistic? That would be something she would just have to find out. But on the flip side, she really did love Tony and she missed being in his company.

"I have an idea!"

"Do tell."

Love Finally

"You mentioned being a detective. What about us spying on Tony?"

"Sounds adventurous. Count me in! When do we start?"

"I haven't thought of that yet. I need to brainstorm and get back to you. In the mean time, what are you doing later?" she asked Tamika.

"Nothing special. Why what's up?"

"You wanna go to happy hour at Pearl Bistro? I need a drink or two to help me think things over."

"It's a bet. I will call Marcus to let him know that I will be running late. See you in a few." *Click.* Just that fast, Tamika disconnected the line and Carla placed the last of her things in the drawer beneath her desk and made her way out the door.

Carla waited on a bench located at the front of the lounge and stood up when she saw Tamika approaching. "It's about time you made it. I was going to get started without you," she teased.

"You wouldn't dare," Tamika responded and they greeted each other with their custom hug. "I'm feeling those shoes," Tamika mentioned of Carla's suede Mary Janes and told herself to pick up a pair the next time she went shopping.

When they finally made it out of the long line, they were told to go inside and the place was jam packed. It seemed like everyone was trying to take advantage of the happy hour drink special. They requested a table but the lady at the front desk advised them that if they weren't going to order a meal, they would get faster service if they grabbed a seat at the bar. Without hesitation, they ran and hopped on the two vacant bar stools that stood before them. The atmosphere was right, the music was popping, but Carla couldn't get Tony off her mind. She also looked forward to playing PI. She needed to find out the truth before she decided if she wanted to take him back in her life.

"They have some fine men up in here," Tamika commented.

"I'm still trying to see who you're talking about," Carla teased.

"Don't be a hater, not all men are blessed with a model figure like Tony."

"I was only kidding. Yeah some of them are cute."

"Yeah, like that guy over there who's been staring at you since the moment you sat down."

Carla looked in the direction which Tamika pointed and thought her secret admirer was sort of cute but he didn't compare to Tony. She quickly rerouted her attention and they continued to scope out the men and the sleazy dressed women who were trying too hard to capture the men's attention. "What can I get you?" the slender looking bartender asked. She had charcoal black wavy hair and dazzling eyes. She was beautiful and didn't appear as the type to work at a bar. She looked like what most would classify as a video chick. Tamika ordered grey goose and cranberry and Carla ordered a cosmopolitan.

"If I wasn't engaged, I would probably be going home with one these fine ass brothas tonight," Tamika claimed after taking a sip of her drink.

"Now that I know is true. For one, you can't handle liquor too well so I hope that's your only drink for the night. And two, your ass is a nympho," Carla said through an outburst of laughter.

"Whatever, I can't help the fact that I enjoy having sex and that's why Marcus ain't going nowhere. I got skills girl." They continued to joke around with each other and Tamika excused herself to the ladies room.

Carla continued to survey the room and caught a younger looking guy staring at her. He barley looked old enough to drink. *I wonder how he got up in here. He probably has one of those fake IDs. I bet he still lives with his mama.* Carla didn't want to be rude and give him the evil eye that she usually gave men to let them know she wasn't interested, so she flashed him a smile instead. He definitely was not her type so she quickly looked away. Seconds past and she could still feel the young guy's eyes on her.

She once again looked in his direction and gave him a smirk. Although she wasn't interested, she found the idea of having a secret admirer to be cute. Her smirk must've made him excited because he then gave her a huge grin. Carla covered her mouth with her hand and tried her best not to laugh out loud. The young guy was missing a front tooth and three of his top teeth on the left side were rotted. It would've served him more justice to keep his mouth closed because he was ten years late for a dental appointment. The comedic sight made Carla laugh inside.

"What did I miss? Anything interesting happen while I was gone?" Tamika asked when she returned. "And why are you covering your mouth?"

Carla knew that if she told Tamika about what she'd just seen, Tamika would make it obvious that they were laughing at the guy's teeth, so she decided not to share it with her. "Nothing, this drink has a bad after taste," Carla lied.

Tamika ordered her second drink and promised Carla that it would be her last. "I'm not driving your ass home if you get drunk," Carla warned.

"I can handle two drinks. Besides, I'll have Marcus pick me up if it comes to that," Tamika spat. The DJ was doing his thing and before she knew it, Tamika was on the dance floor. Carla was not in the mood for dancing, so she stayed at the bar and watched her friend make all the other women envious of her dance moves. All the men stopped and stared when Tamika did an actual split in the middle of the dance floor. *That girl will do anything when she has liquor in her system*, Carla thought and shook her head at Tamika's radical moves.

Two songs later, Tamika made her way back to the bar and Carla filled her in on all the attention her dancing gave her. They watched on as other women tried to gain the same attention that

Tamika did. They looked on and saw a tall, shaved head, brown complexion man approaching them. He looked like Boris Kodjoe and he wore a crisp grey Armani suit. "May I buy your next drink? By the way, my name is Kenneth." he said in a smooth tone and introduced himself to Carla.

She was flattered, but quickly turned down his offer. Under normal circumstances, she would've said "yes" but she couldn't deny that Tony was the only apple in her eye at the moment. Kenneth had a friend with him who was dressed just as nice and Tamika quickly flashed her engagement ring so that it could be seen by both men. The friend turned his head in the opposite direction once he noticed the huge diamond, but Kenneth continued to pursue Carla. "Well what about a dance?" he continued. Carla quickly ended the small talk and told Kenneth that she was flattered by his advances, and that she had a boyfriend. Kenneth then nudged his friend and they walked off into the crowd.

"He was fine as hell," Tamika squealed once the men were no longer in their view. "There is just too much temptation up in here. I need to get home to my man so I can get some good loving. You ready?" Carla nodded her head and they made their way out the front door and into the parking lot.

Chapter 12

Carla stood her naked physique in front of her floor length mirror and inspected her flawless body. The two drinks that she had earlier at the lounge were now making her hormones run wild. She caressed her breasts and imagined that Tony was standing behind her. She ran her hands back and forth between her thighs and her pussy instantly became wet. Fondling herself wouldn't give her the satisfaction that she desired. Carla interrupted her show. *I have an idea. Why don't I call Tony over to make him believe that I wanna make up? It would be perfect to carry out my plan. If I get back close with him, then it wouldn't be obvious.* She grabbed her house phone to dialed Tony's number.

He answered almost immediately.

"Hello."

Hearing his voice for the first time since their argument made Carla breathless. She became aroused more than she was before and asked him to come over. *Damn. Tamika was right. I can be vulnerable, but oh well, I want some sex. And who is best to have it with than Tony?*

She threw on her black silk robe and sprang to the door when she heard Tony's knocks. And even with the door closed, she could smell his fragrance. Carla pulled the door opened and he looked debonair. He wore a black nylon shirt that revealed his muscular build with a pair of blue jeans. Even though he was somewhat dressed down, Carla still found him to look astounding. It didn't matter what Tony wore, he will always be fine in her eyes.

The moment he laid his eyes on her, Tony pulled her into his arms and devoured her mouth with his. Carla pushed the door shut and the sexing began. They started in the living room and then made their way into the kitchen. Some of the positions he had her in, would be considered illegal in some states, but Carla allowed the freak in her to get loose and from the kitchen, they ended up on the bathroom sink and then they ended their night of passion in the bedroom.

The smell of bacon and eggs woke her from her deep sleep. Carla opened her eyes and sat up in her bed. Her body ached and she wondered if it was the effect of the liquor that made her do some of those freaky things she did the night before. She remembered having Tony put her in the sixty-nine position and he sucked on her clit 'til she begged him to stop. *Makeup sex is the best sex,* she thought as she recalled some of the other freaky things they did. She wanted to put the past behind her and move forward, but not so easily. Whether or not Tony was lying or telling the truth about his show at the restaurant, would soon surface. But right now, she was hooked on his dick like it was a narcotic. She still planned on going through with her scheme before she decided to give him a second chance. Having him around may make it easier for her because that way she would be able to get leads on his whereabouts.

Tony appeared in the bedroom wearing a pair of cotton boxers. Carla admired the strides he took. *Damn I love this man.* She hoped she wasn't being naïve about the situation at hand.

"Good morning baby." Tony sat next to Carla and kissed her lips. "Your breakfast is on the table, you better get it before it gets cold."

No man has ever catered to her the way Tony has and she wondered if maybe they were meant to be. Carla quickly pulled on the black robe that she wore the night before and walked out into the dining area. Tony joined her and they enjoyed their meal, feeling like old times. They both decided to play hooky, so Carla called into the office and advised them that she would not be coming in. Tony thereafter made a quick phone call into the restaurant and told them the same thing. After washing the dishes and cleaning the kitchen, they enjoyed each other for a morning dose of where they left off the previous night and ended their expedition in the shower.

When they stepped out of the shower, Tony proceeded to get dressed and Carla strolled into her closet draped in a terry cloth robe and searched for something to wear. She removed a white cotton sundress from the hanger and pulled it over her head.

"What should our plans for the day be?" she asked Tony, who was walking towards her. Carla sat on the edge of her bed and Tony thought that she looked like an innocent teenager with her hair pulled back in a ponytail and a white sundress on.

"I could just lay here and hold you all day to make up for time lost, but I know you would rather enjoy the day outside."

"I have an idea. How about we have a picnic?"

"That sounds like a good idea. So, does this mean that I'm forgiven?"

"Don't push it. I'm taking off today and I need someone to hang out with. You are my only option right now." He had no idea of the plan she had in mind. If she wanted it to be a success as she hoped, she couldn't make him suspicious of her.

"Damn. That's cold." Tony shook his head and laughed.

Carla ran into the kitchen and made turkey sandwiches, filled a cooler with pouch juices, and grabbed a picnic basket from beneath the cupboard. She grabbed a blanket from the linen closet and Tony helped her carry the cooler outside and loaded it and the basket in the trunk of his SUV and then they drove off in search of a nearby park. They found a parking spot at the Atlanta Memorial Park and walked to a quiet area alongside the lake. Carla spread the blanket on the neatly mowed grass and they sat down to eat.

"You ever been on a picnic before?" she asked Tony, who was on his fourth sandwich.

"No," he answered and then quickly swallowed his food. "I've always wanted to experience Mother Nature with a romantic picnic setup, but no girl that I've met was interested in taking picnics."

Carla started to wonder about the choice of women he's dated in the past. "Well you're having the chance to do so now," she responded and leaned over to give him a kiss. They consumed the remainder of the sandwiches like human garbage disposals and before they knew it, they were rolling around on the grass.

Tony always knew how to bring out the kid in her and Carla was enjoying every minute of it. Every now and then, Tony would roll on top of her and show her how excited he was each time he would get an erection, but his erections would quickly deflate when he saw a passing couple. By the time they were through horse playing, Carla had grass stains all over her dress but it didn't matter because she was having the time of her life. She was finally beginning to understand what Tamika meant when she would often tell her to "relax and let her hair down", because she was doing just that with Tony.

Carla stared out at the lake and daydreamed about one day getting married and starting a family. She was definitely ready for marriage and she convinced herself that she was ready for motherhood as well. Tony rubbed her knee and she directed her attention to him. "Where do you see yourself two years from now?" she asked him.

"What made you ask?" he grew curious.

Carla gave her shoulders a slight shrug. "I was just thinking about the future."

"Well in that case, I see myself married to you, the love of my life, and building a successful future." He turned to look at her and she looked at him. Not wanting Tony to see the sudden frustration his words caused her, she quickly turned away.

So now I'm the love of your life? She felt herself becoming upset when she thought back on seeing Tony with that woman, but she was not in the mood to start an argument by revisiting the situation. Carla decided to change the direction of their conversation.

"Have you ever thought about going back to school?", but she also knew that he had plenty potential.

"I did get my bachelors degree in business management, but I don't think I'll go any further."

Carla was shocked to find out that Tony had already achieved a degree, but she frowned upon the fact that there was so much to this man that she doesn't know about. After all, she knew that deep down in her heart; she wanted to be the woman that Tony spent the rest of his life with. What good is it to build something concrete with someone and not know as much as you would like to about them?

"That's interesting. I mean, you never mentioned that you had a college degree before. Well, have you ever thought about owning your own business one day?"

"Yeah, the thought crossed my mind."

"I can't believe that there's so much to you that I really don't know."

"All you have to do is ask."

"Okay. Let me ask you this. Why haven't you invited me to your place?" She turned to face him and Tony stared off into space.

"It just seemed more convenient for you if I visited your place instead."

"See, you're missing the point. I don't have to sleep there, just show me where you live."

"That can be arranged."

"An arrangement should've already been in place." Carla frowned upon the fact that she had to bring that point to his attention. She was beginning to doubt if she should really continue a relationship with this man.

"You never asked. You never seemed interested."

"So I guess I have to initiate everything from now on?"

"Don't talk like that." Tony moved in closer to her and wrapped his arms around her. She pushed him away. The afternoon crowd was rushing in as joggers began to encircle them. They packed up their things and Carla was determined to find out what Tony had to hide.

Chapter 13

Sergio strolled into her office like he was Rico Suave or some damn body.

"It's good to see you, Carla." Sergio greeted Carla with a formal handshake and admired her silhouette through her yellow silk blouse and black pencil skirt. Her round plump ass looked desiring and Sergio could feel his dick pulsating through his pants. He quickly took a seat after she pulled away from their handshake, to prevent her from noticing his sudden erection.

"Same here," she replied and took a seat in her plush leather chair. She immediately pulled out her legal pad. Twenty minutes into their conversation, Sergio leaned in and gave Carla a mild peck on her lips. She was astonished by his actions, but in a sick distorted way, she enjoyed the kissed. On any other day, she would've slapped the mess out of him and kicked his ass out, but for some unknown reason or another, she couldn't find the strength to raise her hand. It was like his kiss froze her.

"What the hell was that?" she finally asked. She was astonished.

"I'm sorry. That move was a little out of line."

"You damn right it was," she snapped, knowing in the back of her mind that she actually loved the way his soft lips felt against hers.

"Carla, I am very attracted to you and whenever I come here to meet with you, you make me feel so alive," he confessed.

"Sergio, what we have is a business relationship. I cannot tolerate such behavior if you plan on using me as your attorney. After all, you are married for Christ's sake."

"My wife and I are on the verge of getting a divorce and my kids are all that I have. Without them I am nothing. And she will not allow me to see them...how fucked up is that?" Sergio threw his hands up in disgust and lowered his eyes to the floor. Carla immediately felt pity for him. She knew that he was probably having a hard time keeping his head above waters, but then again, he brought this whole dilemma upon himself.

"I understand everything that you are going through, but as your attorney, I cannot get personal with you. Do we understand each other?" She knew that she was letting him off easy. How was it that she was in love with Tony, but she was attracted to the man who was sitting in front of her?

Sergio nodded his head and quickly looked away. He was embarrassed that he allowed his emotions to get the best of him. He knew that nothing could happen between them. He apologized continuously.

Two minutes later, her cell phone rang and it was Tony. Carla ended her meeting with Sergio and told Tony that she was in the middle of something and needed to call him back. Truth was, she needed time to think. She became frustrated. Carla buried her face in her hands and wondered if she could really continue to work with Sergio. She was indeed attracted to him or more like lusted after him more than anything else, but her heart belonged to Tony.

"How can I disclose to Tony that I allowed another man to kiss me?" she questioned herself. "I had no business agreeing to represent his case in the first place." She started to beat herself up about the whole thing.

Things were getting stranger and stranger every day. How did her life evolve so quickly into a soap opera? Carla was slowly losing control of her own life and she was determined to get it back. "How could I let things get like this?" she asked no one in particular. "I have to turn Sergio's case over to one of my counter parts or else something is soon to happen that I know I will regret," she spoke into the air. She thought about how disappointed Mrs. Thompson may become if she found out that Carla was no longer defending his case but then again, she had to do what was best for her if she wanted to maintain a relationship with Tony. *She will just have to get over it and understand that it was for the best,* Carla thought as she prepared to search for the best legal attorney to represent Sergio.

The buzz from the intercom distracted her. "Yes, what is it?" she asked, her voice was filled with tumult.

"I'm sorry to interrupt you, but John would like to see you in his office," Sarah informed her.

Carla sighed. "Okay. I will be there shortly." *What does he want now?* She stood up from her chair and her cellular device rang again. She quickly answered when she saw Ellen's name flash across the screen. "Hello."

"Well, I was getting ready to report you missing. I haven't heard from you in what seemed like ages," Ellen said humorously.

It suddenly dawned on Carla that she hadn't spoken to her mother since the night she left for Vegas. "I'm sorry momma...it's just that so much has been happening at work. There are new clients coming in left and right and I have been extremely busy," she exaggerated.

"I know dear. That job of yours sure does keep you occupied. Well at least you're being productive and not wasting your time."

Carla didn't know how to explain to Ellen all the perplexities that were taking place in her life at current. She remembered that John was waiting on her so she promised Ellen a visit on Sunday and quickly disconnected the line.

She took the elevator to the third floor and walked down the long stretched hallway. The third floor was where all the senior partners and a few junior partners' offices were located. John's office was located near the conference room. Carla took a deep breath and then knocked slightly once she approached his door.

"Come in," he instructed.

Carla slowly pushed the door open. "You wanted to see me?" she asked and poked her head inside.

"Come in and have a seat," John motioned. He sat in his huge Godfather chair with an unlit Cuban cigar hanging from his lips. His hair was slicked back and he was dressed in another sleek Italian tailor made suit. His watch glistened on his wrist and his confident poise demanded attention.

Carla walked in, shutting the door behind her and took a seat across from John. She crossed one leg over the other, clasped her hands, rested them slightly onto her knees and gave him her undivided attention. She had no idea what John needed to meet with her for but for him to call her into his office could be good or bad and she hoped for the good.

"Relax, Carla, you look tense. Don't worry, I have nothing but good news." Truth be told, she was holding her breath and she quickly exhaled with his assurance. "Well let's not waste time, I know you have cases to work on and I have a firm to run," John continued. "The fellas of the executive board and I have given some serious consideration to making you senior partner."

Carla's eyes lit up like a light bulb; she wanted to jump out of her seat and scream like she was the winner of *American Idol*. "Oh my goodness…are you serious?" Making partner in a top firm usually required more experience than what she possessed and Carla couldn't believe the promotion she'd just received.

"Look at my face; I am not even cracking a smile," John said in his Italian accent and pointed to his face to display how serious he was. "I have watched you work your ass off. In the past two years, you have gone above and beyond for your clients and this firm. Please know that your late hour stays and hard work have not gone unnoticed. There was a vote and nine out ten people thought you would be the best selection."

Who the hell was the one who cast me out? It was probably that short mothafucker, Kerwin. Kerwin, the only black man on the executive board, was a very married man with three kids, but his egotistic ass thought he was god's gift to women.

Carla begged to differ when she first learned of him and she'd let him know it when he'd ask her out on a dinner date, which he claimed was to basically teach her the ropes about being an attorney.

But Carla saw different when he offered to rent them a hotel room afterwards. She nicely spilled his drink in his pants and told him she would never sleep with him even if he were the last man standing. Kerwin in return yelled that she would never make partner and that she was making a big mistake because he would make an example out of her.

Carla took his threat lightly. She knew he wouldn't dare risk losing everything if he knew she would bring the issue to John's attention and slap a sexual harassment suit on his ass, so after that night, he sent her an apologetic email and used the excuse that he didn't know what came over him.

"I am really grateful for this opportunity," she expressed. And to think that she was getting ready to pitch the idea to him within a couple of months. Since graduating law school, all Carla ever hoped for was to one day make partner, at least before she would retire. One of her dreams were finally coming true and she took it as a sign that others were about to manifest. *God works in mysterious ways.*

"Don't be silly, Carla. You have earned this position. Let me be the first to welcome you aboard, partner." John stood from his chair and extended his arm. "There's a board meeting next Tuesday at 9 a.m. sharp and I need you to be there."

Carla nodded. "No problem. I will be there with bells on."

"You will be relocated to the vacant corner office down the hall within the next couple of days. And again, congratulations."

Carla thanked him once again and departed his office. Walking down the hallway, she wanted to do flips and cartwheels. Her expectations were surpassed because not only was she partner, but senior partner. It seemed surreal. *Who would've ever thought that Carla Milford would be promoted to senior partner? I can't imagine that I am going to be the only black female partner. This is just so unreal,* she thought as she rode the elevator to the first floor. Carla walked into her soon to be old office and glanced at the academic degrees that were mounted on the walls.

"I guess skipping out on parties and staying up late to study is finally paying off. Look how far it brought me." She looked up at the ceiling. "I know this is part of your doing daddy. You are my guardian angel, thank you," she whispered in the air.

Being partner meant more zeros on her paycheck and not to mention the small percentage that she would now own in the firm. She couldn't ask for anything more. Carla counted her blessings and her next plan was to make plans to have her dream mansion built from the ground up. It wouldn't be eight bedrooms like Ellen's, that seemed to be too farfetched, but it would be large enough to create a stable and comfortable home environment for the family she dreamed to have.

Her promotion called for a celebration so Carla pulled out her cell phone to give Tamika the news. She wanted to celebrate over a glass of wine with none other than her best friend. The person who supported all of her decisions, being they were smart or foolish ones. After the fifth ring, Tamika's phone went to voice mail: "You've reached your girl 'Mika, right number, wrong time. Do you boo." *Beep.*

Carla decided to leave a message with hopes that Tamika would call right back. "'Mika, call me back ASAP. I've got some great news and I can't wait to share. I also wanted to know if we could make it a girl's night tonight. Call me back girl." *Click.* Carla scooped up her belongings and her next thought was to give Tony a call, but she knew he was working late, so she quickly disregarded it. She would inform Ellen about the promotion tomorrow because now was not the time for a lecture, assuming she already knew what her mother would say.

It was a beautiful Friday evening and Carla was filled with too much excitement to go home early, so instead, she jumped on the interstate going north bound to celebrate solo. It wouldn't be a first for her.

She recalled the time she'd had to Celebrate passing her bar exam solo because Tamika was away with family, Ellen was too depressed and "what's-his-face" gave her some lame excuse about taking his mother to the hospital, so her only resort was to wine and dine herself at an upscale restaurant. Passing that test required a much needed celebration, even if she did have to celebrate alone. Carla had worked her ass of studying days in and out with sometimes getting no sleep and she was not going to allow anyone to rain on her parade. Had Carl been alive back then, she knew he would've accompanied her. He was her best cheerleader and she knew that he would've been right by her side tonight just the same. But unfortunately, he was not around to share the moment with her, so it looks like tonight would be another solo celebration.

Carla parked her SUV in the garage and walked along the strip to Ra Sushi Bar, a sushi restaurant in the Midtown area. She wanted to enjoy the feel of the cool breeze against her face, so she requested to be seated outside. The streets were busy with what she assumed were college students and memories of her college days instantly flooded her mind. Carla smiled at the fun memories and a waitress approached her.

"Are you expecting someone else?" the woman asked. The Asian female was beautiful. A black knitted cap covered her hair and her defined cheekbones brought instant memories of Tony and Trish together.

"She's not Asian, she's Korean." She recalled Tony saying. He had the nerve to correct her when she classified his so called "business partner" as Asian. *Asian, Korean, who gives a fuck? They all look the same to me.*

Carla informed the waitress who introduced herself as Mindy, that she was dining alone and immediately ordered a strawberry-kiwi margarita. Carla noticed that Mindy had some type of attitude when she walked off and made a mental note that if Mindy should somehow get besides herself, she would definitely report her ass because tonight was not the night and she would be damned if she allowed some waitress to ruin her night of celebration. It wasn't long before Mindy returned with the margarita in hand.

"Are you going to order something to eat?" Mindy tapped her foot against the concrete and seemed irritated.

Okay, that is attitude number two. She has one more time and that is it. She should've kept her attitude ass at home. Carla purposely took her time to browse the menu. She then ordered California rolls and chicken with broccoli. Carla sipped on her margarita and continued to observe the crowd of people as they walked up and down the side walk. There was nothing like a busy Friday night in Atlanta. The mood was right, her drink was on point and all she could replay in her mind at the moment were the words, "senior partner". Carla set her mind on cruise control and crossed her thighs.

Within minutes of enjoying her solitude, sipping her second margarita, and planning on how to decorate her new corner office, Carla heard a familiar voice yelling her name: "Carla, Carla."

She turned in the direction of the sound and wanted to slide down out of the chair and onto the ground, but it was all too late because Sergio was already headed in her direction. "What a fucking coincidence," she mumbled beneath her breath.

"Sergio? What are you doing in these parts?" she asked, her voice changed to a more polite tone and she prayed that he would hurry up and leave. She had forgotten about his earlier charade and seeing him rekindled her memory. That prayer fell on deaf ears because before she knew it, Sergio was pulling out a chair and took his seat across from her. *I like his nerve. After that stunt he pulled in my office earlier today, does he think I want him dining with me? No fucking way.*

"I live in these parts, my condo is three block down from here," he pointed. "What is your excuse for being here alone?" he asked.

"What's wrong with a girl having some *alone* time?" she stressed the word alone, hoping it would hit home and he would get the message, but like a catcher in the outfield, he missed the message ball. "Speaking of which, I never extended an invite for you to join me," she stated to get her point across.

"You didn't have to formally invite me because your eyes did all the talking." He was getting cocky. "And to answer your question, oh, there's a lot wrong with you being here alone, especially a beautiful woman who claims to have a man. If I had a lady with your beauty, I wouldn't dare let her dine alone."

Is he kidding me? "Well sometimes a woman needs her space."

"That's what they all say."

The waitress returned with Carla's order and she had the look of fury in her eyes. "I thought you weren't expecting anyone?"

Carla looked as if to say, "you better slow your roll before I go off on your ass", and the waitress directed her attention to Sergio after getting the message from Carla's expression.

"Are you dining here?" she asked him. Sergio nodded and quickly ordered a bottle of Heineken beer and California rolls.

"What's up with her?"

"I was hoping that maybe you would know. She should've checked the attitude at the beginning of her shift or take her ass home. I guess she won't be getting a tip."

Sergio rested his elbows on the table and leaned across it. "Look, about what happened earlier today…"

"I'm trying to enjoy my night and I don't want to think about your ploy, we will deal with that on a different note."

Sergio nodded his head and sat back in his chair. Carla was no longer becoming annoyed by his presence, she was somewhat happy that she didn't have to dine alone after all, but she still needed to tell Sergio about turning over his case and she sure as hell wasn't going to disclose her promotion to him, but now was not the best time. She was beginning to learn a different side of Sergio, a side that seemed charming and irresistible.

Mindy returned with his order and they talked about sports, (which Carla didn't know much about) World events, and even fashion. She was surprised that a man actually enjoyed discussing fashion. The mood was feeling right and Carla wasn't ready for it to end. She ordered another drink, which was more than she could handle.

"Don't drink those so fast, it will creep up on you fast," he warned. "What are you doing after you leave here?"

Carla shrugged her shoulders. She was feeling the effects of the alcohol that she just downed. Her head was spinning. *I'm not drunk, just mellow...yeah that's it, mellow.* "Home I guess."

"Oh, to the man who allowed you to be out here by yourself?" She gave Sergio a look as if to say, "Mind your own damn business."

"I mean, it's a beautiful Friday night and you're just going to go home? It's not even ten thirty yet. You need to get out and have some fun. You work so hard, you deserve to have fun."

Who the hell does he think he is to tell me what I need to do? But he does make sense. I mean, the night really is beautiful and having fun doesn't sound like a bad idea. I really do need to get out more. But what kinda fun is he talking about? I wonder if this is part of his plan to take advantage of me because he knows I'm tipsy. "What do you have in mind?"

"There's a night club three streets down from here...you wanna go? It's' a really classy set up," he said as if throwing that part in would be more convincing.

"I don't know...I really should be getting home." Carla paused and gave it some thought. "On second hand, I may just take you up on that suggestion. Tonight is a great night to get my party on after all. Besides, I look good, feel good, it's all good." Sergio nodded his head and gave off a grin. He knew it was probably the liquor talking because he knew Carla was more on the reserved side, but he couldn't have agreed with her more. She looked amazing and he wished he could have a piece of her. He paid the tab and they made their way down the side walk.

They walked past the garage and the bold sign that read: *FIRST TWO HOURS FREE!!! $2.00 PER/HR THERE AFTER,* reminded her that it would cost her an arm and a leg if she left her truck parked in the garage.

"Wait...my truck. I am parked in here," she pointed at the garage. "And it's going to cost if I leave it there all night."

"If you don't mind, you can park it at my place if you like. I only live three blocks away and they don't tow. We can catch a cab back to the club instead of walking."

"Great. Let's do it." They climbed up the ramp and hopped in her SUV. Sergio directed Carla to his place and instructed her to park in an empty spot beside a silver Porsche convertible.

"I'm assuming that this you car?" she asked as she put the gear in park

"Yeah. That's my baby." They climbed out of her truck and Sergio pulled out his cell phone to call a cab service.

"This is a nice development. They have some nice condos in the city." She continued to admire the high rise building. "What floor do you live on? I mean, this thing looks like it has over a hundred floors."

"Nah, not quite, but I live way up top," he pointed. "The penthouse. You see that window with the light on?" she nodded. "That's my spot." Penthouses were expensive. The cost to maintain it usually requires that of a mortgage payment. Carla wondered if the expensive car and expensive condo were all acquired with his drug money. But by the looks of it, she knew he had taste. Within minutes, the cab pulled up and they hopped in.

Pulling up to club Opera, the line was wrapped around the building. It seems Sergio had connections because he excused himself to go have a word with the bouncer and next thing she new, they were being escorted into the VIP section by a tall, husky man named T-Dawg.

The music was jamming and Sergio's first stop was to the bar. Carla opted not to drink another beverage containing alcohol because she was still feeling the effects of the last three. She waited in the VIP area until Sergio returned and when they DJ played "Lo" by Flo-rida, she jumped on the dance floor and moved her brick house hips out of control. Sergio watched in amazement as she shook her ass down low to the floor and then back up. She repeated this move throughout the entire song.

The DJ was right on the money with every track he spun because Carla danced to every beat. She finally became exhausted because she marched back into the VIP section and plopped down onto the cushy black lounge chair. "That was fun!" she exclaimed and kicked off her shoes. She lifted her feet and rested them in the chair in front of her and asked Sergio to purchase her a bottled water.

"I haven't danced like this since my graduation party from law school." She took a sip from the plastic bottle and wiped the sweat from her brow. The DJ was slowing down his mixes and Carla knew that was a cue that the party would soon be over.

She gave the club a quick scan and spotted two girls who dressed like they were Siamese twins, but knew they were not blood related. They looked like the type that went to night clubs to hold up walls, you know, the type who thought they were too cute to bust a sweat, wishing that a baller status man would approach them? But these two girls were nothing close to being cute. *Ha, such a shame.* Carla shook her head and the DJ announced the last song.

It was 3 a.m. when she glanced at the watch on her wrist. The cab pulled up and they jumped in the back seat. Sergio gave the driver turn by turn directions to his place.

Carla climbed out of the cab and Sergio handed the cabby two crisp twenty dollar bills. She walked towards her truck and Sergio ran after her and grabbed her by the arm. "Wait...I mean, where are you going. You are in no shape to drive."

Carla snatched her arm away from him. "Don't you dare grab me like that," she spat.

"I'm sorry...I was only trying to stop you from getting behind the wheel. You have been drinking and it's late. Look, you can crash at my place 'til the morning. I won't bite."

Carla wasn't so sure she wanted to follow through with his offer, but she was tired and he did make a point about her driving after she'd had a few drinks. *I could see the headlines now,* she thought. *Attorney Carla Milford arrested on DUI charges.* An image of being on the other side of those jail bars flashed before her eyes. The thought of possibly going down that road quickly changed her mind. "Ummm...okay. I guess crashing here 'til morning would be the wisest choice right now," she said, although she knew that she could've rented a hotel room just the same, but she was already in front of his place and it seemed more convenient.

She walked over the threshold into Sergio's condo and the setting was immaculate. For a semi-bachelor, his place was clean and not one item was out of place. She wondered if he was always this neat or if he had a cleaning service. She walked into the living room and she couldn't believe the size of the thing. He had a remarkable view of the city and Carla had to give him props because Sergio was doing the damn thing. She became a little embarrassed, because truth be told, his condo put hers to shame. She admired the paintings that hung from the wall. They reminded her of the art exhibit she attended with Ellen. Master piece paintings by Van Gogh, Picasso, and Michael Angelo's Sistine chapel, were some of the few that grabbed her attention. Oh the sight was amazing.

"How were you able to come by these?" she asked of the brightly painted master pieces.

"Oh, those? I bought them at an art auction."

"You don't look like the type to appreciate art."

"Well, what can I say? I don't look like a lot of things, but I do have an eye for beauty, that's for sure." Sergio stroked his goatee and as sickening as it sounds, he was turning her on.

Carla took a seat on his leather sectional and Sergio went off to brew some coffee. They sat and talked for the next thirty minutes and he went on to tell her that his penthouse had a game room, three bedrooms and two bathrooms. Carla couldn't believe that penthouse condos had that much square footage. *Maybe that's why they cost so much.* She took a sip of her coffee and before she knew it, her eyes were weighing heavy.

"Where should I sleep?" she asked through a yawn.

"Pick any room you like."

She stood up and walked in the opposite direction of the master bedroom. She remembered Sergio telling her that the two vacant rooms were down the long stretched hallway. She held her shoes in her hand and the wood floor felt smooth beneath her feet.

Carla entered the lavish bedroom. The king sized bed and oak wood furniture stood out like a space fit for a king. Sergio knocked on the door and Carla jumped.

"Would you like a T-shirt or something? It would probably me more comfortable," he yelled from behind the closed door.

"Uhh...yeah. That would be nice," she yelled back. Within minutes, Sergio knocked again and he handed her the oversized shirt through the small crack she made with the door. Carla pulled on the shirt and inspected her facial features in the mirror.

Knock... Knock...

"What now?" she murmured under her breath. "Come in."

Sergio pushed the door open and he strolled into the bedroom wearing silk pajama pants and his bare chest was exposed.

"Yeah? What's up?" she asked and look at his image through the mirror.

"Just wanted to make sure that you're comfortable. Is the temperature okay?" His lips were moving but what he said or asked hadn't registered. It was as if her ears went deaf for the moment, because she was too busy checking out his physique.

"Did you hear me?" he asked after clearing his throat.

"Huh? What? I'm sorry...I missed that."

"Are you okay, Carla? You seem a little distant."

"Huh? Me? Oh no, I'm fine."

"I was asking if you are comfortable."

"Oh, yes...yes I am. I'm probably just tired," she faked.

"Okay. Well good night." Sergio turned to walk away.

"Sergio. Wait." Sergio turned to face her.

"What's up? Are you okay?"

"I'm sorry. Yeah. I'm fine." She dropped her eyes down to the floor and placed her hand behind her neck.

"Are you sure?" Sergio walked closer to her. "What you need a massage or something? Why are you rubbing your neck?"

Carla removed her hand and giggled. "You are more charming than I thought."

"So you think I'm charming?"

"Well..." She sat on the bed and Sergio sat beside her. He took her hand and stared into her eyes.

"You are beautiful, and that's off the record." Carla blushed and pulled her hand away from his.

"That was kind of you. Look, I really need to lay my head down." She attempted to stand up, but Sergio grabbed her by the arm and pulled her beside him. Before she could speak, he leaned in and silenced her with a kiss. Carla tried to pull away, but he placed his hand behind her head to keep her face close to his. When he finally released her, Sergio bit down on his bottom lip and held her by both hands and looked into her eyes. Carla was lost in his gaze.

"Oops. I did it again," Sergio said.

"This time I think you intended to."

He stroked her face with the back of his hand and laid her on her back. He leaned over her and peeled off the T-shirt and exposed her round breasts that stood at attention. Sergio couldn't believe the beautiful sight before him. Her round flesh looked smooth and delicate. He developed an instant hard on and Carla felt the bulge through his pants. She gave off a devilish grin and climbed her naked body under the sheets and Sergio slid out of his pants and joined her. All thoughts of Tony immediately flew out of her mind.

They lay facing each other and she reached down and massaged his thighs. He guided her hand to his manhood and she quickly obliged him. Carla climbed on top and straddled him. Without a condom, he slipped his throbbing dick inside her slippery mound and she rode him like a brand new Ferrari.

Ten minutes into the heat of the moment, Carla switched positions. This time she straddled him with her back facing him. She rode him like they were at a rodeo show each time he lifted his hips and pumped his dick deep up in her until they both climaxed. Sergio indulged in her warmth and within seconds, he slid his dick out of her and held her in the air with his face buried between her nestle. He massaged her clit with his tongue and brought her to another climax. Within seconds, he lowered her onto the bed and they were out like a light bulb.

Carla jumped up and freaked out. This strange bed was not her own and she couldn't believe what she'd done. She glanced over at Sergio, who was sprawled out on his back with his hands folded across his chest and a satisfied smile plastered across his sleeping face. His dick was now limp and his balls sagged between his thighs. A bad taste immediately formed in her mouth.

"This was not supposed to happen. No...not in a million years," she mumbled. Guilt and shame came over her all at once. She clutched the sheet against her naked body and her head was filled with a sudden pressure. She had to find a way to get out of there and not wake Sergio.

Carla allowed the sheet she once clutched against her skin to fall down her body. She quietly eased her way out of bed and looked back at Sergio, whose eyes were now wide opened. She didn't expect to see him awake and her heart fell to her toes, mainly out of shock.

"What's the matter? Where are you going?" he asked and sat up in the bed.

"Sergio, you and I know that this was a huge mistake...I have to go."

"Wait...Carla, we can talk about this."

"Are you fucking kidding me? We fucked each other last night. What the hell is there to talk about? That's not something that can be undone." She quickly hauled on her clothes and made a run for the front door, barefooted and all. Sergio attempted to go after her, but he was too late. She was already in her truck and he watched her speed off.

Chapter 14

Carla raced to her shower and turned the shower knob to the hottest temperature and tried to burn away her guilt. She lathered her washcloth and attempted to scrub away her shame, but she stopped when the water stung her skin. Carla looked down and saw blood mixed with water washing down the drain. She'd scrub herself so hard that some of the skin on her chest, arms and thighs was removed, which caused the blood to flow. Tears streamed down her face and she slid down against the shower wall until she reached a curling positing. How was she going to reveal to the man she loved that she had unprotected sex with another man? Her thoughts ran wild and she just wanted to die. She was devastated. She'd let herself down and it was no one else's fault but her own. There was no way around it. Keeping this a secret was not an option and she wished she could take it all back.

It was going on 6 p.m. on a Saturday afternoon and the skies looked just how she felt, gloomy. Carla was stretched across her bed in a cotton pajama set and she stared out the window. She had no energy and all she wanted to do was sleep away her misery. There was only one explanation for this type of feeling, depression.

She'd lost her appetite for the entire day and her head spun out of control due to stress. Tony must've called her phone a thousand times before she finally powered it off. She couldn't find the guts to talk to him. Not in her current state. She closed her eyes and harked back to the night before. A knot formed in her stomach and she wondered why she allowed Sergio to talk her in to going to some damn night club and crashing at his place afterwards. Why didn't she just pick up and go home like her mind told her to? If only she could press rewind like a tape player. But the truth of the matter is, what's done is done and it was something she would have to live with.

Sunday morning. The skies looked brighter, but Carla's mood was nowhere near bright. She dragged herself out of bed and headed to the kitchen. She poured herself a cup of coffee and sulked in front of the blank TV screen. She grabbed her phone from the center table and decided to power it back on. When it finally booted up, she had twenty-three text messages from Tony asking if she was okay and if he should come over, two voicemails from Tamika asking about the good news she wanted to share, and one message from Ellen asking if she still planned to give her a visit. *Oh shit. I did promise momma that I would pay her a visit.* Carla threw the phone across the carpet and sunk lower in the sofa. "I can't let her see me like this. I'll have to visit at another time."

Her cell phone rang and, she stood up from the sofa and walked across the floor to answer it. She knew that she have been avoiding her loved ones and pretty soon, they would need answers why.

"Where have you been?" Tamika questioned. "I have been blowing your phone up like I was a possessed boyfriend. Did you get my message?"

Carla sighed. "Yeah I just listened to it."

"Okay what's up? This is totally not like you to not return my calls and I do not like it one bit. Is it Tony again?"

"No." She hesitated and wondered if she should tell Tamika about her dealings with Sergio. She needed advise about her recent actions and she trusted no one else but her best friend. Usually she would've tried to work it out on her own, but she's never put herself in such a predicament as this before.

"I did something horrible and I need to talk to you about it."

Tamika paused. "What is it Carla? You don't sound like yourself."

"'Mika, I...I. I don't know how to say it."

"What did you do? Did you cheat or something?" She'd hit the nail right on the head and hearing those words come out of her mouth stung Carla like inflicted pain.

She hated to admit it, but she had to own up to her actions one way or another. "Yeah." Carla's voice was almost a whisper and her tone was sullen. She was not proud of what she'd done.

"What? You are fucking with me right? Is this when you're going to shout 'I gotcha'?" Tamika paused but got no response. "Wait, are you telling me that Ms. goodie too shoe who saw immorality in people who cheat has turned hypocrite to her own judgments? This is a real shocker. I'd never thought that a good girl would go bad, but seeing a nigga cheating on you will surely make you do it."

This was not the response she expected. Tamika was not making this easy for her, but the truth was the truth and Tamika was always the person to deliver the truth whether she liked it or not and that shit hurt.

"Yeah, I slept with someone else last night and I am so regretting it."

"Why? Was he that bad?"

"No, No, No. It has nothing to do with his dick size. I mean what about Tony?"

"What about him? I mean, you practically caught the guy cheating on you so what are you so mad about? It clearly has to be more to this story if you feel so much regret."

"It's complicated. How am I going to tell Tony about this?"

"Don't."

"You can't be serious. I can't walk around with this guilt and continue to sleep with him and look him the eyes like I did nothing wrong," Carla protested.

"Why not, men do it to women all the time. He'll just be getting a dose of his own medicine."

Carla couldn't believe the words that were coming out of Tamika's mouth. Who was this woman on the other end of the phone and what did she do to Tamika?

"Look Carla...I'm sorry. It's just that I hate seeing you get hurt by these humans who call themselves men. I love you like the sister I never had and I'm hurt when you're hurt. It's time to get tough and start thinking like a man, but you're right, you should tell Tony about this. I mean, do you like this other guy?"

"No."

"Well if you really love Tony like I think you do, then yes; you have some explaining to do."

"And that's the part I'm afraid of. I mean, I don't know how he will react."

"Let me just be real with you and look at the situation, not as your best friend, but as an outsider looking in. We all make mistakes, but it's learning from them that makes all the difference. If you were woman enough to lie down and get screwed, then be woman enough to tell the truth. I'm not taking sides, but I said that to say this, if the shoes were on the other foot, you too would like an honest explanation."

Carla let off a sigh of relief, glad to have her friend come back to her senses. She knew that she could always count on Tamika for advice, even if it was advice that she didn't want to hear. But she knew that Tamika was right. *Damn. I hate when she's right.* "Thanks 'Mika". She knew there was a phone call to be made as soon as she ended her call with Tamika.

"Oh you're not getting off that easy. So who is this mystery man? He must be one helluva brotha if you let him hit the skins on the first night," she teased and turned the mix of their conversation into a whole new flavor.

Carla feared that she would be faced to answer that question. "Not merely, but he's no one you know."

"So, who is he?" Tamika pressed for an answer.

"Ummm...he's a guy that I ran into last night when I was having dinner downtown. We've ran into each other a few times before at different gatherings, but I just had too much to drink last night and the situation just got out of control," she half lied.

"Oh...so we're just going to 'blame it on the alcohol' like Jamie Fox, huh?"

"Not entirely, but yeah. If I were sober, you know that that shit would've not happened."

"Well was he any good? I mean you have to air your dirty laundry."

"I truly can't remember." It was sad, but true. Her sexual encounter with Sergio had no meaning. And then it hit her like a ton of bricks that she'd corrupted her soul and now the joke was on her.

"Damn. Did you have that much to drink? If you can't remember, then you clearly wasted your time. You mean to tell me that you fucked this man in vain?"

Ouch. That was a low blow, but again, it was the truth. She never knew the truth could hurt this much.

Carla was not up for discussing her promiscuous act any further so she blew off Tamika's question and told her that she would call her back later.

"Wait...what about the good news you wanted to share. That message you left on my voicemail."

"Oh...nothing. We can talk about it over lunch next week or something." She ended the call and lay across the sofa. To talk about her promotion was no longer exciting. She had a decision to make and she might as well let the cat out of the bag if she wanted to free her conscience.

Tony rushed over the moment Carla told him that they needed to talk. He knew there was something wrong by the tone of her voice and the fact that she avoided all of his calls the day before made him more concerned.

"What's wrong baby?" He'd asked her for the one hundredth time. It had been over an hour since he'd been sitting on the sofa next to her and Carla has not opened her mouth once. She just sat there with a blank look on her face.

"Did someone do something hurtful to you?" He'd asked her that question repeatedly but it didn't hurt to ask again since he'd run out of questions. He'd already asked her every question that he could possibly think of.

After a million questions unanswered and two hours later, Carla finally broke her silence. "I cheated on you," she blurted.

Tony's concerned look turned into that of a deranged serious killer and Carla could see him balding his fist as if he were about to strike her. She wished she could've taken it back. He then hopped up off the sofa and dashed to the other side of the room like he was a raging bull running from a plague or some type of infectious disease. Carla didn't know if she should've made a run for it and seek help or wait to see his next reaction.

"No, No, No. Maybe I didn't hear you correctly. What did you just say?" He used his finger to push his earlobe forward.

Not wanting to add pain to injury, Carla decided to remain silent and not repeat herself.

"You heard me correctly. Tony...I'm sorry. I didn't mean for this to happen."

"So who is this sorry ass mothafucka that you let run his dick up in you? Huh?" His chest quickly heaved up and down with each breath, showing his anger, and she could see his veins protruding from his neck. "I swear to God, Carla, if you ever give me a disease I will fucking kill you and him."

She has never seen this side of Tony before and it was beginning to scare her. Tears welled up in her eyes and poured down her face like a burst of rain.

"You think crying is gonna change anything? You think it's going to make me feel sorry for you? I bet you weren't crying when you were lying down and got fucked. Were you? I mean what was it? Was I not man enough for you? What…one man can't satisfy you?"

His words made her stomach churn. She wanted to answer his questions and tell him that yes he was all she needed, but her mouth felt like it had been glued shut and her body fell numb.

"Since cat got your tongue, tell me one thing. Did you ever think about me during all of this?"

Her tears flowed harder and Tony rammed his fist into the wall and nearly punched a hole through it. Of course he was pissed. He was raised not to lay hands on a woman, and he wouldn't dare catch a charge over a cheating ass woman, so hitting things was his only outlet.

He was told by the woman he loved that she'd cheated on him and he wanted to break something, but he also want her to see that her words stabbed him like a knife. Crying at this point was not an option because his anger surpassed any tears he would muster up. He hated to have called her out of her name, but her words got the best of him and fuck it; the relationship was now over anyway. How could he trust a woman who just confessed to cheating? Yeah he liked her honesty, but that wasn't good enough to keep him around.

"Was this done out of spite because you still think that I had an affair with Trish? I mean if that was the case, there are a hundred and one ways to get revenge, but sleeping out on your man, that was a whorish move."

"All I ever did was loved you, and I thought you loved me. But I guess I thought wrong. You are no different from the rest." He was now breathing normal and his voice became calm. "You know what, I'm outta here...and while you're at it, lose my fucking number. And I'm serious about what I said earlier. I'm going to the doctor in the morning and you better pray that everything comes back normal." He pointed his finger at her and his voice was serious. He walked out the door and Carla fell to her knees.

Three days passed since the episode with Tony and Carla did not go into the office. She was in no shape or form to conduct any productive work. She had buried herself in bed.

Hours later, she managed to force herself out of bed and checked the answering machine that beeped every ten seconds, letting her know that there were un-played messages. Sarah and John left several messages about her no show status and when the CEO calls, then you know that there's a problem.

She was just promoted to senior partner and now she wished she wasn't because it was the promotion that led her to celebrate in the first place. Had she not gone downtown to celebrate, she wouldn't have run into Sergio under those circumstances and her relationship would not be in shambles.

She called John and apologized for her behavior; she also told him that she came down with some unexpected illness but was certain that she would show up to work the following day. Tamika called and left messages, threatening to come over and kick the door down, but Carla knew it was a front and Tamika never showed. Ellen left a message and complained about her no show behavior on Sunday and told her how disappointed she was and that they needed to have a serious talk the next time they see each other. The one person she hoped would call didn't call and that made her more depressed. For the past two days, she would block her number and call Tony's cell just to hear his voice. He knew that it was her calling but little did she know that he missed her just the same or even more. She knew that she'd made a big mistake and she had to get her soul mate back. A few weeks ago, she'd given him the third degree about having dinner with some jeweler and she turned around to do what she did.

Carla walked into her office; still feeling like her heart was ripped out of her chest. She didn't want to be there, but she still had to make a living. It was 9:00 a.m. and she was already hoping that the day was over. Sarah buzzed the intercom and told her that Sergio was on his way into her office. Before Carla could tell Sarah to turn him away, he walked through her door.

"Are you okay? Where have you been? I came here every day looking for you since you stormed out of my condo."

"Sergio, please. It is too early and I really don't want to be bothered. You can't keep showing up here unannounced and without an appointment."

"Are you serious? You weren't saying that shit when I was blowing your back out."

Ouch. This was what she was afraid of. She knew that sooner or later, her reckless actions would come back and bite her in the ass. She stood up from her chair and the scorn of hell filled her eyes.

"I want you to get your ass out of my office now."

"Oh. So you come on to a brotha and now I'm the one to blame?"

"You are ridiculous. You made a move on me."

"But you didn't stop me either."

"You know what? You are absolutely right. But I'm stopping you now. Get the hell out before I call security to haul you out."

"So it's like that?"

She didn't respond. Carla pointed her finger towards the door. As he exited, she yelled, "And don't worry about your case; it will be turned over to another attorney."

Sergio had forgotten all about his case and then her words hit home base. He stopped in his tracks and turned around. "Carla, I didn't mean it like that. I was just concerned about you and I wanted to make sure that you were okay," he pleaded.

"Do I look okay to you Sergio?" Tears filled her eyes and she plopped down in her chair, rested her elbows on the desk and buried her face in her hands.

"I am not against you Carla. I really want to help. I take the blame for all of this. I don't know how to say this, Carla, but I'm falling for you."

She raised her head and her eyes were blood shot. "Wha...wha.. you what?" She couldn't believe her ears. "Sergio, you can't be serious. How could you be falling for me and you don't even know me?"

"I can't explain it, but the way you make me feel is beyond the imaginable. The heart can't control who or what it feels for."

"I really can't handle this right now," she spoke through her tears and buried her face in her hands once again.

"Let's talk about this over lunch."

She looked at him and yelled, "You don't get it, do you? Sergio, my relationship is ruined because of our fiasco. It's affecting my job and I can't handle it. You need to leave now or else I will be forced to call security. Do not show your face in my office again or you will end up behind bars."

Without a word, Sergio made his exit, but he was determined to fight for the new found love of his heart and that would not be last time she laid eyes on him.

Chapter 15

It had been a month now since Carla last saw Sergio and she had yet to speak with Tony. Two days ago when she left work, she was on her way to the grocery store and she had a feeling that someone was following her. She'd notice that there were times when she would look into her rearview mirror and a white sedan followed her every turn. The person driving the unknown car looked like Sergio, but whenever she would try to get a good look at his face, the unknown man held his head down or looked in another direction. Carla wanted to park her truck and walk up to the car, but she feared putting herself in danger. She made a mental note that if she should ever bear witness to such a suspicious act again, she would notify the authorities. That was the first and last time that she'd notice that strange event so she convinced herself that maybe she was paranoid, and pushed the event to the back of her head.

On this particular day, Carla couldn't wait to step foot in her condo. She was stressed at work and she wanted to flush her stressful day out of her mind. She planned to watch a movie and relax. She'd eaten a large salad for lunch, so she wasn't really hungry, but she had a craving for ice cream.

Carla took a hot, calming shower and threw on a laced negligee. She was excited about her solo movie night so she anxiously ran into her living room and popped the *Love Jones* DVD into the DVD player.

While the previews were showing, she retreated to the kitchen and grabbed the quart of Haggen Daz cookies and cream ice cream, which she bought for this moment, from the freezer and returned to the living room. She took a seat on the sofa and indulged in the calorie filled treat.

She was relaxed and for the first time in weeks, she was actually enjoying her solitude. Carla laughed and cried throughout various scenes of the movie as she snuggled on the sofa and memories of Tony filled her mind. Living without Tony was by far the hardest thing she'd have to do for the past month. She'd moved into her corner office and business was picking up and clients kept rolling in. As far as her career was concerned, that part of her life was perfect, but whenever she would come home, Carla was filled with emptiness and needed Tony by her side more than ever.

The movie was nearing the end and so was her ice cream. She shoved the last spoonful down her throat and then there was a sudden knock at the door. "Who the hell is that? They better have mistakenly knocked on the wrong door because they are interfering with my movie time," she fussed and sat up on the sofa. She placed the empty carton on the floor beside the white leather sofa and ran to the bathroom to retrieve her robe. There was another knock, which was louder than the first and now she was annoyed. Carla pulled the door open, ready to release the venom from her tongue about pounding at her door, and what she saw left her speechless.

Sergio stood in front of her and she didn't react fast enough because before she could shut the door, he barged in.

"How the hell did you know where to find me?" She spun around to follow his every move as she stood by the door and contemplated her next move.

Sergio was now sitting on her couch and Carla couldn't believe his nerve. "I have my ways." He crossed his thighs like he was some big shot and ran his tongue across his teeth.

"You need to get out before I call the police and considering your current state, I know you wouldn't like that very much."

"Are you threatening me?"

"Just know that I am serious." Carla walked over to the phone and Sergio leaped from the couch and grabbed her by the hair, pulling her head back.

"Put the phone back before I hurt you." Carla became fearful and did what she was told. Sergio walked her away from the phone and pinned her back up against the wall.

"Did you think that you would just throw my case over to someone else and turn your back on me?" Carla was too afraid to respond. Sergio licked her neck and started to grope her.

"Stop. Get away from me you son-of-a-bitch!"

He muzzled her mouth with his hands and probed between her thighs with his hand. "Shhh."

Carla's screams were scuffled as she tried to yell obscenities.

"Don't I make you feel good?" Sergio reached for her breasts with his free hand and Carla tried to move her body but he made it difficult because of the position he had her in. Her mind raced. When Sergio took his eyes off of her and looked down to attempt to unbuckle his pants, Carla noticed that he'd become distracted and saw it as her chance. She thrusted her knee into his groin area and Sergio cried out for pain and released his hand from her mouth and curled up, grabbing his crotch.

"You bitch!" he spat and looked up at her.

Carla ran across the room for the phone and bobbed her body from left to right like a boxer in a boxing match, getting ready to jab his opponent. "Who feels good now?" She now felt macho. She couldn't believe that he tried to rape her, but the fact the he didn't succeed and she was able to defend herself, gave her a sudden adrenaline rush. She made the mistake of turning her back to pick the phone up from the floor after it fell out of her hand, and by the time she grabbed the phone to call the police, Sergio managed to run out.

Chapter 16

Carla gave the police a report on Sergio, but it has been weeks since the incident and they have yet to make an arrest. This bothered her and she now regrets the day she decided to sleep with him. She needed a vacation. What was really going on with her life? It was times like this that she wished Tony were around. Why did she have to cheat and ruin things? But how was she so sure that he hadn't cheated on her? She didn't make mention about the incident with Sergio to anyone, not even Tamika. She got herself in this mess and she needed to get herself out. As she continued to weed through her thoughts, there was a knock at her door. Carla paused and was skeptical about answering. She ran to the kitchen for a butcher knife because she refused to have what happened to her happen again.

When she pulled the door open, she raised the knife above her head and was surprised to see Tony standing in front of her. She quickly brought the knife down to her side. Her legs felt weak. That very feeling made her understand what the group SWV meant when they sang the song, "*Weak*" because she felt like fainting. He was the last person she expected to show up on her doorstep, but she was happy he did. Carla felt relieved. His presence somehow calmed her. She stared at his chocolate skin in awe and everything she's ever felt for him, rushed through her and filled her insides to the tenth power. Her earlier thoughts vanished and she was always amazed at how quickly this man could change her mood from stressful to calm. His effect on her was unbelievable.

Tony spotted the knife in her hand and stepped back as he held up his hands in a surrendering motion. His eyes widened.

"Hey! Be careful with that thing. I came unharmed."

"I'm sorry." Carla looked down at the knife and thought about how paranoid she probably was. But then again, she had to make sure she protected herself and she would be damned if Sergio ever stepped foot inside her home again.

"Is everything okay?" Tony looked down at the knife and hesitated getting close to her. "What's up with the knife?"

"It's nothing. Come in."

"Are you sure that I will be safe? I didn't come here to lose my life," Tony joked as he walked past her and entered through the door.

"I didn't mean to scare you. I wasn't expecting anyone and I wasn't sure about who was at the door."

"So you answer the door with a butcher knife?"

"I was just frightened, that's all."

"Well, maybe you need to install a security system or something. You may end up hurting someone if you continue answering the door with that thing every time you hear an unexpected knock. I'm sorry to embark upon you without notice, but I was in the area and decided to stop by. I figured that if I called, you wouldn't answer, so I just took a chance. If you want me to leave, it's okay...I'll understand."

If I want you to leave? Is he fucking crazy? I don't ever want you to leave again, she thought. She knew that he was lying about being in the neighborhood, because he had no reason to be. And like Whitney Houston in the movie, *Waiting to Exhale*, Carla exhaled. She beamed from ear to ear and offered him a seat beside her on the sofa. They talked for a couple of minutes about how much they missed each other and before she knew it, Carla was sucking on his neck, making her way down to the dick that she missed so dearly and sucked him into ecstasy. They ripped each other's clothes off and Tony had her bent like a pretzel as she commanded him to have his way with her.

They'd sexed themselves into exhaustion for the latter part of the night and Carla woke up feeling like a brand new woman. Daddy was home and she refused to let him go again. She sang the lyrics to "*Daddy's Home,*" by Shep and the Limelites as she flipped the omelet in the skillet. It's funny how good sex can make a person forget their worries and sing a new tune. Tony walked into the kitchen and admired her ass through her robe. He shook his head and smiled as he watched her work the skillet.

"That's right baby, daddy's home for good." He walked up behind her and wrapped his arms around her waist. Carla leaned her head against his chest and nearly dropped the skillet on the floor.

"You're about to make me burn this place down. You know you can't be feeling on me when I'm cooking. You get my hormones all riled up and dangerous things can happen," she teased.

Tony laughed at how cute she was and walked back into the bedroom to let her handle her business in the kitchen. Shortly after, breakfast was served and Carla ran into the bedroom with the intention of hauling Tony out of bed so that she could seat him around the dining table. She'd slaved over the stove to create a five star omelet and she wanted to him to enjoy it while it was still hot.

When she walked into the bedroom, Tony was talking on his cell phone and he rushed to hang it up when he saw Carla walk in. She thought his actions seemed suspect, so without hesitation, she questioned him.

"Who was that?" She did indeed feel insecure, because in the back of her mind, she believed that Tony was seeing someone else during their one month split. She couldn't blame him if he did because her thoughtless ways initiated it. Tony was fine as hell and what woman wouldn't want him in their bed? He was the complete package. But she would be damned if he was talking to the next bitch while in her home and lying in her bed.

He looked at her as if to say, "Why are you doing this?"

"Tony was that another woman's voice that I just heard? Are you seeing someone else?" The truth was Tony has never laid eyes on another woman since he met Carla, not even during their temporary split. Snagging a woman wasn't difficult for Tony. Women practically threw themselves at him every day, but his heart belonged to Carla just as much as hers belonged to him. Tony saw that she was getting pissed off so he told her what he knew she wanted to hear, just to ruffle her feathers.

"Yeah, that was a woman's voice," he answered in a nonchalant tone. "And?"

"Look, I know that I made a huge mistake and I have apologized and suffered long enough. But I will not stand here and allow you to disrespect me in my own home."

Tony stared at the TV and pretended to ignore her. He could see her blood boiling and as he watched her from the corner of his eye. Her face was turning red and he just loved how sexy she looked whenever she got upset. He didn't mean for her to go over the edge, but he would ruin the surprise that he planned for her if he'd told her the truth.

"This was probably a big mistake...I think you should leave," she said calmly.

"But what about breakfast?" he asked and continued to play his little game.

"You have some fucking nerve. You know that? Tell that other chick to make you breakfast. Call her ass back and tell her you're on your way." Carla was upset at his nonchalant attitude and his disrespect. *He is taking this shit as a joke, but I am not playing with his ass.* She grabbed his clothes from the floor and threw them at him.

"Take your shit and get out," she screamed as the garments landed on his chest.

Tony climbed out of the bed and walked towards her. He tried to pull her close for a warm embrace, but she pulled away from him and a tear rolled down her cheek. "I don't think I can take this Tony. Things may never be the same between us again and I can't live with the fact that you might use my cheating against me so that you can have an excuse to mess around with other women."

He pulled her into his arms and this time she didn't pull away. "Carla, I would never do that to you, baby. Yes that was a woman on the phone, but it's not what you think. I only behaved the way I just did because I love to look at how sexy you are when you're mad. I didn't mean to hurt you and I am sorry." *Give me a break. Is that the best he can come up with?*

He held her face between his hands, parted her mouth with his and explored her mouth with his tongue. His dick sprang forward like daylight savings time. When she felt his hardness through her robe, Carla couldn't resist. Sex was her weakness. His sex. She pulled him down on top of her as she fell back on the pillow top mattress. She no longer cared about the woman's voice she heard on the phone because Tony was making love to her and not the other woman. *If it were serious, he wouldn't be here with me right now.* Was she really being naïve or have her hormones rushed to her brain? How could someone as intelligent as Carla fall so weak for one man's love? Was her guilt about cheating causing her to believe whatever Tony told her, even if she didn't believe him? Whatever it was, it didn't seem to matter, because she guided his baton to her love tunnel and they explored each other's insides and climaxed over and over again as she got lost in his love.

Chapter 17

Carla opened her eyes and Tony was sprawled out beside her. She lay quietly beside him and quickly scanned her bedroom. When she looked at the nightstand and spotted Tony's cell, the thought of yesterday suddenly came back to her. Was Tony playing her like a fool? Was he cheating? Who was that woman he was on the phone with? The questions became overwhelming without answers. She felt foolish for sleeping with him after contemplating the idea that he could be possibly two timing her. Carla needed leverage. She needed to know what was going on. If she wanted answers, she would have to find them on her own. Today was the day she hoped to shine some light on the truth, if there was a truth. Carla hoped her thoughts were wrong, but there was only one way to find out. She eased out of bed and grabbed her cell from the dresser. "Tamika," she whispered. "It's time to put our plan in action."

When Tony left out this morning, Tamika came to pick Carla up in Marcus' car. They didn't want to take a chance and blow their cover. Both women wore hats and disguised themselves with sunglasses. Tamika came well prepared with a pair of binoculars. Carla cracked up at the sight.

"Look at us. Never in a million years did I think that I would be trailing behind some man, just to see if he's cheating or not."

"Girl, love can make anyone do some crazy things. But look on the bright side, you'll discover the truth and not to mention that this is going to be exciting."

Carla looked at Tamika in disbelief. "Are you serious? 'Mika, this is not something to be taken lightly. This is my life. My relationship. My heart. What if I see something that I wish I hadn't? I'm starting to wonder if I should really do this."

"I wasn't trying to make a joke out of it, Carla. But it's your call. Either you want to find out sooner or later or not find out at all.

The choice is yours, but you better choose fast because he's pulling off and we're going to lose him if we don't hurry."

"Huuugh. Let's go. There's no sense in turning back now. After all, I called you out of your house and I didn't take off from work for nothing."

"Are you sure you're ready for this?"

"Tamika, don't let me second guess my decision. Let's go."

"Okay. Here goes nothing." Tamika drove off behind Tony and was careful to keep him in sight.

"So why did you decide to do this today?"

"I heard him on the phone with another woman."

"No!"

"Yes."

"Are you sure?"

"Very."

"When you called, I did not hesitate to call my boss to tell him that I was taking a sick day. I would not miss this for the world. If Tony knows what's good for him, he will be on his p's and q's."

"No. I wanna catch him red handed so that I can quit wondering what if."

"There's nothing like knowing the truth."

Carla nodded as her heart raced and kept her eyes on the back of Tony's truck. Ten minutes into their drive, they followed him to his first stop, Starbucks. They waited until he came out of the store and marveled at how oblivious he was to his surroundings. Not once did he look around. When Tony got back into his truck, they followed him to the restaurant. They staked out for a while until hunger was obvious. Both women had growling stomachs. They looked at each other and laughed.

"We should've thought this through more thoroughly. How are we going to leave and get something to eat? What if he leaves when we're gone?"

"We'll just have to risk it because I am hungry," Tamika said. "We'll go somewhere that's close by." Carla agreed and they drove off to a nearby McDonalds.

Hours passed and not once did Tony leave the restaurant. Tamika and Carla took turns napping and between breaks, they would sing along to the music that they played or they would make fun of the people going and coming out of the restaurant.

It was nearing closing and they couldn't be more relieved. Carla was somewhat disappointed that she didn't see anything suspicious, but it persuaded her that she must learn to trust Tony again, to some extent. When Tony walked out of the restaurant, they paid attention and observed the other staff members, who were leaving out to their cars. None of the women seemed like his type. All he did was wave good night and hopped in his truck. When he pulled off, Tamika started her engine and followed closely. They almost missed him at the red light, but were pleased that he stopped on yellow. They stopped three feet behind him.

"Where do you think he will lead us next?" Tamika asked.

Carla shrugged and hoped that she wouldn't see the unexpected. When the light changed, Tony picked up speed and they did the same. He was headed to the highway and once he drove onto the ramp, he sped down the freeway and just when they were about to do the same, an eighteen wheeler cut them off and they lost him.

"Damn." Tamika slapped the steering wheel. "We were so close. We were doing well, up until now. Damn that truck driver."

"Maybe it's a sign. What if he is innocent?" Carla was secretly thankful. She didn't know if her heart could really take the truth.

What she saw was enough. She didn't catch him doing anything and that's how she would like to keep it. She would just have to learn how to control her negative thoughts, if she could. She already messed up once. As much as she was curious to know the truth, she convinced herself to let it rest, for now.

"Are you okay with it?"

"What else can we do?"

"We can try again on another day? Don't you want to know?"

"Who wouldn't want to know if their man was cheating? If you seek, you will find, but what if I'm not ready to face the possibilities of what I may find?"

"So, are you comfortable with what you saw thus far?"

"Perhaps. But since we don't have other options, let's go home."

Chapter 18

It had been weeks since the undercover investigation with Tamika. The fact that she came up empty handed, caused Carla to agree that she would past behind her so that she and Tony can move on with their lives together. She decided to take it one day at a time and see where the relationship leads them. Tony and Carla have been spending more time with each other since then and he hasn't had any more suspicious phone calls since. He even allowed Carla to search his contacts one night and that made her believe that he had nothing to hide. Actually, when she looked through his phone, she was surprised that there were hardly any female names in the log. This morning, as she was getting dressed for work, Tony told her that he had something planned for her when she got off. He told her to meet him at Aja, an Asian restaurant where many of Atlanta's well known socialites dine from time to time, by 7 p.m. sharp. Ever since Tony came back into her life, he wined and dined her like no man has before.

Enjoying her new position, Carla sat in her new corner office and anticipated the surprise that would be awaiting her. She planned to leave the office early today because she did not want to be late. Her office had a wonderful view overlooking the city and every now and then, she would gaze out the window and watch the many cars drive by. There was nothing like the city life, but she preferred to work in the city and live in the suburbs. It was easier for her to separate her personal life from her work life that way.

Carla rushed home just in time to beat the rush hour traffic. She couldn't wait to see what Tony had planned. She pulled out a black satin wrap dress, designed by Chanel, from her closet and paired it with black pumps. Diane hooked her hair up the day before with fresh curls and Carla looked fierce. She was ready to take this special night by storm.

She suddenly felt out of breath from running back and forth from her closet, but this feeling felt foreign. Whatever it was, it hit her like a ton of bricks and she had to sit at the edge of the bed to catch her breath.

Within minutes, she felt better and continued her preparations. She soaked in a warm bubble bath for nearly thirty minutes and when she suddenly felt chills, Carla gladly stepped out. She massaged her skin with body oil from the Carol's daughter collection and selected the sexiest pair of thongs that she owned. If Tony was on his best behavior, which she knew he would be, she would sneak him into the ladies room and run his mind wild.

She did her final twirl in front of the mirror to make sure that everything looked perfect and it did. Carla looked like a princess and she was on her way to meet her prince charming. She grabbed her clutch purse and headed out the door humming the tune to *"It's too late to turn back now,"* by Cornelius Brothers and Sister Rose. She'd never felt as good as she did tonight. Things were starting to flow in the right direction again and Carla couldn't wait to see what the night had in store for her.

The drive to the restaurant was a smooth one, which was a good sign that nothing would go wrong. Everything was going her way. Traffic was light, which allowed her to make it there in record time; considering that she lived almost an hour away from the area.

Carla parked her Range by a vacant parking meter and inserted two handfuls of quarters. She wasn't sure of the length of her stay, but the five hour time reading should be more than enough. She glanced at her Movado watch and she had ten minutes to make it inside. She tried to guess what the surprise was because Tony gave her no leads. She was so deep in thought that when she attempted to cross the street, she didn't notice the bright yellow Lamborghini, with California plates, speeding down the one way street and nearly did her in for the kill. Carla quickly jumped back and the only reaction she was able to muster, was a gasp. It all happened so fast and she was terrified.

She attempted to cross again, this time checking for speeding cars, and when she saw that the course was clear, she dashed across to the other side. As she walked down the sidewalk, Carla received stares from every direction. The dress was indeed flattering, and her luscious curls would make any man bow at her feet. She needed no one to tell her how gorgeous she looked, because her confident strides showed that she already knew.

Carla made her grand entrance and gave her name to the cute heavy set woman behind the desk. The woman was dressed in a crisp white buttoned down shirt tucked into black slacks and Carla figured it was uniform when she noticed some other staff member dress in the same attire. The woman carried herself well and her makeup was beyond beautiful. Carla had time to observe the woman because she was too busy looking for Carla's name on a ten page list. She noticed the woman making a circle when she flipped to the fourth page and then she looked up at Carla and smiled.

"Mr. Simmons is awaiting your arrival. Follow me."

Carla did as instructed and followed the woman's lead. She was guided to a secluded area and what she thought was supposed to be a beautiful night, didn't seem so beautiful anymore. She almost had a mental break down and she could feel her heart splitting in two. She felt humiliated and wanted to turn around and leave with her dignity, but it was too late. She was already seen by him. She wanted to know if he took her for a joke. How much longer will she be put up with the games? When will she be able to open her eyes and stare the love that she often desired in the face? The man she believed to be was Mr. right, was proving himself as Mr. wrong.

Enough was enough and she needed answers. She was filled with fury and if she didn't know the consequences of breaking the law, Carla would've slapped the life out of both of them and then find his car and do some serious body damage. *Where the fuck is Tamika when I need her?* Tonight was her battle and she was not going down without a fight. At this point, it was either all or nothing. Besides her career, she had nothing else to lose. As far as she knew, she'd already lost the man she loved with all her heart.

Carla marched over to the table where they were seated and her devil horns were shooting out through the top of her head. She stood before Tony and Trish and her poisonous words began to flow uncontrollably.

"You fucking bastard. Is this why you invited me here? To make a fool out of me Tony...is that it?" Tony tried to explain himself but she gave him no room to speak. Trish was shocked by Carla's sudden outburst and she was delighted that other customers were not in view to witness the embarrassing commotion.

Carla was like the energizer bunny because her mouth kept going and going. "You claimed that this slanted eye bitch was a goddamn business partner and I was so stupid to believe you. Are you doing this to make a point? Why didn't you just break up with me instead of humiliating me like this in front of this sleaze ball? I knew that you were up to no good when I first saw you two together and you know what? I'm glad I cheated on you because you deserved it." Trish's mouth flung wide open.

Tony buried his face in his hands. Not out of embarrassment, but because Carla's words slapped him in the face. Hard. He was not pleased that Carla just insulted him in front of his jeweler, and on top of that, she put their business out on front street. No, he was not pleased, not one bit. He knew they would have to have a serious talk when they leave the restaurant, but for now, he had to stop her while she's ahead and save her from further embarrassment.

Carla was going bonkers and Tony had never known her to be so foul mouthed. He had to stop her before management got involved.

Even though her words hurt him, Tony remained cool and collected. She was embarrassing herself and him and he wished she knew how much of a fool she was making of herself. "Carla, stop." His voice was commanding.

"Don't you tell me to stop," she spat and looked down at Trish, whose eyes had grown wide.

"Why can't you find your own man? I know he told you that he had a woman, but you just had to keep throwing yourself at him huh?" Trish sat there with a confused look and Carla was too angry to notice it.

"You know what? You two can have each other. I don't need this." She was out of breath. Carla turned to walk away, but Tony quickly grabbed her by the arm and stopped her in her tracks.

"What is wrong with you? I've never seen you lose your cool like this before. Did you have a bad day at work?"

"Oh, so you think this shit is funny? No Tony, my day was fine, that is until I got here and saw you dining with her. But as soon as you loosen my arm so that I can leave, my day will be better when I am out of your life for good." She was now emotional. Her words echoed in her mind and she couldn't imagine being without him for good. She tried to be strong, but it was no use. Tears sprayed down her face like a broken fire hydrant.

Tony managed to calm her down and then he dried her face and held her in his arms. She still wanted to put up a fight, but her ranting and raving made her weary. Carla gave in and he walked her over to join him at the table.

She managed to quickly pull herself together and pulled out her compact mirror. Her flawless makeup was now smeared from wiping her face and her mascara was mixed with her tears and left a black line under her eyes. She felt ashamed of her recent behavior and she was adamant about apologizing until she got some answers.

Trish sat upward in her chair and avoided making eye contact with Carla. The mood was tense and the tension was thick. "Are you okay now?" Tony asked. Carla nodded and he began to set the record straight.

"Carla, I invited you here as well as Trish because I wanted to surprise you and Trish was the bearer of the gift." Carla looked confused and she tried to make sense of what Tony was saying. She attempted to speak but he continued with his explanation before she could utter a word.

"Before I explain any further, I guess it would be appropriate for me to introduce you two to each other and then, Carla, you owe Trish an apology for your defiling outburst."

Carla looked at Tony as if to say, "You must be out of your damn mind, because I am not apologizing to anyone."

Tony read her expression but quickly dismissed it. He introduced both women and Carla was the least thrilled. Trish extended her hand but Carla refused to shake hands because as far as she knew, Trish was out to steal her man from under her nose. Her behavior was childish and she knew it, but then again, love can make a person do some crazy things.

Tony realized her stubbornness but he decided not to push it. He continued to explain to Carla who Trish really was and what their business dealings was with each other, but Carla didn't give a flying fuck and wished he would just get to point about why he chose to humiliate her.

He was through with his speech and then she saw Trish place a black leather briefcase, the same one she carried the last time, on the table. Trish punched in a code and the briefcase flew open and revealed the least expected.

Carla's eyes widened at the glitter and sparkle. Tony smiled at her reaction and wondered how dumb she was going to feel once he executed his plan. Carla gasped at the sight of the five diamond rings than shunned so brightly. They were neatly placed beside each other, forming a straight line. Her mood was now changed from being irate to feeling like a jack ass. She knew that she now had some serious apologizing to do and became angry at herself for allowing her emotions and her assumptions to get the best of her. She was out of character and she made a fool of herself in front of Trish and Tony and hoped they would forgive her for such tyrant behavior.

She loved that man and love made her act a fool.

"So, what do you think?" Trish asked with much hesitation. To see that Carla had calmed down, Trish felt at ease.

Carla looked up at Trish, who show cased the rings like Vanna White on *The Price is Right,* and gave her a warm smile. She then looked at Tony and did the same. It was the least she could do for now. "They're absolutely beautiful," Carla said and then paused.

"Trish, I am so sorry for my behavior earlier. But I came here expecting to see Tony sitting here alone and when I saw the two of you, well...I just flipped. Being a woman yourself, I hope you understand where I am coming from."

Trish held out her left hand to show Carla her wedding ring. "You see this? I've been married for five years and I've been through hell and back with my husband, so I definitely know where you're coming from."

Carla was shocked by Trish's response and realized that Trish had some sista-hood in her. Trish turned out to be the complete opposite of what Carla expected and finding out that Trish was married made her feel more like a dummy.

Tony was pleased to see that things were getting back on the right track. Everything didn't go as smoothly as he planned, but seeing the women make amends was a good start. Trish went on to explain that she's known Tony for quite some time and he often gives her business with his jewel requests. Carla's mind backtracked to the night Tony took her to Morton's and she remembered the nice diamond bracelet that he wore. Oh she felt like such a fool.

"Tony has worked extremely hard to make sure that the finest platinum bands and diamonds were selected, so I chose the top five and he asked me here to show the pieces so that you can select the one you desired most. He figured that since you would be the one wearing the ring, he wanted you to be happy wearing it," Trish said and then smiled.

Love Finally

Carla turned to face Tony. "Why are you doing this when I don't deserve it? I can't believe that after what I did to you, you still choose to go above and beyond to make me happy."

"Carla, I love you and when I said that I wanted you to be my wife, I meant it. I am not saying that what happened was right, but I believe that everyone deserves a second chance. You are my soul mate. I didn't invite you here to embarrass you or have an argument, but to allow you to choose your wedding ring."

Carla selected the princess cut, five carat diamond embedded in a platinum band. Trish wished them well and left, as her job there was done. Tony then took the ring and got down on one knee. He looked up at Carla, stared in her eyes, and popped the question that she was so longing to hear. "Carla Milford, will you marry me?"

If there was enough space, she would've done a thousand back flips. Tears filled her eyes and she finally blurted, "Yes...Yes. I will marry you." With that said, Tony slid the prestigious diamond ring down on her finger and they embraced each other. Carla prayed that tonight would be the last night that she shed a tear; until her wedding day that is, but that day will be tears of joy.

Chapter 19

"I can't believe that we are now both wives to be," Tamika squealed. "Now that you've been promoted and Tony is soon to be your husband, you can start shopping around for that dream house you always wanted."

"I know. I don't think the reality of it has hit me yet. I feel like I am dreaming." It has been two days since Tony proposed and Carla has been trying to persuade him to move in with her, but Tony thought it would be too rushed and assured her that they will soon be living under one roof. Why the wait? She didn't know, but she wouldn't tolerate it much longer.

"You're damn here at my place almost every day. So I don't see why you just can't move in with me," she'd told him two days ago.

"I'm kinda glad that we didn't discover any real findings during our investigation. That woman was a part of his plan all along and it's good to know that he wasn't cheating after all. We are going to laugh about this in the future."

"Yeah, I'm sure."

Carla sat back in her rolling chair and admired the sparkling rock that was on her finger. Carla still couldn't believe that she was engaged to be married and it wouldn't be long before her last name would be changed to Simmons. Tamika was right. It wouldn't be a bad idea to plan on building her dream house after all because she was no longer a bachelorette and she knew that it wouldn't be long before she and Tony started a family together.

She'd told Tamika about the proposal, but intentionally skipped over the whole dramatic scene that she created.

"I'm glad that you two were finally able to work things out. This is definitely called for a celebration."

"Maybe we can get together this weekend?"

"I was thinking that maybe we can get together after work today."

"Today is not a good day. I really haven't been feeling well." Carla did notice that for the past couple of weeks, she has been feeling quite crabby. Most of the time, she would have to force herself to have a peppy attitude. She's almost always tired and then a sudden light bulb went off in her head.

"Tamika, I have to call you back, but I promise that we'll catch up this weekend."

"You better keep your promise. Bye."

Carla placed her cell phone on her desk and her head began to spin. The thought of possibly being pregnant gave her an instant migraine. "Maybe it's just stress," she said aloud to convince herself to think differently.

She needed to get fresh air. She informed her new receptionist, Michelle, that she was stepping out for lunch and should be back shortly. Now that she was a senior partner, John gave her a personal receptionist. Michelle was nothing like Sarah. In fact, Sarah was always prompt and knew the firm like the back of her hand. Michelle still had some learning to do and her lack of promptness irritated Carla. If Sarah hadn't violated her that day, she would've considered giving her the position. Carla grabbed her bag and headed for the elevator.

She pulled into a nearby Starbucks and purchased a blueberry muffin and a grande caramel frappuccino. She took a seat in the back of the coffee shop and tried to relax her mind, but it wasn't working. Carla knew that something was definitely up because her recent behaviors were nothing like herself. She thought back on how emotional she's been lately, but figured it was all because of what she was going through at the moment with Tony.

She needed to know the truth. The suspense was killing her. Carla stood up to exit the building and suddenly plopped back down on the chair when she saw Sergio walking in her direction. "What in the..." Her eyes grew wide. *What are the odds of us meeting here?* She did not expect to run into him; and today had to be the day of all days. *When will my drama ever end?* She was prepared to knee him again he wanted to try anything stupid.

"Hey, Carla," Sergio waved to her as he continued to walk in her direction. She couldn't believe how Sergio acted as if everything was okay between them. *This asshole has a Dr, Jekyll and Mr. Hyde personality going on. Does he not know that the entire Atlanta police department was in search of him? How the hell can he act so calm?* Carla pulled out her cell phone.

Actually, Sergio showed up at the coffee shop on purpose. He'd been following Carla around ever since that day he ran out of her house. He'd staked out her condo several times since then and watched her going and coming on a daily basis. He knew what time she made it into the office and what time she left. He often parked across the street from her office building and followed behind her whenever she would leave on her lunch break. He'd discovered her favorite lunch spots whenever he would watch and see who she would be having lunch with. He'd even trailed behind when Carla and Tony were out on dates and he would get pissed to the eighteenth power whenever he would catch them kissing. There were many close calls when he almost revealed himself, but he was only waiting for the perfect opportunity to approach her. On this particular day, he'd followed her to the coffee shop and when he realized that she was there alone, he decided to make his move.

"Looks like we're thinking alike," he said and sat in the chair next to her. It had been a little over a month since Carla saw or spoke to Sergio and she wondered why the police haven't found him yet. Carla cringed and wanted so badly to be out of his presence

"I was in the mood for coffee and I decided to stop in. I thought that was your truck parked out front," he continued. "So how have you been? You still look great. Look, we need to talk."

He is fucking psychotic. "Listen, you dirt bag, *we* have nothing to talk about. I should've mutilated your ass for trying to rape me. The police are after your ass and I'll be damned if they don't find you."

"Oh so you're gonna turn me in? They can try and catch me but I doubt they will."

"Let me warn you, if you ever come anywhere close to me again, your ass may not be so lucky."

"Ooooo. I'm scared. Good luck trying to prove that I tried to rape you. You threw your pussy on me. Remember?"

"You remember this, I am a lawyer. I know how to get around the system. Keep on playing with fire and your ass will get burned." She snarled her lips at him.

"I don't have time to entertain you, but I promise that they will catch your ass." Carla threw her bag over her shoulders in preparation to leave.

"Oh c'mon, you mean to tell me that you can't spare two seconds of your time to chat with an old friend? I mean, it's been like what...a month or two? It can't be that bad."

"You are fucking crazy."

"Yes, you are right. I'm crazy about you."

Carla stood up and when she tried to walk past him, Sergio grabbed her wrist and told her to sit down. His tight grip showed Carla that he was serious. She didn't want to draw attention from other customers, so she did as she was instructed. Sergio's behavior was scaring her. He looked like he hadn't showered in days. His once neatly trimmed goatee was grown out, his hair was in need of a comb and he just looked a hot mess.

"Did you think that the incident at your house was going to be the last you saw of me? I know you're smarter than that. I told you that I loved you and you just shut me down like a broken car."

" I..."

"Shut up, Carla...just shut up. You're not going anywhere until you hear what I have to say," he said through clenched teeth. Carla folded her lips and listened as he spoke. The dark look in Sergio's eyes and his disturbed demeanor caused a sudden fear to come over her.

"I have been following your every move for the past month." She was shocked and wanted to slap him but she knew he would probably strike her back.

"You just don't understand how much it hurts every time I see you hugging and kissing that punk you call your man. Dammit, I told you that I love you so why is that so hard for you to understand? Raping you was never my intention, and I didn't know what came over me that day. I got so thinking back on the day we slept together and I had to have more of you. When you tried to resist me, I just lost it. Look, I'm sorry, but can't you see what you are doing to me?"

Carla wondered if Sergio was suffering from some type of a mental problem. How could he claim to love her? He didn't know much about her, they only had a one night stand and she couldn't make sense of it. Sergio was overwhelming her. This was not the time for her to be dealing with this.

"I really need to be going," she said in a whisper. Sergio saw the fear in her eyes and he released his grip from around her wrist and when he did, the imprint from his fingers remained.

"See what you're making me do? I need you, Carla."

She wanted so badly to get away from him so she told him what she believed he wanted to hear. At this moment, she was willing to do anything to get away. "Sergio, I promise that we can talk about this over lunch tomorrow."

Love Finally

His voice was instantly filled with hope. "Really? Are you for real?"

Then it was refilled with anger. "You better not be bullshitting me or I swear, you will regret it."

Carla shook her head. "No...no. I'm serious. Call me at the office tomorrow at around noon and we can go from there. But please, it's urgent that I get going now."

"Don't go trying nothing stupid." Carla nodded her head and ran all the way to her truck. The moment she hopped in, she started the ignition and sped off.

Chapter 20

Tears poured down her face as she continued to drive. She couldn't believe all that was happening to her. Her thoughts were all over the place. With no intention of returning to the office, Carla was unsure of whether or not she should go home. Knowing that Sergio was following her, made her paranoid. She needed to tell someone because she wasn't so sure that she was safe. But who would she tell? This whole thing was obviously her fault and she needed to fix it. What the hell was she going to do? She slowly regained herself and her earlier thoughts invaded her mind. Her current thoughts suddenly took priority over the situation with Sergio. She couldn't battle both at once. She needed to free her mind from her existing assumptions first, and deal with Sergio later. If her assumptions proved to be true, how can she handle the two? To try and alleviate one of her recent stresses, Carla decided to stop into a nearby Rite Aid pharmacy. She got out of her truck and scanned the parking lot for any suspicious vehicles.

Carla walked into the store and located the aisle she was looking for. She walked up and down the aisle countless times eyeing the product she planned to purchase. She couldn't believe how expensive they were. This was her first time purchasing such product, so she was a bit nervous. An employee walked past her several times and gave Carla a weird look each time she saw her pacing. Not wanting the clerk to get the wrong idea, Carla finally grabbed the box from the shelf and headed to the checkout counter. Carla paid the cashier, who wished her luck when she saw item, and bolted out of the store. She gave the parking lot a quick scan and hopped in her truck. It's funny how she wasn't as observant of her surroundings before now. Sergio really had her mind going.

She quickly turned the key and unlocked the door. Carla pushed the door opened and the bathroom was her first stop. Her heart pounded as she read the instructions from the packet. She peed on the stick just like it said, replaced the cap on the wet end, and placed it on the counter. The instructions told her to wait five minutes and it was the longest five minutes of her life.

Carla paced the passage way between her bedroom and bathroom. She has never been so nervous. Assuming that five minutes was up, she returned into the bathroom, picked up the plastic content and saw two red lines. *Oh my god.* Her heart picked up speed and she knew what those lines indicated because she'd read the meaning of the results from the instruction sheet.

Her world has taken a sudden curve ball and Carla didn't know if she should be happy or sad. She always thought that the day she discovered she was pregnant, was supposed to be a happy moment. But didn't she feel happy. If anything, it seemed more like a curse than a blessing. There was no way a baby would fit into the equation of her life. It would only make matters difficult for her. She crawled into bed and dragged the sheet over her body. Tears soaked her pillow and countless thoughts filled her mind. How was she going to tell Tony? Things were just starting to get back on track for them and she doubts he was ready to be a father. This was not how she planned her life.

It was supposed to be marriage first, then house, then child. Why hadn't she been more careful and used protection?

The whole thought pained her. Just when she thought she took two steps forward, something happens to pull her four steps back. Yes, she always wanted a child, but not now; now was not the time. She'd just gotten engaged and she needed time to plan the wedding. She'd just made partner and having a baby now would ruin everything that she worked so hard for. With her busy career, there was no room for a baby. What was she going to do? And to top it off, Sergio was stalking her. She needed to vent, but who should she call? Tamika would've been her first choice, but she couldn't reveal what she just found out to any one, not yet. She had to make up her mind fast and figure out a solution.

Carla tried to fall asleep so that she can forget everything, but it was a failed effort. Her house phone rang and it was her mother. "Hello."

"Oh my, you sound horrible! Is everything okay?"

"Yeah. Just a little tired, that's all."

"Are you sure that that's all? Carla you have been acting a bit strange lately. I haven't seen you much since we left that exhibit and this is clearly not like you. The last time I spoke to you was when you told me about your promotion and if I hadn't called into the office to check in on you, I probably wouldn't have found out about it then. Is there something going on that I need to know about?" Carla told Ellen about her promotion just days after she moved into her new office. Of course Ellen was furious that Carla had kept it hidden from her for as long as she did, but it was just like Carla suspected. When Ellen found out about the promotion, she'd given Carla this drawn out speech about using her money wisely and to make sure that she settles down with a man of the same rank.

"Momma, everything is fine. It's just that with my new position and all, I've been a bit busy," Carla lied. Truth was, Ellen knew that Carla was hiding something from her and Carla always knew how to keep her worries hidden. But it wouldn't be long before Ellen would add pressure that would leave Carla no choice but to open up and explain herself. But Carla figured that Ellen wouldn't understand what she was going through.

"Well, if you say that's what it is, then I have no other choice but to believe you. So how is your new office coming along?"

"I still can't believe that you kept your promotion from me for an entire week. I should've been the first person you notified. How do you think your father would feel?" Carla knew that she probably should've notified Ellen sooner, but she also knew how anal her mother could be at times. She didn't even tell her about the engagement or Tony for that matter and if Ellen was upset about not finding out about a promotion, how would she feel when Carla dropped the bomb on her?

Carla sighed. This was all weighing heavy on her. "I'm sorry momma, you're right. Speaking of daddy, I sure wish he were here." Carla knew that if Carl were still alive, her life would've probably been in a better condition. Carl always knew how to work himself around any situation. Carla would often go to him with her problems, which made Ellen jealous of course, but Carl always had the answer. Her father was not judgmental like her mother and that's what she loved about him. She knew that Tony and Carl would've gotten along great, only if he were still alive to meet him.

Carla didn't know how to fill Ellen in on all of her latest drama. Ellen wouldn't understand and she'd only know how to judge the situation instead of trying to give Carla comforting advice. How on earth was she going to tell her mother that she was engaged and expecting a child? She wouldn't tell her. It would make things more complicating. As if her life wasn't complicated enough.

"Carla I want you to promise me that you will not conduct this behavior anymore. You are my only child. With your father gone away from us, you are all that I have and we need to stay in touch more often."

"Okay. I promise."

"Love you. You're still my little angel. Bye." Carla smiled through the phone. Her mother's words brought comfort and guilt at the same time. While Ellen confessed to loving her, Carla had dislike for the unborn child inside her.

Carla's stomach growled. She climbed out of bed and retreated to the kitchen. The thought of eating for two suddenly dawned on her. There were some serious decisions to be made and they had to be made fast.

She grabbed a frozen dinner from the freezer and heated it in the microwave. The chronologics of her day played in her head while she stood by the microwave. "Oh shit," she suddenly blurted. "I promised Sergio that I would meet up with him tomorrow. What the hell was I thinking?" Carla had obviously forgotten about it. She'd been too focused on getting a pregnancy test when she'd left the coffee shop. She contemplated calling the authorities and she knew that with him being out on bond with a pending case, he was bound to do time if she reported him.

Things just wouldn't make themselves easier for her. The microwave beeped, signaling that the food was ready, and Carla pulled on the handle to open the door and removed the hot box from the glass tray. A spell of nausea hit her once she was done eating and Carla didn't know if she could get use to the illnesses that came along with being pregnant.

She took a hot shower, allowing the water to massage her tummy. While thinking of her current state, Carla blamed the embryo for the hell she believed it will cause, when in actuality, she brought hell upon herself.

Chapter 21

Carla slept uncomfortably throughout the night. She had a hard time coping with her new findings. She didn't even know the first steps that she needed to take. This was all too much. None of what she planned for. She promised to make a doctor's appointment before the end of the week. Relieved that her nausea subsided, Carla dragged herself out of bed, showered, and quickly got dressed for work. Tony must've called her over a hundred times the night before, but she didn't know how it would've been possible for her to talk with him without giving off any signs that something was wrong. Tony was quite an observer and he was always in tuned with her emotions. She needed to talk him, but wouldn't allow herself to. Not until she thought things through. She stared at herself long and hard in front of the mirror, trying to imagine what she would look like with a baby bump. Thinking about the baby suddenly disgusted her. The thought of losing her shape and having stretch marks besieged her. She wanted it to go away. She planned to. Carla let out a sigh and then slipped her feet into a pair of deep brown pumps that compliment her red and brown attire, and then dreadfully headed out the door.

She'd promised Sergio that she would meet him for lunch and although she knew that she was really taking a dangerous risk, Carla decided nevertheless to follow through on her promise. Carla sat at her desk twirling a pencil between her fingers and watched the clock that hung on the wall. When the hour and minute hands both pointed on twelve, her office phone rang and startled her. She subconsciously jumped back in her seat as the pencil fell out of her hands and landed on the carpet. Carla grabbed the receiver, took a deep breath and reluctantly answered. "Hello."

"I see that you kept your word. I'm parked down stairs waiting for you."

His voice gave her the creeps, which instantly brought her back to her senses. *What the hell am I thinking?* Carla slammed the receiver back on the holster and her heart felt like it wanted to come through her chest. The phone rang again, but this time she just stared at it until the ringing stopped. She would've been out of her mind if she chose to meet up with Sergio, not knowing what he was capable of doing.

He'd called back a total of seven times, within the past hour and Carla was now afraid of leaving the building. She had to think fast. She refused to give Sergio control of her life. As much as she was going to hate doing it, Carla called the police and reported that someone was stalking her.

Later that evening, she'd asked one of the security officers to walk her to the parking lot. She didn't notice any suspicious vehicles lurking around, so she felt relieved and hopped in her truck after thanking the wrestler built guard. Carla pulled out of the lot when her cell phone rang. She shuffled through her bag for the device and when she finally retrieved it, the caller hung up. Carla thumbed through her call log for the last missed call and Tamika's number popped up. She quickly touched the screen to call her back.

"I just tried calling you," Tamika blurted before Carla could even say "hello".

"That's why I'm calling you back. My phone was lodged in my bag between my stuff and by the time I finally turned it free, you'd already hung up."

"Oh. Well you know the wedding is in two months and I wanted to do a little shopping."

"I thought you hired a planner."

"I did and I'm not shopping for the wedding silly...I'm shopping for the guests."

"Huh?"

"I decided that I would do the unusual and provide appreciation bags for those who are going to come out and celebrate the day with us."

"I see." Carla's mind was far out and Tamika noticed.

"Are you listening?"

"Yeah."

"So what do you think?"

"It's a nice gesture."

"So will you come shopping with me?"

"When?"

"Now!"

Carla looked at the time on her custom made clock that was installed in her dashboard. "Okay. Where do you want to meet?"

"Party City off of Lenox Rd."

"Okay. See you in a little while. I may get held up in traffic though."

"Didn't I teach you about taking back roads?"

"I haven't mastered those streets yet."

Tamika let out a short laugh. "Alright, call me when you make it. Bye."

Carla pushed the end button and placed the phone in the cup holder for easier access. She let out a sigh and made a U-turn since she was no longer going home as she'd planned. Traffic was crazy just as she'd imagined it to be and her eyes started to burn. Fatigue was kicking in and she knew that it was a result from her pregnancy. However, she managed to stay awake and after her thirty minute drive, she safely made it to her location. Carla called up Tamika to inform her that she was looking for a parking space and she would meet her inside the store as soon as she was able to park.

"It's about time." Tamika gave Carla a hug when she approached her. "Look at these...what you think?" Tamika asked about a set of decorated pens.

"Those are cute," Carla answered dryly. She was tired as hell and shopping was the last thing on her mind.

"Hmmm. Maybe I should keep looking." Tamika replaced the pens on the shelf. She noticed that Carla wasn't her usual self and knew that something was wrong. They'd been friends for as long as she could remember and she definitely knew when something was bothering her friend.

"Are you okay?" she turned to ask Carla.

"Huh? Yeah I'm fine."

"Don't lie to me Carla. I've known you long enough to know when something is wrong, so now you better fill me in."

"'Mika, I promise...I'm fine."

"Carla Milford, I've never known you to lie to me so don't start now."

"You sound like my mother," Carla said and laughed.

"So, what is it?"

"You just never let up...do you?"

"Never have and never will. I'm all ears."

"I swear, you should've been the lawyer instead of me." There was brief silence and Carla avoided eye contact with Tamika. She browsed the shelves and without looking at Tamika she said, "We can talk after we get out of here." She knew that she owed

Tamika an explanation. Besides, Tamika has always been there and it was the least Carla could do.

They walked the aisles a little while longer and Tamika decided to get the pens after all along with paired white doves and phrased decorated photo albums. She decided to get each pen engraved with her and Marcus' name along with their wedding date so that the guests will have them for remembrance.

They finally checked out and Tamika suggested that they go to a nearby deli to grab a bite to eat and catch up. They sat at a vacant table toward the back of the shop and Tamika took a bite out of her sub. Carla kept her eyes glued to the door as she watched for anything suspicious. She wasn't sure if Sergio was still following her, so she tried to play it as safely as possible.

"I love this place," Tamika complimented and swallowed her last bite. "So...what's up?"

Carla shoved a spoonful of her cheddar and broccoli soup down her throat and then let out a sigh. "Where do I start?"

"I guess I better brace myself because this seems heavy." Tamika scooted her chair forward, so that she would be closer to the table.

"I probably won't be able to keep this as a secret much longer, but I took a home pregnancy test yesterday and the least expected resulted."

"So are you telling me what I'm thinking?"

Carla nodded. "Yup...I'm knocked up."

Tamika couldn't believe what she'd just heard. "Wow! Congratulations. I'm finally going to be a godmother. So does Tony know?" she asked with excitement.

Carla fell silent. "No, he doesn't. You are the first person I've told this to since I found out."

Tamika noticed that Carla didn't seem too happy. "What's the matter? You don't seem excited about it."

"It's not that I'm not excited…it's just complicated."

"'Mika, I don't think that now would be a good time to have a baby…with trying to plan for the wedding and my promotion and all. I just think that there's just too much going on for me to deal with pregnancy and its effects. I already have nausea and I can't stand that queasy feeling."

"Don't be foolish. Children are a blessing from God and he will not put more on you than you can bear. Trust me when I say that everything will work itself out. If you think that things are a little stressful, why don't you cut your hours at the firm and plan the wedding after you have the baby? I mean, it's not like you'll be losing pay and I've known people to be engaged for years before they actually make it official."

Once again, Tamika was right and everything she said made perfect sense. *Damn she makes me sick.* Carla hated when Tamika was right because it gave her no room for a debate. Of course she knew that she had those options if she really wanted to go through with the pregnancy, but she was just looking for an excuse so that she wouldn't feel guilty about having a possible abortion.

"Everything you just said makes perfect sense, but…I don't know. I'm scared 'Mika."

Tamika reached across the table and held Carla's hands. "Carla, you know that I am always here for you. I am your number one supporter. You have nothing to be afraid of. I got your back one-hundred percent. I'm sure if you talk to Tony about it he'll understand. I know that he will be excited to know that he will soon be a father. Just promise me that you will not consider abortion as an option."

It was like Tamika read her mind. The guilt trip hit her and without warning, the tears began to flow. Tamika figured that Carla was probably overwhelmed with the new changes in her life and that being pregnant made her emotional so she hugged Carla and consoled her. That was only part of the reason behind Carla's tears. Tamika didn't know the whole story behind it.

"How am I going to explain this to my mother? I can handle Tony, but Ellen will not let me hear the end of it. You already know how she feels about me dating men that are 'below my rank', as she so puts it. This is just too much for me. What have I gotten myself into?"

"Carla, what's done is done and it's too late to play the blame game. This is not the time for shoulda, coulda, woulda's. You have to learn to accept the facts and figure out the best way to deal with them. Besides, you are a grown woman for crying out loud and your mother needs to realize that you have your own life to live."

"Ha...try explaining that to her. Ellen and I have gotten into numerous arguments about me living my life the way I choose to, but she still thinks that I am that thirteen year old Carla that she can control."

"If you explain to her that it's your life and that she needs to allow you room to make your own decisions, I think she will understand."

"I would like to believe that just as much as you, but I know my mother."

"Do you know how many women try to have babies but are unsuccessful? You should consider yourself blessed. This may be your only chance to bear a child. You never know what God has planned for this child and your life. I once did a research on women who have abortions and did you know that it can make some women sterile and cause them to no longer conceive the natural way?"

Carla was surprised at Tamika. She never knew that Tamika took that much interest in pregnancy. Tamika released Carla's hands and leaned back into the chair. There was a moment of silence between them and Carla noticed Tamika staring at nothing in particular, as if she were in deep thought. Without giving eye contact, Tamika spoke.

"Carla, I never told you this before..." Tamika paused. "But Marcus and I have been trying to get pregnant for the past year and I read in an article that partners who try within a twelve month period but are unsuccessful, are probably infertile. Anyway, Marcus and I decided to get checked and the doctor said that I was the problem...something about not being able to ovulate." Tamika went on to explain to Carla that Marcus and she planned to do in vitro fertilization and that they are also considering adoption.

"Oh my god! Tamika, I had no idea. I'm sorry...I know you will make a wonderful mother someday."

Tamika smiled. "It's okay, I never expected for you to know that. It's something that I have been dealing with but I've learned to accept it and moved on with my life."

Learning about Tamika's secret made Carla analyze her situation with a different state of mind. She now realized that she had a lot to be thankful for and was disappointed at herself for thinking selfishly. She was only thinking about herself and not about those who would've been hurt by her actions.

"Listen, Marcus is going out of town next weekend and I was thinking about inviting some friends over and just have a girls get together."

"That sounds like fun. I'm game." They spent the next hour discussing ideas for the event and they both cheered up and temporarily forgot about their complicated issues. Tamika suggested that Carla go home and get some rest. She thanked Carla for joining her and told her that she promised to give her a call. They said their good-byes and went their separate ways.

Carla relaxed in her bed and she never felt better. The only thing missing was Tony by her side. There was a special event at the restaurant where he worked. He'd told her earlier that day about some celebrities renting out the place and that he had to stay over until the event was over…whatever time that was. Carla wanted to wait up for him, but her body wouldn't let her. She closed her eyes and reminisced about what Tamika told her back at the deli and it saddened her to know that her best friend had to go through such an unfortunate circumstance. Carla gently placed her hand on her stomach and said a quick prayer to thank God for the blessing that was growing inside of her and she then asked God to work a miracle for Tamika to be blessed with a child and then she apologized for her earlier egotism. Before she could complete the word, amen, Carla was out like a light bulb.

It was going on two-thirty a.m. and Tony was just walking through the door. He managed to take a quick shower and pull on his cotton pajamas without waking Carla. He eased himself under the sheets next to her and kissed her on the cheek. He hoped not to wake her because he had a long day at the restaurant and he was extremely tired. His eyes struggled to stay opened but he couldn't resist staring at her. He loved how peaceful she looked in her sleep and each time he would watch her sleep, he would often say a silent prayer to thank God for bringing her into his life. *Man I love this woman.* He kissed her cheek once more and attempted to roll over and drift off into la la land, but Carla felt his breath on her cheek and opened her eyes.

"Hi babe. When did you get in?"

Damn. Just what I was afraid of. Please let her go back to sleep. Now.

Tony faced Carla. "I just got in babe." He gingerly put his arm around her waist.

"How did it go?" Her eyes were now closed and Tony noticed that she wasn't entirely awake.

"It went well. Go back to sleep and we can discuss it in the morning. Okay?" He kissed her forehead.

"Okay." Carla rolled over. Her back was now facing Tony. He pulled her into him so that her ass rested against his groin. Carla placed her hands over his and as much as he was getting turned on from the warmth of her ass against his now growing package, Tony was too tired to even think about sex.

"I love you Mrs. Simmons," he mumbled. Carla heard him mumbling to her as she was trying to go back into a deep sleep and she mulled over whether or not she should tell Tony about Sergio.

Love Finally

Chapter 22

Since her run in with Sergio at the coffee shop, Carla has not heard from or saw him. He was nowhere to be found but she made sure that the Atlanta police department stayed on their hunt for him. She would not be entirely comfortable until she knew that he was found and locked away. With Tony back, she felt more secure in her home. The thought weighed heavy on her and she decided not to tell Tony. This was something she needed to handle on her own.

The sunrays beamed through the window and forced Carla to roll over. The warmth felt good against her skin but her eyes were sensitive to the light. Carla turned her back to the window and sat up in the bed. Tony was no longer lying beside her. The digital clock on her night stand read 9:00 a.m. She remembered Tony coming home late so she knew that he did indeed sleep in her bed. Not only that, but his clothes were thrown over the chaise beside her bed. There was no delightful aroma in the air so she knew he wasn't in the kitchen. Carla got up from the bed and went to search for Tony. She figured that he was probably watching sports center in the living room, like he usually did when he didn't want to disturb her from her sleep, so she walked into the living to see if he was there. She was surprised when she stumbled upon an empty couch and a blank TV screen. She walked out onto the back terrace, and again, no luck. *Hmmm. Where could he be?* Carla walked back into the living room and spotted his keys on the center table. *He can't be far because his keys are still here. Maybe he went for an early walk or something.*

She gave up on her search and hurried to the bathroom as her bladder felt like it was about to explode. Carla rushed through the door and let out a startled scream. "Ahhh." She didn't expect to see Tony in the bathroom. He sat on top of the closed toilet lid with his head held down, his eyes probing the floor tiles and held the used pregnancy test in his hand. The lines were faded, but visible enough to read the results. *Shit.* Her urgency suddenly disappeared as she stood perpendicular to him with a puzzled look on her face. She couldn't believe that she'd forget to get rid of the evidence. She didn't know what to say. She twiddled her thumbs and thought about how she would explain everything.

After two minutes of silence, Tony looked up at her. "What's this?" he asked and held out the plastic stick towards her.

"It's a pregnancy test." She held her head down.

"Dammit, Carla, now is not the time to be a smart ass. You think that this is funny? I know exactly what it is but can you explain to me whose positive results it is?" He threw the stick in the wastebasket beside the toilet.

Carla paused. She contemplated telling him a lie: that the test belonged to Tamika and she didn't want Marcus to find out so she asked to come over and take the test there, but Carla knew that lying would only make matters worse. She said a silent prayer hoping that Tony wouldn't go about things the wrong way. She held up her head and matched his stare.

"Those are my results," she said solemnly. She didn't know how he would react.

Tony ran his hands back and forth on his close cut head. "So when were you planning to tell me?" He didn't sound angry and that made Carla feel good about answering his question.

"Tony please don't be upset. I just found out the day before yesterday and I was going to tell you this morning."

There was silence. She waited for him to speak, but he gave no immediate response. *This is not looking good.* Carla grew nervous.

Within minutes, Tony managed to say, "I'm stunned. I can't believe that I am going to be a father." He reached out to grab her arm and sat her on his lap. He rubbed her stomach and planted kisses on it and held her close as he allowed his thoughts to marinate.

Carla kissed the back of his neck and her urgency returned. "Tony, I gotta go," she said and bounced up and down on his thigh.

Tony knew what that little dance meant so he jumped up off the toilet and excused himself to allow her some privacy.

Carla washed her hands and walked into the bedroom. Tony was lying on his back across the bed with his hands folded behind his head. She climbed on top of him and he threw his arms around her, bringing her into a tight embrace. Carla rested her head on his chest and listened to his heart beat. The prolonged silence was awkward.

"So when are you going to the doctor to get checked?" he asked.

"I'll call tomorrow for an appointment. You wanna come with me?"

"I wouldn't miss that opportunity for the world. This is my seed we're talking about and I plan on being at every visit."

Carla's face lit up and she leaned in and kissed him with her morning breath. She had yet to brush her teeth, but her breath smelled like cherries. She was pleased to know that Tony took it better than she thought. Seeing how happy he was made her decide to keep the baby after all. There were adjustments to be made, but she would do what was necessary for both her and the baby's health.

"You just made me the luckiest man," Tony said and stared in her eyes. His stare melted Carla's heart.

"I can't wait to start our family together. I think we should get married sooner. What you think about going to the city hall and after the baby is born, we can plan that big wedding you want."

"Are you serious?" She was not expecting that. "Tony, you are the man I want to be with forever and I think that's a great idea."

"Okay. After your first doctor visit, we will go and sign the papers." Carla beamed from ear to ear.

Tony rolled her on her back and made sweet passionate love to her. Carla oooh'd and ahhh'd as he brought her to one orgasmic pleasure after another.

A week passed and Carla was now legally Mrs. Simmons. She didn't have the traditional church ceremony and glamorous reception that she envisioned, but none of that mattered anymore. She was married to the man she loved and that meant the world to her. There was no word from Sergio and she wondered if the police ever caught up to him. Tony spent most of his time at her place as usual. Instead of staying some nights, like he normally did when they were courting, he even moved in most of his clothes. This marriage thing was new to her and she was still trying to cope with the whole idea. She hasn't yet told Tamika or Ellen about the great news, but she planned to update Tamika once she attended the girls retreat that they had planned for the upcoming weekend. Ellen on the other hand, would have to wait until Carla could come up with the perfect way to explain everything without her mother going over the edge.

Tony accompanied her to the doctor the previous Wednesday and Carla found out that she was six weeks pregnant. They viewed the ultrasound and all they could see was a hollow space in her stomach, which was described as a yolk sac. The doctor informed them that it was too soon to see any prominent features, but assured them that on her three month visit, they would be able to hear the baby's heart beat as well see some of its developing organs. They were so excited about the new bundle of joy and after they'd left the doctor's office, Tony expressed to Carla that he would be counting down the months. Since finding out about the pregnancy, Tony spoiled Carla more so than before. He catered to her every need and made sure she ate healthy and avoided stress. Each day that she spent with him made her fall in love with him more and more.

Carla stood in her closet and browsed the racks as she contemplated on what outfits to pack. She was getting ready to visit Tamika and planned on having a good time at the event. She was spending the night and Tony told her before he left for work that he was going to miss her but he wanted her to enjoy her stay with the girls. Tony would be at work as he always was ninety-three percent of the time and Carla figured that he spent so much time at the joint.

She settled for a loose fitting cotton dress that was green in color and fell right above her knees. The dress graced her curves but didn't reveal too much. Now that she's pregnant, Carla tried not to wear clothing that fit too tightly. She gathered a sleeping shirt, her toiletries and an outfit to wear home the next day and placed them in her overnight bag. She made sure that she didn't forget anything and anxiously walked out the door.

She didn't want to show up empty handed, so Carla stopped at Publix to pick up drinks, and finger foods that she knew everyone would enjoy. She even purchased a bottle of wine. She was excluded from drinking it, but that shouldn't be a reason why her friends couldn't drink and be merry. She made her purchase and loaded the items in the back seat of her SUV. She climbed into her truck and spotted a white sedan that slowly drove past her. Carla's heart skipped a beat. She knew that it was Sergio because that was the same car that was following her a month ago. She locked her doors, started the engine and peeled out of the parking lot, careful not to hit passing pedestrians.

She managed to get on the highway and while she constantly checked her rearview mirror, there was no white sedan behind her. Carla couldn't be too sure, but she still played it safe. Oh she wanted to tell Tony about this because she knew that Sergio was capable of doing some serious harm, but how could she explain it? Would they understand? Would they be angry at her for deceiving them? How did Sergio know where to find her? Why must he continue to stalk her? Carla called the police and reported it. Why aren't the damn police trying harder to find him? She was starting to think that they weren't doing their job. Carla wanted it all to end so that she can live a peaceful life.

She checked her mirror one last time and the course appeared to be clear. The silence was killing her. She needed something to take her mind off of her problem so she powered up the CD player and enjoyed the sounds of India Arie that sang out at her. Tamika lived an hour away from Carla's house and with thirty minutes left before she arrived, Carla had some time to think.

Carla wondered how Tamika would react when she discloses that she and Tony were officially husband and wife. The mere thought of her being his wife sent tingles down her spine. *"Brown skin, you know I love your brown skin, I can't tell where yours begin..."* Carla sang in tune with the lyrics. The music was definitely setting her mind at ease and she reflected on her first doctor's visit: *Six weeks! I'm further along than I thought. I was expecting them to say three weeks.*

"OH SHIT!" Carla nearly swerved her truck into the lane on her left and nearly side railed the car next to her. She had to regain her composure before she caused a terrible accident. She instantly felt sick and her stomach was in a knot. She wanted to pull over on the side of the highway, but decided against it. Her chest heaved heavily and she felt like she was about to have a sudden anxiety attack. She decelerated her speed and took deep breaths. She remembered the doctor explained to her that stress can affect the baby and could possibly result in a miscarriage. Tears formed at the corners of her eye and Carla fought to keep them from ruining her makeup. She was ten minutes away from her destination and spilling tears at this point was not an option. Her friends would definitely know that something was wrong and she was not in the mood to explain herself. Her life as she knew it was now over. How would she tell Tony that the baby she was carrying inside did not belong to him, but resulted from her one night stand affair? She suddenly lost her vibe and thought about turning around to go back home. But if she did that, she would have to face Tony and explain to him why she changed her mind from attending the party, but worst of all, she would have to lay with her husband knowing that her child was not his. Facing him right now was not in her best interest. Carla continued her drive and figured that she would have time to think things through by spending the night at Tamika's.

The door swung open the minute Carla pressed the buzzer. Renee, a friend of Tamika's and also one of the bridesmaids, answered the door.

"Oh, hey Carla!"

"Hey Renee. It's been a while girl where you hiding?" she asked in the most friendliest voice she could muster up. She didn't want the way she was truly feeling to be noticeable.

"Girl I'm always working. We were all waiting for you. Everyone is already here so now that you finally showed, the party can begin." Carla's hands were full with grocery bags so she was unable to give Renee a hug. She stepped over the threshold as Renee went to retrieve the rest of the bags from the back seat of the truck.

Tamika ran up to Carla and noticed that she needed help so she gladly took some of the bags off of Carla's hands. She thanked her for the food and Renee joined them shortly. Carla gave Tamika a longer hug than usual and Renee ran off to join the other girls in the living room. Tamika was curious about the long hug, but she decided to question it later because now was the time to unwind and have a ball.

"Hey Carla! Glad you can make it," Sherise, another bridesmaid hollered.

Carla flashed her a gingerly smile and said, "I'm glad to be here." Carla wasn't too fond of Sherise because she was known to be whorish and slept around with married men. Carla met Sherise in college and introduced her to Tamika. The three became cool with each other until Sherise tried to hit on Carla's ex-boyfriend behind Carla's back. Carla was livid when she found out through a third party and nearly caught a charge for whooping Sherise's ass in front of the entire student body that was present on campus that day, but Tamika managed to talk her out of it and this was their first encounter since then.

Tamika turned up the volume to "Brick House" and they all started doing the bump. Carla's mood was definitely better but she knew that once this was all over, she would have to stare her problems in the face once again.

They danced until they were all exhausted and after the last song on the old school album, they gathered on Tamika's sectional. "That was fun," Renee said and poured herself a glass of wine from the bottle that stood on the coffee table.

"This reminds me of our old college parties," shouted Sherise.

"Yeah I bet it does with yo' hot ass," Tamika said and then they all burst out with laughter.

"So how has it been going, Carla?" Sherise asked.

"I can't complain. Things are really picking up at the firm. God has truly been blessing me."

"Amen to that," the other three said in unison and clinked their wine glasses together.

"Why aren't you sharing a glass of wine with us, Carla?" Renee asked curiously.

"Oh no I'm fine. I had an upset stomach earlier so I'm just gonna cool out until I feel better."

"Okay well I guess that means more wine for me," Sherise blurted.

Tamika shook her head. "You haven't changed one bit with yo' alcoholic ass, 'Resee." Everyone laughed and after they were rested, they continued to dance, crack jokes and have a good time.

Hours later, they were getting tired. It was late. Sherise stated that she was sorry she couldn't stay overnight to finish the party, but she had an urgent meeting to attend. Tamkia, Carla, and Renee knew that Sherise kept multiple partners and that she came up with an excuse so that she could end up in bed with one of her many lovers. She forgot that tomorrow was Sunday and they all knew that Sherise does not work on the weekends. They pretended as if they didn't know the deal, but thanked her for coming anyway. Renee was married with two kids and she had to get home because

Love Finally

her husband had to get up early for work and she needed to be there to watch the kids.

When both girls left, Tamika and Carla were left to enjoy each other's company. Tamika was one who didn't forget things easily so she decided to ask Carla about the hug she received earlier.

"Are you okay?" she asked Carla, who was laid out across the couch.

"Yeah. Girl I had so much fun tonight. Marcus needs to go out of town more often so we can do this more often."

Tamika cracked a smile at Carla's comment, but she really wanted to have a serious talk. "Carla, I noticed that you gave me a long hug earlier when you got here. I know that we always greet with a hug, but this hug was different. I felt your vibe. It felt like you are asking for help without words."

Damn. I hate coming around her. She always figures me out. Carla sighed. She sat up in the couch and the smile she once wore disappeared. "You got me. I hate the fact that you know me so well. I hope you're not too tired. After you hear what I have to say, you're going to be glad that you're sitting down."

Carla began to explain to Tamika about Sergio's attempt to rape her and him stalking her.

"Oh no, Carla, I can't believe you kept that from me. Did you notify the police?" She stood up and walked over to Carla and gave her a hug. "Does Tony know about this?"

Carla shook her head. "No, Tony doesn't know. I'm afraid of what could result if he finds out. Besides, this is something that I need to handle."

"You know I know some people who can make that nigga disappear right?"

Carla managed a chuckle. "That will not be necessary. The police are already on him. It disturbs me how he always knows how to find me when he wants, put the police can't find him. If they don't get him soon, my hands may be forced to do something."

"Hell, if they don't get him, you should have all their damn badges revoked. That is just ridiculous. These police spend so much time worrying about the wrong things at times. If something happens to you, that will be their asses."

Carla explained to Tamika about how things got started between her and Sergio. She explained how Sergio showed up at her office, requesting her to be his lawyer, and that a former client referred him. Tamika expressed that she understood. Carla dropped the bomb when she revealed that Sergio was the guy whom she had an affair with and Tamika was in shock.

"No Carla. Why did you do it? How could you have allowed that to happen?" Tamika told Carla that she was disappointed in her actions and that she should've used better judgment but then told her that she understands that people make mistakes.

She went on to reveal that she and Tony got married last week at the courthouse and Tamika nearly flipped out of the couch. "Carla Milford! I thought we were best friends. You have done a great job holding out on me. Wow. I am so happy for both of you. So I guess you told him about the baby?"

Carla nodded and then she quickly looked away. There was something else she needed to get off her conscience but she didn't know how to get it out. "Is there more? You have a weird look on your face. What is it?"

"I don't know how to say this and you're probably going to flip when I tell you, but the baby belongs to Sergio and not Tony."

"WHAT!" Tamika buried her face in her hands. "How can you be so sure?"

"Tony and I went for my first check up on Wednesday and the doctor calculated that I was almost seven weeks. Tony and I just got back together a little over four weeks ago and before we started to have sex again, Sergio was the last person I slept with."

"Did you use protection?"

Tears poured down Carla's cheeks. "No."

"Oh no. What have you gotten into? Did you ever think that maybe you could have contracted a disease? You don't who or where that man has been laying."

"I know. I don't know what I was thinking...or more like I wasn't thinking. How could I be so foolish to put myself in such a disastrous predicament?"

Tamika embraced Carla and assured her that everything will work out.

"So I am assuming that Tony isn't aware of this?"

"No. I just realized it today. And he is so damn happy about me having what he thinks is his baby."

"Well you need to tell him before it's too late."

"What if he tells me that he wants a divorce?"

It wouldn't be long before her skeletons would have to be revealed. Carla spent the night trying to conjure a way to break the news to Tony. You know what they say, "what happens in the dark, will eventually come to light"

Chapter 23

Saddened that her girls retreat was over, Carla entered her condo to the delightful smell of grits, eggs and sausages. She dropped her bag by the door, kicked of her sandals, and snuck into the kitchen, where she saw Tony slaving over the stove. He looked so sexy in his black sweats and plain white T-shirt. She has never met a man who looked sexier than her husband. When Tony settled the pan on the burner, Carla walked up behind him and wrapped her soft arms around his waist. This startled Tony briefly because he didn't hear her coming in. He swung around to face her.

"Hey baby. You snuck up on me. How did it go? Did you have a good time?" he asked her in between each succulent kiss he planted on her lips and cheeks.

"Yes. It was great but I missed you," she said, still locking him into a tight squeeze.

"I missed you too. You know I'm not going anywhere. You came just in time for breakfast." Tony pulled away from her and removed the pan from the burner and then clicked off the burner.

He fixed Carla's plate and then his. They sat at the table and demolished the food on their plates. Tony noticed that Carla was extremely quiet. Her heart was tearing apart as she thought about the dreadful bomb she was about to drop on her husband. He expected her to tell him all about what took place when she visited Tamika. This was unlike his wife. He's always known her to be upbeat and full of conversation. He pushed his plate to the side, drank the last of his orange juice and leaned into the table.

"So how did it go with the girls last night?"

"It was great," she responded and kept her eyes on her plate.

"That's all? I would imagine that you would tell me about all the wild stories you all shared or something or how Tamika flipped out when you told her about us getting married," he said and sat back in the chair with his arms folded across his chest.

There was a temporary silence between the two. "Carla, baby is everything okay? You look tense," he asked and unfolded his arms to lean into the table once again.

Carla's gaze was fixed on the wall unit. "Yes, Tony, everything is fine....look we need to talk." She could no longer bear the guilt. This was something she needed to do. Tony needed to know the truth and she was ready to deal with the consequences, or at least that's what she told herself. What would he do? Would he leave her? Will this be the end of the road? Her brain was overloaded with questions.

What is it this time? The last time I heard those words, things did not end on a good note. This better be good, but based on her somber attitude, I know it won't be. Tony sighed. *Here we go.* "I'm listening." He rested his chin in both of his palms as he planted his elbows on the dining table.

Carla still avoided eye contact. "Tony, I love you so much and I never want to hurt you our ruin what we have together." She began to sob. Telling him the truth was killing her as much as she expected it would hurt him. Tony walked over and held her in his arms.

He rubbed her back. "Baby, you are my wife and there is nothing that we can't get through together."

Carla looked up and stared into his eyes through her tears. "Are you sure about that?"

"Okay Carla what's up?"

"I think you should sit down."

Tony returned to his chair. "Tony, I hate that this happened and whatever you decide to do after I tell you this...is just something

I will have to learn to deal with." She paused and then said, "No, I can't do this." More tears flowed.

"Stop crying, babe. Remember what the doctor said about getting stressed out? It's not good for the baby. Now whatever you have to tell me, just go on and say it. There is noting that can't be fixed." Tony reached across the table and motioned for her to place her hands in his, but Carla refused.

"Tony..." she lowered her eyes to the floor. Her voice was now a little above that of a whisper. "This baby is not yours."

Tony's eyes widened and he looked like he wanted to jump across the table. "WHAT? Wait. What do you mean? Carla please tell me that you are fucking with me right now."

She shook her head.

Tony held his head in his hands. "I can't believe you Carla. So if it's not mine, whose is it?" he asked in an angry tone. "No...don't even answer that." Tony stood up from his chair and pushed the table forward, almost knocking Carla out of her chair.

This made Carla cry harder. She wanted to explain everything to Tony. She wanted to tell him that Sergio stalking her and how he tried rape to her. She wanted to tell him how sorry she was for sleeping with Sergio and how she wished she could take it all back, but she cried so hard that she was unable to speak. Tony was now furious and Carla sat there looking helpless. He picked up his empty plate and threw it against the wall. Carla flinched with fear and covered her head with her hands as the ceramic shattered. She could hear Tony swearing as he lividly stormed off towards the bedroom. Seconds later, he returned without saying a word and walked out the front door, slamming it behind him. Carla slid out of her chair and unto the carpet with her knees bent upward and buried her face in between her thighs. She was clueless as to whether or not her marriage was over. She believed with all her heart that on that day she has officially lost the love of her life.

Love Finally

Chapter 24

Two weeks passed and Carla has yet to see or hear from Tony. She has been slacking at work and lost a few clients behind it. She was a complete wreck. She withdrew herself from Ellen and Tamika and made it a habit to go home and drown in her tears. She'd lost weight and on her last visit, the doctor told her that she was putting herself at risk for a miscarriage.

Today when she showed up for work, her receptionist, Michelle, tried to stop her from entering the office.

"No Mrs. Simmons," she'd pleaded, pulling on Carla's arm trying to stop her. "Please don't go in there. There's…"

Carla told Michelle to save it. She was not in the mood to hear Michelle's whining. Michelle was really trying to warn her. Carla was in a daze and she always thought that Michelle was sort of wacky anyways so she disregard Michelle's plea and walked past her. Carla turned the corner to enter her office. When she laid eyes on him sitting with his legs crossed in her chair behind her desk, she wanted to turn around and run for dear life…but her legs fell numb and she found it hard to move.

"Come in. You look scared…don't be. I won't hurt you unless you force me to. You have been avoiding me on all counts and we need to talk. So what better time than now?" Sergio walked over to her, took her by the hands, leading her into the office, and then shut the door behind them. Carla was trembling. *Oh God.* Sergio sat her down across from him, in front of her desk. *Was this what Michelle was trying to tell me?*

"What happened to lunch? I told you not to try anything stupid now didn't I?" Carla nodded. She was filled with fear and was unable to speak. Sergio walked over beside her and stood over her. He ran his hand down her cheek. Carla wanted to bite his arm and make a run for it, but he had her cornered and she was too afraid. All the male executives were out of town for a conference, where she was supposed to be if it weren't for her personal problems, so there was no one to call out to. Michelle and Carla were the only two workers in the building. Michelle would be of no help. Carla sat quietly and played his little game. Her mind couldn't think fast enough. She couldn't plan her next move. Sergio continued about how much he loved her and that if he can't have her he would kill himself.

"I'm not trying to scare you, Carla. I just want you to see how much I need you or else I wouldn't be doing this," he'd told her.

"But what about your wife and kids?"

"They are gone...can't you understand that? The crazy bitch picked up and moved away," he yelled. "By the way, if you were wondering, I've been indicted and my sentencing is within a week. So you see, that's why I need you. I know for sure that they are going to lock my black ass away for good. And with you in my life, I know that I will always have someone in my corner."

This son-of-a-bitch is crazy. Had she brought him stalking her before the court, they would've snagged him when he was arraigned. She was so disappointed that the police didn't work harder in pursuing his arrest sooner. Based on the report he'd just given, Sergio would be behind bars eventually.

Minutes later, Michelle burst into the office with the police. Carla was relieved. She didn't think Michelle had it in her and she felt stupid for not listening to Michelle in the first place. "Are you okay Mrs. Simmons?" Michelle asked. "I knew he was up to something so I informed the police right before you showed up."

Carla nodded and watched as the police handcuffed Sergio and read him his rights. He was gone and she hoped for good. She wanted to scream at the officers for their lack of hard work, but she was exhausted by the time they were hauling Sergio out. This was too much to swallow in one day. Sergio turned to look back at Carla and the truth to what she knew no longer mattered. There was no sense in telling Sergio about the baby. What he didn't know won't

Love Finally

hurt him and besides, things were already turned upside down enough.

Later that evening, Carla reclined on her chaise. Knowing that Sergio was finally behind bars led her to believe that a chapter of her life was now closed. But not completely. She was still carrying his child. This gave her probable cause to seek an abortion, but she wasn't sure if it was the right thing to do. She considered giving the baby up for adoption, but she was already bonding with the fetus and it would break her heart.

A warm shower would always relax her so Carla briefly put her thoughts on pause and headed to the bathroom. She never expected her life to turn out this way: Her husband ran out on her and the father of her child tried to rape her and was now behind bars for his irresponsible ways.

Carla toweled off and stared at herself in the mirror. She noticed that her pregnancy has changed some of her features. Her washboard belly no longer existed; her breast grew a cup size and she gained a few pounds. She was now ten weeks pregnant and she had to cope with it alone. Carla shook her head and walked into her bedroom. She no longer felt sexy so she found herself sleeping in extra large T-shirts. She sat at the edge of her bed and her house phone rang. Without looking at the caller ID, she answered. "Hello."

"Carla? Oh my god where have you been? I have called your office, cell and house for the past two weeks. What's going on?"

Carl broke down in tears. "Tamika, I don't know what to do."

"What happened?"

Carla sighed. "He's gone and I don't know if he's coming back."

"Who?"

"Tony. I told him about the baby after I left your house and he got real angry and walked out."

"Oh, Carla, why didn't you call me? I'm sorry I haven't been checking in on you like I should have."

"It's not your fault. You have your own life to live."

"Did he put his hands on you?"

"No. But the look he had in his eyes told me it took everything in him not to. He just smashed a plate against the wall, said a few cuss words and left."

"Oh, Carla, I'm sorry. Do you need me to come over?"

"No. I'm getting ready for bed anyway."

"Well have you at least talked to him since then?"

"No. He changed his number. I tried calling him."

"Why don't you go down to the restaurant?"

"Why? So he can embarrass my ass? No way."

"I mean he's still your husband and you guys need to work it out and do what's best for the baby."

Carla sighed. "We'll see what happens."

Chapter 25

Two months later. Tamika's wedding was less than a week away and Carla along with some of the bridesmaids planned to throw her a bridal shower. They rented out a ballroom at the Intercontinental hotel in Buckhead. They invited a few of Tamika's closest family and friends to attend and they were expecting fifty people. They came up with a plan to lure Tamika out of the house without her becoming suspicious. Of course, Carla was the mastermind behind the plan.

Now at four months pregnant, her life was still missing a piece to the puzzle. However, Carla stopped crying over spilled milk and learned to move on with her life and was slowly getting back to her old self again. She was beginning to learn how to love herself and depend on the love of others. She hasn't been served with any divorce papers, so legally she was still Mrs. Simmons, without her husband by her side. She loved her husband and she wished things between them could be different. She was not willing to give him up, so if anything called divorce were to take place; it would be all on him. She hoped that wasn't the case. Carla looked at herself in her visor mirror as she waited for the red light to change to green. The shower was scheduled to start at 3:30 p.m. and she was right on schedule. It was 1:15 p.m. and she needed to swing by the hotel to drop off the cake she'd just picked up from the bakery. She called up Tamika and told her that she made an appointment for them to enjoy a day at the spa, so she needed to be dressed and ready upon her arrival. Tamika expressed her excitement with the endless screams that sang out in Carla's ear and stated that she was super anxious about getting a relaxing massage. However, Carla knew that Tamika was in for a big surprise and would probably be disappointed that the whole spa thing was a mere ploy. But nevertheless, Tamika would be more appreciative about the shower once she found out about her awaiting surprise.

She pulled up in the driveway, turned off the ignition and stepped out of the truck. She shut the door and straightened her cotton sundress. She walked up the walkway and before she could ring the bell, Tamika swung the door open. "How did you know I was here?"

"Don't be silly. I am so excited, I couldn't wait. I have been looking out the window for the past thirty minutes waiting for you to show up."

"Girl, you act like we're about to go and pick up a million dollar win from the lottery."

Tamika fanned her off. "Come in. I have to go and grab my purse from up stairs and put on my shoes." Tamika dashed towards the stairway, leaving Carla by the door. Carla smiled and shook her head. *She is going to be in for a rude awakening.*

Tamika gracefully walked down the semi-circle stairway sporting a black top and a blue denim jean skirt. Carla wondered why she suddenly went from being speedy Gonzales to being as slow as the hare and realized that Tamika's heels were too high for her to walk in. Carla chuckled as Tamika struggled to climb down the stairs. "That's what you get for trying to be cute. Hurry up because we don't have all day."

"Oh sush!" Tamika said as she held on to the rail and walked down each step one by one, careful not to fall. The sight had Carla tickled.

"'Mika? Why the hell are you wearing those heels anyway? Girl you already have a man...who you trying to look cute for?"

"Shut up Carla. I wanna look cute for me...okay?"

"You look like you need help. Do I need to hold your hand?" Carla laughed.

Tamika finally made it to the bottom of the stairway and stood still for a second, trying to maintain her balance. "So, how do I look? You like?" she asked with a huge grin.

Carla nodded expressing her approval. "Not bad. Not bad. You look great! Too bad I won't be able to dress like that for another five months."

"Don't worry fashionista. You will get your killer bod back in no time. I am sure of that."

Carla looked down at her cantaloupe sized belly and ran her hands over it. "I guess so. Anyways, we need to get going."

"Okay baby momma...let me grab a pair of flats because I doubt I'll be able to survive in these heels all day," Tamika giggled and slowly walked to the utility room to retrieve her shoes.

On the drive to the hotel, Tamika bobbed her head to the beat of 50cent's new album, looking like a teenager who was getting ready to purchase their first car. Carla often peeped in her direction and smiled at how excited her friend was. Carla turned her Range into the entryway of the hotel and Tamika immediately turned down the volume. "Oh my gosh. This is going to be great! The Intercontinental? I heard that they have some of the best masseuses," Tamika screamed and clapped her hands as she bounced up and down in her seat.

"Calm down, girl."

"You just don't understand. I am in dire need of relaxation. This is a getaway that is well overdue and *I* don't have to pay for it," Tamika laughed.

Carla sneered at her and pulled up to the valet. The man handed her a ticket and they hopped out of the truck and proceeded towards the entrance. "C'mon 'Mika! You're walking too slow...hurry up. Oh my bad, your heels are too high," Carla said teasingly.

"That is not funny," Tamika tried to whisper through clenched teeth, not wanting her voice to echo throughout the hallway. Carla laughed as she watched her friend struggle to walk in her shoes.

Carla stopped and waited for Tamika to catch up to her. "Why don't you change into your flats?"

"Um Um I might see a celebrity walking through here, girl. You know how the Atlanta Housewives love to frequent this place," she chuckled.

Fifteen minutes later, they managed to reach the ballroom. Carla opened the door slowly and allowed Tamika to enter first. When the crowd yelled: "SURPRISE!" Tamika gasped with astonishment and covered her mouth with her hand. She couldn't believe that Carla had her fooled. She turned to look at Carla as if to say, "I'm gonna get you for this." And with a big smile, she walked over to her friend and gave her a big bear hug. The room was filled with at least fifty people. Tamika mingled with her friends and family and thanked them for coming. She was still shocked at how tight lipped everyone was about the surprise.

Carla stood by the buffet and fixed her third plate as her cravings got the best of her. Sherise spotted Carla and walked over to where she stood. "Aren't we looking pregnant?" she asked and eyed Carla up and down. "That explains why you were acting all funny that night we were all at Tamika's house…how do you plan on fitting into your gown for the wedding?"

"Sherise, please don't start with me. You know I only respect you because you're going to be in the wedding. This is for Tamika's sake, but don't push it. I am here to have a good time and I suggest you get out of my face before I embarrass your ass and tell everyone how you fucked your boss to get to your new position. Don't test me." Sherise held up her arms as if she were under arrest and without a comeback, she eased away from Carla and joined the crowd.

Carla chomped down the last of her buffalo wing as she at the table by her lonesome and looked on at the crowd. She was pleased to see that her plan was successful and everyone was having a good time. The DJ was doing his thing and when he played the "Electric Slide", Carla jumped up out of her seat and joined everyone on the dance floor. She danced next to Tamika, who had taken off her heels and slipped on her flats, until the music ended. The party was winding down and it was almost time to vacate the ballroom. Carla only rented it for five hours. The DJ made an announcement that the guest of honor would like to make a toast. Everyone took their respectable assigned seats and Tamika held up her wine glass. She commanded their undivided attention through the microphone that she held in her hand and then cleared her throat to begin her speech.

"I would first like to thank everyone who came out. You guys really did a good job with surprising me. My best friend over there in the corner," Tamika pointed, "Tricked me into thinking we were going to have a relaxing day at the spa. But honestly, this was better than any massage." Tears filled her eyes. "You guys are gonna make me cry damn it! But these are tears of joy. I'm so excited that I will be married in less than a week and all of you will be there to share with me. I wanna make a toast to love, friendship, and a longevity marriage." Tamika raised her wine glass and her guests, minus Carla, did the same and in unison, they lowered their glasses and drank their wine.

Tamika and Carla stood by the door to thank the guests for coming as they made their exit. When the DJ packed up his equipment and left, they exited right behind him with the bundle of gifts that Tamika received. They waited for the valet persona to pull up and when he did, he assisted both girls as they loaded the gifts in the trunk. Carla then handed him the ticket along with a tip before climbing into the driver's side and then they drove off into the night.

Chapter 26

Carla stared at the phone as she contemplated on giving Ellen a call to give her the news. She knew that Ellen would be more than upset when she found out that Carla kept her marriage and pregnancy a secret. The guilt burned Carla up inside, but she knew that her mother deserved the right to know. She finally built up the courage and dialed Ellen's number. "Hi mom."

"Well, it is about time. What have I done to make you treat me like a stepchild? I tell you what, I got so tired of calling you and when you never returned my calls, I promised myself that I would just give you your space. I knew you would eventually call when you were ready to talk."

"I'm sorry momma. I just had so much going on and…I want to know if we can go someplace and talk about some things?"

"Of course we can baby. Where do you want to go?"

"Can you meet me at Twist in like an hour and a half?"

"Sure. Let me get ready. I'm glad to have my baby back. See you soon." *Click.*

Carla nervously walked towards the umbrella shaded table where Ellen sat. Ellen had on a straw hat with shades and sipped her lemonade from the straw. She looked like she should be sitting on some tropical island somewhere. The day was sunny and beautiful, so Carla didn't mind the outdoor seating. She walked up to Ellen, who almost didn't recognize her, and waved. "Hi momma."

Ellen peeled off her shades and did a double take as she looked Carla over. "What in the world? Did you gain weight? Why is

Love Finally

your darn stomach so big? Sit down and tell me what's going on because you are not the Carla I know."

Carla pulled out the chair and took her seat. She leaned into the table and directed her gazed off into the busy street. Ellen leaned to the side and intercepted Carla's gaze. "What's going on Carla? Are you pregnant?"

Carla let off a sigh and looked at her mother. "Yes," she answered and sat up in the chair with her hands in her lap and held her head down, looking down at the ground.

"Well, why didn't you tell me this before? How far along are you?"

"Four months," she answered somberly with her head still lowered, afraid to face her mother's eyes.

"Carla Milford, I can't believe you! Why are you doing this to me? So who is this young man that I have yet to meet? Does he work at the firm?"

"No... he doesn't." Carla finally looked up and barely matched her mother's stare. "His name is Tony and he's a waiter at a restaurant...and we...we...we're married." Carla held up her hand to display her ring.

Ellen threw her hand on top of her straw hat that covered her head. "WHAT? YOU ARE WHAT TO WHO?" her voice escalated and Carla immediately looked around to see if anyone was watching.

"Could you quiet down your voice? You're going to draw attention."

"Don't you dare tell me about what I need to do."

Carla grew bold and took control of the situation. "Look momma. Before you have a cow, just please hear me out." Ellen calmed down and nodded. "I have been seeing this guy for quite some time and yes he is a waiter, but he really makes me happy. I never brought him around because I know how judgmental you are." Ellen gasped. She was shocked at the way Carla spoke to her.

"How on earth can he afford to support you and a baby on a waiter's salary? Huh? You want to explain that part to me? For Christ's sake, Carla, you are now a partner with the firm. Don't you see that this man is after you for what you have? Of course he's gonna jump and marry you because he plans to take half of everything you earn if you ever decide to leave him and having this baby is only going to make things worse. How could you be so blind not to see that?"

She never stops. "Momma, you are going about this all wrong...."

"Carla Milford, I believe that I lived enough years and have enough experience to know what I'm talking about. This Tony person is looking for a woman like yourself to leach off of."

"If you should know, Tony has never asked me for a dime. He does very well for himself and I wish that you will stop being so one track mind and listen to what I have to say."

"I'm going to be honest, Carla. I am not comfortable with the idea. Why couldn't you have a normal wedding instead of running off to the courthouse? Because it's obvious that's what you two did. I never received an invitation in the mail," Ellen said sarcastically.

"Now I think you are overreacting. This is the same reason why I am reluctant to share anything personal with you. When things don't go the way you think that they should go, you are so quick to go off the deep end." Carla was becoming frustrated. "As my mother, I would expect you to be more supportive and have more faith to believe that you raised me well enough to make intelligent decisions."

"Yeah you proved that when you got mixed up with that fool who had a baby with another woman behind your back, right?" Carla couldn't believe that Ellen just threw that up in her face.

"I don't even know why I tried talking to you, this was pointless. It is my life and I am going to do what I want to do whether you like it or not. I am not a little girl anymore."

"Carla, I'm sorry, I shouldn't have said that. But you have to understand how I feel to know that you hid something so important from me."

"Yes, I admit that I was wrong, but I also thought you were better than this, momma." Carla did not expect to engage in such a heated discussion with Ellen. It was a good thing that they were the only ones dining outside. The cars driving by couldn't hear them and there weren't any current passersby.

"This is all too much right now. Maybe I should go." Carla stood up and walked off. Ellen didn't even bother calling after her because she knew she'd said some hurtful things and she only wished that Carla would soon find it in her heart to forgive her.

It was going on nine-thirty p.m. and Carla felt lethargic. She curled up on the sofa and watched BET's *comic view* to get her mind off of the day's earlier episode. She missed Tony's voice and now would've been the perfect time to talk to him. He always understood her and always listened to whatever she had to say, no matter how dumb she probably sounded. Carla closed her eyes and reminisced on the days when she and Tony would lay on that same couch and how she enjoyed his touch when he would hold her in his arms. Damn, she missed her husband and she wanted him back. She messed up big time and had to find a way to fix it.

Chapter 27

"You look so beautiful," Carla told Tamika, who was beaming with joy. It was finally her wedding day and her sequined Mia Solano wedding dress made her glow like a queen. The makeup artist touched up Tamika's makeup as she batted her eyes, forcing the mascara to dry. The bridesmaids were all busy trying to get things in order and Carla helped to straighten out Tamika's cathedral style train, which extended about nine feet from her waistline. Tamika look absolutely stunning and Carla wished she would've waited to have a grand wedding.

"I hope I don't cry and ruin my makeup," Tamika said as she felt tears stinging the corner of her eyes.

"You better wait until you say 'I do'," Carla told her as she clipped the laced veil through Tamika's curls. Tamika looked like a bride that you would see doing a photo shoot for a bridal magazine.

"Marcus is waiting at the altar you guys," Renee squealed. She'd peep out the door to see all of what was going on inside the church. She was always the nosy one. "The church is packed from wall to wall. I hope no one else shows up or else they have no choice but to stand. How many people did you invite? The entire state of Georgia?"

"You are so funny Renee," Tamika retorted. "You know that I have a big family and I can't help it if I know a lot of people." Tamika teasingly stuck out her tongue at Renee and they all bust out in laughter.

"You all look so wonderful," Tamika complimented her bridal party once she stood up from the vanity chair. The bridesmaids were coordinated in a Tiffany blue satin tube dress with silver shoes to accessorize. Because she was the maid-of-honor, Carla wore a silver dress with lace front and she almost gave Tamika a run for her money at her own wedding, even in her pregnant state. They did their final look in the mirror and the wedding planner came in to alert them.

"Take your places everyone. The wedding is about to start." Everyone took their places and Tamika took a deep breath. Today would be the start of a new beginning and she couldn't wait. She held Carla's hand and without words, they both new that nothing would surpass their friendship.

"I'm so happy for you," Carla said and walked off to go to the altar to wait on her best friend to walk down the aisle.

The ceremony was the most beautiful thing that Carla has ever seen. She shed a few tears when the bride and groom read their written vows to each other. She wished her husband was there to share the moment. They pulled up to the country club town hall and the reception hall was beautifully decorated. Carla made sure that she would get the wedding planner's number from Tamika because she absolutely loved his work. It always seemed like the not so straight guys always had a keen eye for elegance. Everyone was seated at the bridal table with Tamika and Marcus in the middle. Some family members stood up and gave speeches about the wonderful couple that the bride and groom made together. The groom made a toast and the DJ played "You" by Kem to allow the newlyweds their first dance. Everyone looked on in awe until the dance was over. Shortly after, everyone else was allowed to join the dance floor. Everyone, including Carla danced themselves into exhaustion, but most importantly; they all had a good time. Before the party ended, Marcus and Tamika were the first ones to make their exit because they had an early flight the next day to start their honeymoon in Hawaii. Carla knew that she would have to go two weeks without seeing her friend and she wished them well and left shortly after.

The door bell rang and Carla woke up startled. She'd taken a three week vacation from the firm after the wedding. Lord knows, her pregnancy kept her more tired than anything else and she planned to sleep in as late as she could each day. She wasn't expecting company and with Tamika out of the country, she wondered who would be ringing her doorbell at ten O'clock in the morning. She thought it was probably her mother coming over to talk about the argument they had the week before, but Carla was over it and wished not to revisit that discussion. She unexcitedly dragged herself out of bed and walked into the bathroom to pull on her robe. Carla walked towards the front door and quickly pulled it open. The moment froze her and she was now wide awake and lost for words.

"May I come in?" Tony asked her. Unable to speak, Carla nodded and made room for him to enter. "Where's your knife this time?" Carla chuckled inside as she thought back on that day. If only Tony knew the real reason she'd greeted him at the door with that butcher knife. Tony stepped inside and walked past her and sat on the couch. With her hands still on the door handle, she paused, took a deep breath and said a silent prayer before turning around. She walked over to the couch and sat about twelve inches away from him. This moment was just so weird. Yes, he was her husband for crying out loud, but he walked out on her and not once did he try to reach out to her. Then again, she really couldn't blame him because she was part to blame. They sat in a discomfited silence that was longer than what they were accustomed to. Carla checked him out from the corner of her eye and she recalled checking him out the same way when they first met at the restaurant. *Who would imagine that we would ever get to this point?* Tony smelled like heaven. His scent reminded of her of the very first time when he showed up at her door and took her out for ice cream. Oh how she wished she could turn back the hands of time and start everything over...but she knew that was impossible. She continued to sit quietly and waited for him to say the first word.

"So how have you been? I see that you've gotten a little bigger...the baby I mean."

Carla smiled and touched her stomach. "Yeah. I've been okay for the most part," she lied. She was missing him like crazy like that song by Natalie Cole.

"So I guess you told the other guy that he's the father of your baby? He must be wondering how much of a sucker I am for marrying a woman who is not pregnant with my child." Tony shook his head and then lowered it. If only he knew that Sergio was in jail and had no idea about the baby being his. "You really had me fooled, Carla. Why didn't you say something before we got married? Huh? I was so excited and looked forward to starting a family with the woman I loved with all my heart...my wife. And when you told me some Jerry Springer shit, I just lost it. I didn't know if I could handle it. I know I was wrong for staying away and cutting you off like I did, but I was really hurt, Carla. Really hurt." Carla saw a tear roll down Tony's cheek. She's never seen him cry before. Her guilt trip hit her once again and then she too started to cry. If only she could undo the wrong she had done. She never meant to hurt him. She loved him just as much as he said he loved her.

Carla hesitantly placed her hand on Tony's knee. He didn't pull away like she expected he would. "Tony, baby I love you so so much. There is not another man that can take your place in my life. What I did was inconsiderate and wrong, I know, but I need you back in my life. You don't know how miserable I've been not being able to have you by my side."

Tony slid closer to Carla and gently wrapped his arms around her. Magically, his touch made her tears suddenly disappear. Carla hugged him back. "Promise me that you will never leave me again."

"I promise." Carla pulled away from him and cupped his left hand into hers and used her free hand to stroke his cheek. She fell silent and tried to get her thoughts together.

"Tony, there's something that we need to discuss." At that point, it was all or nothing. Carla made up her mind to set her skeletons loose and lay it all out on the table. She wanted her husband back in her life and she no longer wanted her secrets to keep them apart.

Tony cleared his throat. "Okay. I'm ready when you are." Carla turned her body in a position where he could see straight into her eyes and she into his. Her mother always told her that the eyes never lie and she wanted Tony to understand and see the truth in all that she planned on telling him.

"I believe that as your wife, I need to be totally honest with you. I never told you this before because I didn't want you to think any different of me and I figured that if I'd told you, then it probably would've ruined everything." Tony did not interrupt her. He sat very attentively, glaring into her eyes as he prepared himself for her to pour her heart out to him. "That guy, who I slept with, followed me home a couple months ago and tried to rape. He was even stalking me." She could see that he felt her pain as the word left her lips. Tony's body tensed and Carla wanted to stop right there and tell no more, but she had to get it out. "The baby I'm carrying...belongs to him." Tony tried to constrict his emotions, but her words pierced him harder than the bullet wound he received in Vegas. He pulled his hand away from hers and buried his face in them. He wanted to get up and walk out, wishing he never showed in the first place...but his body suddenly went weak. The horrific and heart breaking news he'd just heard, sucked the air out of him and left him feeble and short of breath. A nauseous feeling came over him but he found it hard to vomit. Carla reached out to touch him but he shook her off.

"Maybe I shouldn't say anything further." Tony removed his hands from his face.

"No. I want to hear all of what you have to say. I don't want any more surprises...you've surprised me enough."

"Alright then. Please believe me when I say that I didn't plan any of this." There was no response from him. Not even a blink of the eye. The rage and anger in his eyes put fear in her, but Carla silently persuaded herself to stay strong and continue what she started. "Well, a former client of mine who turned out to be his godmother referred him to me to represent his case." Tony nodded his head as if to say, "I can understand that." And Carla continued.

"I decided to take the case for her sake. Everything was fine and I was handling the situation well until the day I got my promotion. I was so excited and wanted to celebrate the occasion. I mean, I've been busting my ass in hopes that that day would come soon and when it finally came, I was overjoyed. You were working late that day and Tamika never answered her phone when I called so I decided to celebrate alone."

Tony parted his lips like he wanted to speak and pop her bubble with a pin. The words that were coming out of her mouth no longer made sense to him. Everything was now a blur and he was deep in his own thought. As far as he was concerned, if she wanted to celebrate, she should've called him instead of assuming that he wouldn't have left work and if he weren't able to leave, she could've waited until the following day. *If she'd waited one more fucking day, it wouldn't have been that big of a deal. I mean one damn day. What was so hard in waiting? I would've fucking celebrated with her...shit maybe throw her a party even.* Tony had to shake it off because he could feel his blood boiling and didn't want to lose control and do something he would regret. He wanted so bad to tell her to just shut up, but decided against it and allowed her to finish.

"I went to Atlantic Station to grab a bite and he spotted me sitting outside in the outdoor seating area. I had too much to drink that night and I allowed him to talk me into going out to a night club. He then convinced me to crash at his place since I'd been drinking...and I don't know what came over me. I don't know why I even listened to him. If I would've come home like I planned, none of this would've happened." Carla was now bawling and laid her head in Tony's lap.

Tony wanted to comfort her, but he found it hard to touch her at that point. His thoughts were racing and all he wanted to do right then was get his hands on Sergio. "Where is this son-of-a-bitch now?" he asked as his chest heaved rapidly. Carla raised her head.

"He's in jail. He showed up at my office couple months ago and my secretary called the police. They arrested him on the spot and the fact that he was convicted of a crime, I doubt he'll be out anytime soon. I never told him about the baby though."

Hearing that Sergio was locked away gave Tony some relief. He didn't care to know why Sergio was in jail. He pulled Carla into his chest for a tight embrace.

"Carla, why didn't you tell me all of this before? We could've avoided all of this if you would've just opened up to me. Baby, I can't read your mind. We have to learn to communicate better."

Carla nodded. "I'm sorry, Tony." Carla then came to realize how important communication really is in a relationship. Miscommunication can cause such havoc and she regretted not coming forward sooner. She decided that she would never keep secrets from her husband again, especially those that can jeopardize their marriage. Tony promised that he would never walk out on her and the baby again and that he would take full responsibility and father the child even though he knew it wasn't his.

"It's not fair that our child grow up without a father. He didn't ask to be brought into this world so we need to be the best parents that we can be." He went on to tell Carla that he would treat the baby like his own flesh and blood and he wanted the baby to have his last name. Carla hugged him tight.

"We are forever going to be a family now and I will never allow anyone to hurt you again." He wiped Carla's face with the back of his hand and kissed her damp cheek. She was no reason why she could stop loving this man. Tony dangled his keys in her face and his attitude changed to that of excitement.

"Let's go for a ride. I have something to show you."

Chapter 28

They drove through the city and Carla recognized the highway once Tony turned onto it. She's never driven that route before. Carla realized that it was the same direction where he led them when she and Tamika followed him the night they were staking him out, before that trailer cut them off. She continued to look on and wondered where he was taking her.

Twenty minutes later, they pulled up to a beautiful three story house. It was bricked all around and the yard space was huge. There was a Bentley parked in the driveway. It was dark, so the view wasn't very visible. As Tony pulled into the driveway, Carla turned to him.

"Where are we?"

Tony put his truck in park. "You said you wanted to know where I lived right?"

"You mean that this is your house?" Carla gasped. "Oh my! This is huge! You live here alone?"

Tony nodded. "It is *our* house now." He held her hand and they continued to sit in the truck.

"Why haven't you brought me here before? That still puzzles me. You led me to believe that you had something to hide."

Tony shook his head. "No. That is not the case. Carla, there is something that I need to share with you as well." She pulled away and sat up to face him.

"I've been keeping some information from you. I wanted to tell you this before, but there was so much going on between us and every time I wanted to bring it up, the timing was never right. "

Carla's heart skipped a beat. She braced herself because she's never known Tony to keep secrets from her. Or so she thought. She knew that she'd made her mistakes, but only hoped that she would be able to handle whatever he was about to tell her. For some reason or another, she felt like crying again. Whatever Tony had to say to her may be too much and she probably wouldn't be able to bear it. No matter how hard she tried, tears would not flow. Carla guessed that perhaps she was just all cried out.

"Remember that day we were at the park and you asked me if I ever thought about owning my own restaurant?" She nodded. "Well, the truth is...I own the waffle joint where we first met." Carla's eyes widened. This was far beyond anything she expected to hear from him. She always suspected that something was up, but never in a million years did she suspect that he'd owned a restaurant.

"WHAT?"

Tony nodded. "Yes. See, my father started the business when I was younger and when I first learned about his illness, I went to college to earn my degree so that I would have the education it required for me to take over the business. There are three chains of them. My mother's sister owns the one in California and we franchised the beginning restaurant that is currently in Philadelphia. When my mom died, she left me as the sole owner to all of their assets here in Atlanta. I didn't know how to tell you this at first, because I promised myself that I wanted to fall in love with a woman who sees me for who I really am and not for what I have to offer. I know you doubted me in the beginning because you thought that I was just some lousy waiter, but what intrigued me about you even more was that you were able to look beyond that and see me for the person that I am within." Tony pointed to his heart. "Carla, that day when we first locked eyes at the restaurant, my heart told me that you were the one I've been looking for all along. All I ever wanted was to be loved and love in return. And I now have that love...love finally, with you."

Carla was speechless. It was all making sense now, all those times she wondered where his finances came from. *It's all coming together now. Why did I ever misjudge him?* She felt like she owed Tony an apology "Tony I'm sorry for ever judging you." Tony placed his finger over her lips to quiet her.

"Shhh. That's all behind us now." Carla couldn't have prayed for a better husband. He was all she ever dreamed to have and more. She learned a valuable lesson: be slow to judge and do not cast a stone if you're living in a glass house. She promised herself from that point on; she would never judge a book by its cover until she knows all of its content. She hoped her mother would learn the same thing once she finally got the chance to meet Tony and learn all about him.

"Tony, I'm curious about something."

"What is it?"

"If you own the restaurant, why do you present yourself as an employee?"

"I was waiting for you to ask. Well, part of the answer to that question is, I've watched my father put his sweat and tears into making sure that his business grew successfully and when I decided to take over, I promised that I would continue to make sure that it was ran in a successful manner. The other reason is because too many times, I've dined at restaurants and you never see the owner. Mangers always work their staff to death but you never know what your workers go through until you have walked in their shoes. Working in the restaurant allows me to bond with my customers as well as relate to my staff. I never want them to think that I believe I am better than them because I own the place. And they respect me for that. I get the chance to see what takes place on day to day basis and I love being involved."

Carla had a higher level of respect for her husband. She would have never looked at it from that perspective. She exhaled deeply. "Wow! That is absolutely commendable. You are going to be the perfect father and role model. Our child is going to be the luckiest kid in the world."

She gave the exterior of the house another look and then her eyes traveled in the direction of the Bentley. "So, whose car his that?" She pointed towards the prestigious automobile.

"Do you really want to know?"

"Please Tony, no games."

"It's yours."

Carla's mouth flew open. "What?! Mine? But how?"

"I was meaning to surprise you with it as a wedding present, but I never had the chance." She gave Tony a kiss. "I love you so much. When do I get to try it out? She laughed.

"The keys are already inside."

"Before we hit the road in my new whip, may I get a tour of my new home?"

Tony pulled her face into his and kissed her again. "Anything for Mrs. Simmons."

Chapter 29

Tamika returned from her honeymoon two weeks later and she called up Carla to have girl talk over lunch. She couldn't wait to dish the details about Hawaii and all of what went down. "Girl, we have to vacation on that Island, just you and I. Carla, the place was unbelievable. I swear, if I didn't have a decent job and a beautiful home, I would pack up and make the island my permanent place of residence and I would drag your ass right along with me too." Carla giggled.

"I can tell that you had a really great time. I mean, look at you...girl you are glowing! Marcus must've really handled his business in Hawaii." Tamika had a devilish grin on her face and Carla definitely knew that she was up to something. "What? Don't tell me that your ass went out of the country and did some freaky shit?"

"Only if you're talking about being freaky for my husband in that romantic suite we rented," Tamika said and laughed.

"I am so glad that you are back. I was missing our talks like crazy," Carla confessed.

"So, what's up with you?" Tamika asked. "I see that you are getting bigger every day." Carla rubbed her stomach.

"I just want this thing to be over and done with. Pretty soon I won't be able to look down and see my toes."

"So you and Tony back together?" Tamika sipped her ice tea through a straw.

Carla inhaled a forkful of salad and nodded. "Yes and our marriage is getting better every day!"

"That's great. Now we can do couples retreats."

"That shouldn't be so bad...matter of fact, that sounds like fun. Maybe we can rent out a log cabin in the mountains like they did on Tyler Perry's, *Why did I get Married*."

"Yeah! That's right. I never looked at it like that. That movie was the bomb too!"

"Umm hmm." Carla sipped her lemonade.

"Well I was trying to wait to tell you this, but I can't hold a secret. At least not from you anyway." Tamika's face lit up and a KOOL-AID smile plastered across her face.

"What is it?"

"I'M PREGNANT!"

Carla gasped and nearly choked on her lemonade. "WHAT...OH MY GOD! Tamika, that's great news!"

"Tell me about it. Marcus is so excited. I guess what we really needed was to take a break from our stressful lives and relax...and girl that break in Hawaii seemed to do the trick."

"So it looks like I'm going to be a godmother too!" They held hands and took a moment of silence to marinate in their joy. Surprisingly, they didn't shed a tear. They just looked at each other with smiles on their faces.

"I didn't believe the results when I took the home test the first time so I went out and bought a few more tests of different brands and when they all showed up positive...I knew then that my mind wasn't playing tricks on me."

"I am so happy for you...no wonder you're glowing like that. Well, I have a secret of my own."

"This time it better be good," Tamika warned.

"Oh it is, trust me." Tamika leaned into the table and stared into Carla's mouth, wanting to capture every word, letter and syllable that she spoke. Carla shared the news with Tamika that her used to be waiter husband was actually the owner of the restaurant.

"WHAT? Carla, are you for real?" Carla nodded and smiled. Girl you struck gold...no you stuck diamond and didn't even know it! I tell you one thing, God sure works in mysterious ways."

"Tell me about it."

Forgetting everything she said in the past months, Tamika looked at Carla, but looked like she was staring off into space when she said, "Girl, Tony is a good man. I mean, look at all of what you both went through and he chose to stick around and man up to something that he could've easily turned his back on. I sure wish they made more men like him. The average Joe probably would've given you his ass to kiss and turn around and serve you with divorce papers and then have the nerve to ask for half of everything plus alimony and claim infidelity. Girl you were blessed with this one." Carla couldn't have agreed more. When she look back on everything, she realized how easily she could've ruined her chance at true love and losing a man that loved her with every being in his body. Carla drank the last of her lemonade and crossed her ankles.

"Guess what?"

"What?" Tamika asked excitedly.

"I quit my job!"

"WHAT!"

"Yeah! Tony told me that he wanted me to chill out...you know because of the pregnancy and all. But I told him that I wouldn't feel right just sitting at home doing nothing. So I decided to open a small practice representing business owners and securing their contracts, preventing them from being scammed. And Tony is my first client! He wants me to handle the restaurant accounts and he's even referring some other business owners that he's good friends with."

"Carla Milford, you have out done yourself again. I am so proud of you." They continued to chat and catch up on the latest events and when that conversation bored them, they did some baby talk. Everything that seemed bitter in the beginning was starting to become sweet.

One month later. Carla and Tony showed up at Ellen's door unannounced. When Ellen opened the door, Carla could tell that she was not pleased at the sight of Tony. Instead of greeting them, Ellen hooted her nose in the air and walked off, leaving the door open for them to let themselves in.

"Are you sure about this?" Tony asked nervously.

"Don't worry. It'll be fine...my mother can be stubborn at times." Carla held his hand and led him as they joined Ellen in the family room. Before they sat down, Carla introduced Tony to Ellen and she barley looked in his direction. Ellen picked up the remote to mute the TV and Carla motioned for Tony to have a seat.

"Momma, why are you making this harder than it needs to be?" Carla asked as she sat next to Ellen.

"Carla, how dare you show up to my house unannounced ...with him?"

"Momma, that 'him' is my husband and your son-in-law whether you like it or not."

"Oh no he's not. Any son-in-law of mine will not get my daughter pregnant and then marry her behind my back...better yet, he will not work as a dead beat waiter."

Tony was astonished at Ellen's reaction and he never expected Carla's mother to be so unyielding. *Carla definitely takes after her father because she is nothing like her mother,* he thought.

"Momma, you are going about this the wrong way. Will you at least give him a chance? You don't even know him."

Ellen looked at Tony sneeringly. "And I don't have to," Ellen spat.

"Momma for your information, Tony is a business owner and he takes very good care of me. He helped me to start my own law practice." Ellen's eyes widened and her mouth fell open.

"What did you just say? Carla Milford, I know that you did not quit your job for a scam that he's trying to bait you into."

"You just never get it...do you? Momma you have a lot to learn." Carla turned to Tony. "Come on babe...let's go. I'm sorry about this. I didn't intend to bring you here to face this humiliation."

Tony stood to his feet. "It was a pleasure meeting you Mrs. Milford." He attempted to shake hands with Ellen but she just looked away and left him hanging. Without saying a word, Carla walked off from her mother and followed behind Tony. She headed out the front door and never looked back. It pained her inside that of all people, Ellen was not supportive. Carla forgave Ellen in her heart, but she didn't know if their relationship would ever be the same. She had a lot of thinking to do. Just when she thought the drama in her life was over, it never ended. She was thankful to have a supporting and loving husband in her life as a well as a best friend she knew she could always count on. Now that she had the love she always dreamed of, Carla was more than determined to do whatever it takes to keep that love alive.

Epilogue

One year later. Carla and Tony were blessed with a two month old baby boy who they were honored to name, Tony Simmons Jr. Tony Sr. opened up two more restaurants in the bay area of Atlanta and one of which Carla is the owner. Her practice was booming and her clientele was made up of Atlanta's rich and famous. She managed accounts like that of Ludacris' restaurant, *Straits*, P. Diddy's, *Justins*, just to name a few. Tamika was quickly brought on board as the chief executive marketing operator and was soon due to have her baby girl.

Carla was planning to have that grand wedding she always wanted with Tamika as her maid-of-honor. She decided to wait until Tamika had the baby so that they would both look glamorous in their dresses. Before any wedding would take place, Carla made plans for her and Tony to meet with a contractor, along with an architect, so that they can work on the drawings for their new home. Tony agreed to put his current home on the market so that he and Carla can have a fresh start. Carla had it all figured out: A seven bedroom, eight bathroom estate with a four car garage and a large yard for the children to play in. Yes, children. She and Tony planned to bring new additions to the family and they would get right to it once Tony Jr. reached a year old.

Although she didn't talk to her mother much, Carla would phone Ellen every now and then to check up on her and make sure that she was doing okay. Ellen; however, did apologize for her behavior and she told Carla that she planned to give Tony a chance. She saw how happy he made Carla and that was all she really wanted for her daughter. Ellen thought she could've protected Carla from heartbreak, but she learned that she had to eventually allow Carla to live her life. Now that she was a grandmother, Ellen wanted nothing more than to be in her grandson's life. Carla would visit her every so often with Tony Jr. and Ellen totally adored him.

Love Finally

She realized that she did a fine job raising her daughter and couldn't be more proud. When all was said and done, Carla, Tamika, Tony and Ellen all learned that they needed love in their lives.

The Melodians couldn't have said it better when they sang, "Love Makes the World Go Round."

LaVergne, TN USA
04 March 2010
174941LV00001B/4/P